Fool's Last Dance

Book 3 of System Apocalypse: Kismet
An Apocalyptic LitRPG

By

Tao Wong & David R Packer

Copyright

Published by Starlit Publishing
PO Box 30035
High Park PO
Toronto, ON
M6P 3K0
Canada

www.starlitpublishing.com

Ebook ISBN: 9781778551833
Paperback ISBN: 9781778552298
Hardcover ISBN: 9781778552304

Books in the System Apocalypse Universe

Main Storyline

Life in the North

Redeemer of the Dead

The Cost of Survival

Cities in Chains

Coast on Fire

World Unbound

Stars Awoken

Rebel Star

Stars Asunder

Broken Council

Forbidden Zone

System Finale

System Apocalypse: Kismet

Fool's Play

Fool's Bond

Fool's Last Dance

System Apocalypse – Relentless

A Fist Full of Credits

Dungeon World Drifters

Apocalypse Grit

System Apocalypse: Australia
Town Under
Flat Out
Bloody Oath

System Apocalypse: Liberty
Head of the Class

Anthologies & Short stories
System Apocalypse Short Story Anthology Volume 1
System Apocalypse Short Story Anthology Volume 2

Valentines in an Apocalypse
A New Script
Daily Jobs, Coffee and an Awfully Big Adventure
Adventures in Clothing
Questing for Titles
Blue Screens of Death
My Grandmother's Tea Club
The Great Black Sea
Growing Up – Apocalypse Style
Interdimensional Window SHOPping

A Game of Koopash (Newsletter exclusive)
Lana's story (Newsletter exclusive)

Debts and Dances (Newsletter exclusive)

A Tense Meeting (Newsletter exclusive)

Comic Series

The System Apocalypse Comics (7 Issues)

Table of Contents

Chapter One 1

Chapter Two 17

Chapter Three 37

Chapter Four 45

Chapter Five 57

Chapter Six 71

Chapter Seven 83

Chapter Eight 97

Chapter Nine 111

Chapter Ten 121

Chapter Eleven 137

Chapter Twelve 151

Chapter Thirteen 165

Chapter Fourteen 177

Chapter Fifteen 191

Chapter Sixteen 203

Chapter Seventeen 213

Chapter Eighteen 227

Chapter Nineteen 239

Chapter Twenty 251

Chapter Twenty-One 255

Chapter Twenty-Two 263

Chapter Twenty-Three 273

Chapter Twenty-Four 283

Chapter Twenty-Five 293

Epilogue 303

Author's Note 309

About the Authors 311

About the Publisher 313

Glossary 315

Chapter One

The ache in his bones wasn't real, but Fool felt it anyway. Sitting down was a road well-traveled by this point, but that didn't make it smooth. He could still feel the grate in his joints that matched the grate of the gravel he sat on, even if the feeling in the bones wasn't real.

Thanks to the System and its tweaks, he looked as if he was in his early thirties, and performed as if he was a superhero in his late teens. However, the body still remembered. Coming up on seventy years of rough living and poor self-care? A couple of years of awesome couldn't entirely stop the momentum of neglect he'd built up.

His muscles felt warm and liquid. The fight had been hard enough to make him move. He rolled his shoulders and closed his eyes for a moment. Remembered the good bits.

A sharp claw that had almost nailed him, and the rushing joy of the pirouette he'd spun into, that had turned into a leap and a smashing downward blow. The heavy blow from the body of the beast that had driven him back, hard, and the brief flicker of rage had made him grit down and shove back.

Fool should be bruised. Battered. Dead, if he wanted to really think about it. Instead, he was looking out over his favorite valley, enjoying the contrast between the body that was his now and the body he'd used up getting to this stage in his life.

The sun was warm, and even if the world had changed for the worse, he was still in a better place. Didn't mean he could completely shake off the old life, but he was getting better all the time at embracing his second chance.

Maybe that was the difference. He'd lived a full life, lived to feel the regrets for all his mistakes. Maybe that made it easier for him to see the opportunity, having come from a place of pain and loss.

If someone had just gotten a new body, that was a dream come true, but if they hadn't seen the crippling emotional pain the old one would have caused them in the years to come? Maybe the gift might feel a little hollow. More likely though, Fool had just forgotten what it was like to have a fresh young brain that hadn't been through the wringer yet.

With a final shake of his wrists, he turned to see how his partner was doing.

Jackal was carefully wiping the gore off his outfit, sporting a cheery grin. Fool wasn't entirely convinced by it. There was a hollowness behind the smile, one that had been sneaking its way into Jackal over the last few months. They hadn't talked about it. At first, Fool had figured the big man was tired, but now he was getting the sense that Jackal was wondering where all of this was going. Fighting monsters and working for a secret organization was fun and all, but even Fool could feel it was getting old. It was a living, but it wasn't a real, full life by any stretch of the imagination.

There wasn't much either of them could do about it. That didn't stop Fool from trying to cheer up his friend in his own way.

"You missed a spot," he said.

That at least got a raised eyebrow from Jackal. "Do you want a faceful of bug guts? Because that's how you get a faceful of bug guts."

Fool couldn't stop the laugh from bursting out of him, and the grin that shone on Jackal's face in response was a proper one, from the heart.

"No," Fool said, flopping down on his back for a moment. "And sorry. I didn't mean to splash you."

Jackal barked out a short laugh and sat down next to Fool, after relenting and using a cleansing spell to get rid of the rest of the goo.

The remnants of the giant insect lay scattered about on the ground in front of them. The thing was huge, but even so, an errant gust of wind was enough to lift one of its wings a respectful distance up in the air. It had taken them longer than they'd expected to bring down the beast. It hadn't been a butterfly when they'd found it.

When they'd tracked down the rampaging beast that had been carrying off the local livestock, it had looked like a giant segmented caterpillar, almost like a beetle. It was swift, for all its bulk, and had led them on a merry chase down the valley and up a mountainside. The transformation had been its final ace in the hole. Just as they'd knocked its health all the way down, it had curled up into a ball and formed a hard shell all around itself.

It had taken most of Fool and Jackal's combined attacks to crack that shell. They'd attacked with desperation, sensing that something far stronger would come out if they gave it time, and they'd been right.

They'd finally cracked the shell seconds before the transformation into the beast's flying form had completed. It was mostly done, so they still had a fight on their hands, but in its weakened state, the monster never really had a chance.

Fool's last blow, powered by his Hammer of Loki Skill, had pulped its head almost clean off.

He wasn't ready to get up just yet and glanced over at Jackal. The big man was staring off into the distance.

"Butterfly," Jackal said.

He didn't follow up on that, so Fool sat up with a grumble and looked around.

It was a warm day, with the Fraser River giving off a clean, damp smell to balance the sticky-sap smell of the nearby woods. Fool couldn't see any butterflies around. Lots of flowers floating about on top of the tall grass, but no butterflies.

Then he saw it. The carcass. "Oh. Yeah. I guess it was. Mothra-thing, maybe? That would have sucked."

The wings of the beast they'd killed were cracking open a little in the sun, drying and spreading out. The wings had a speckled sheen to them, and Fool could even see small scales all over them, just like a butterfly's wing.

Jackal nodded and walked a little closer to the dead monster. "Transformation, but only outwardly. No matter what it might have wanted to be, the System would still make it a monster."

"The more things change, the more they stay the same." Fool stood up using only one leg, just for the fun of it. "Even in a new world, the powers that be still get to force the same shit down on everyone."

Jackal looked at the thing for a silent moment. "Maybe. But maybe not. Might just be that we are only seeing things the way they want us to. Perhaps there's a layer of reality we aren't seeing yet."

"What, getting all 'matrix' on me now?"

Jackal grinned. "No, not like that. Just that it's a big universe. Even with the breadth of the System, it's not everything. And we're only being exposed to one minor part of it."

Fool could only nod.

The sun still shone, the wind still ruffled the trees and grass, the smaller birds still flew, but it felt as though time stood still for a bit. Just the two of them, and the corpse of the creature that had died trying to change itself.

A timeless moment, and too many thoughts, but it still passed.

Fool shook off the remnant bits of gore and dirt. The grin hadn't really left his face, but it flared a little brighter. "Time to head back. Party should be getting started."

Jackal grinned back, and for a moment, whatever thoughts were in the back of his mind seemed to flit away. "Right! The Grammas were going to make strudels with the new crop."

"Cherry," Fool said, his mouth suddenly watering. "I was promised cherry strudel. With glaze."

"Not if I get it first." Jackal was off like a shot.

Fool cursed and followed. The two of them pulled out every trick they could, and in less than an hour, they were back in McBride.

The smell of food and the thumping ring of music led them to the heart of the party. Main Street was overflowing with people, and it took Fool and Jackal a while to work through the gathering folk. The little village had grown into a small town over the last few years. It hadn't been easy, with the high-level monster spawns all around them. The Foundation, Fool and Jackal, and the recruits they'd brought in, had been instrumental in keeping McBride on top of any attacks. Passing through the town, Fool felt as though he'd had a moment to fight side by side with almost everyone.

It hadn't been just them though. The entire village had risen to the challenge the System had brought, rallying together, hunting constantly to keep their levels growing, keeping a constant and active Artisan community going. The village was a lot like it had been before the System, only more so.

A tight community working hard to support each other and looking constantly to a better future.

Which was the reason for the party today. The hard work was paying off, to the point where the village finally had a little excess. They'd put together a well-trained combat unit to hire out, and now they had their first potential contract. The City of Vancouver had recently come under new management and found themselves a little understaffed in some aspects.

The McBride Flying Cavalry had put in a bid, and it had been conditionally accepted, details to be worked out in person. Tomorrow they would be taking to the air for the trip to Vancouver. Fool and Jackal would go along to assist in the negotiations.

Today was a going away party, and also an excuse to celebrate not just survival, but how well they'd prospered in the face of a potential extinction event. Fool was enjoying every bit of the attention, and it was reminding him of how much this place had become home.

McBride was in a beautiful and auspicious location, but it was the people who really made it home for Fool. Some of the folk he couldn't remember the names of, but he knew enough about them to greet them and ask how whatever thing they were working on was going. Or how their family was doing, or hobby, or crafting. It was a comfortable web of connection all around that nestled him into comfort, like feathers in a nest.

A roaring laugh ahead kept his feet moving through the crowd and toward his destination.

The library greens had a small gazebo, and Yagnar barely fit into it. She took up a whole bench by herself, and even sitting, her head almost reached the eaves. Roger was across from her, and Olivia was sitting between the two, watching their animated conversation. Yagnar was still laughing when

Roger noticed Fool and Jackal coming through the crowd, and he waved enthusiastically at them.

Fool was about to wave back, but Yagnar spun about to see who Roger was waving at, and when she saw the two of them, she jumped out of the gazebo with a speed that belied her size. She spread her arms wide for a hug, and Jackal was already there before Fool had even started to grin.

Yagnar looked great, as did the other two. They were all dressed for the party. Roger was wearing, of all things, a suit. It looked good on him, and Fool noted that he'd grown substantially in the last while. Physically, Roger had gotten a little more brawn on him and a few more inches in height. He didn't look like a buff teenager anymore, but more like a confident young Hollywood action star.

Fool had seen Roger's mental growth in the last while as well. After their adventures in Wells Gray Park, Roger had mostly ditched the spoiled brat approach. The last time Fool had seen him in battle, they'd been repelling a wave of monster attacks on the west side of town. Roger had taken charge of a cadre of youths and was ably directing them, guiding them to finishing off monsters wounded by older fighters, sending them out in squads to take on smaller and weaker monsters. He'd become a leader, and one that cared about his followers.

Olivia wasn't so formal looking, but she'd ditched her adventuring gear of bone fetishes and ragged leathers for a stylish look that was still somewhat casual. Big shoes, black tights with coastal art in black and green running down the sides, and an oversized black hoody with some kind of cartoon face on it that Fool didn't recognize.

Yagnar, though… she'd gone all out. The long red dress she wore wasn't an evening gown, but it was almost as eye-catching. Fool recognized the style as being based on a fifties-style housewife classic, but it had been cut and fit to flatter. The arms were bare to show off her muscles, but the cut of the rest, along with the heels, gave more of a pinup impression.

The contrast to her usual military uniform was startling, but also the clearest sign of the progress the town had made. Yagnar was now in charge of logistics for the Foundation. Her inherent skillset had been pushed to new levels with the Foundation's backing and access. What she was wearing was the clearest sign of the future of McBride that Fool could look for.

It was a sign that the worst had passed. Better times, if not good times, were ahead.

Home was finally a place he could relax.

Lucy felt the sound even before her hand touched the door. The door almost buzzed from the pulse of it, and an atavistic shiver ran up her spine in anticipation. She paused just long enough for a single breath, already feeling the luscious pulse that would shiver the little horns on her head.

There was no one to watch her, but the show never ended. She set her shoulders just right, let her favorite predatory grin rise like a moon through the fog, and flung the door open.

The floor was packed. She could tell even before she stepped out on the gallery, just from the way she should see bodies milling about on the edges, in the dark places. Thieves' Heart was on the stage, the house band driving a last beat so hard she felt her hoody popping against her body as the song ended.

They didn't pause between songs, a lone guitar wailing quietly for a moment before the drums started back with a rock-steady beat. She leaned over the railing as the vocalist let loose with a seductive wail. Eyes looked up at her.

Not everyone. Just the regulars. Those who knew that this gothic rock staple was her theme song. It always marked her entrance to the dance floor, her nightly hunt for a partner or two to make the night less lonely.

The song hit its bridge, rising in intensity, and she felt the lovely taut and swollen muscles of this body longing to move, to dance. Hungry, sparkling eyes met her gaze from below, and she grinned down on them.

She loved this. Loved this city, this Vancouver. These people who had let her build this home for them, this secret enclave where they could dance, where they could free themselves and be themselves and find those fleeting secret moments that made life worth living.

And tonight, she was going to show them that love as best she could.

"You're not supposed to be here."

Lucy didn't spin in surprise. This was her club, after all. And she wasn't that surprised. But it was good to show some surprise. Didn't want to give away all her secrets. She stopped. Then slowly turned and tilted her head at the figure leaning against a pillar farther down the dwarf gallery.

Red and white armor, with fine wisps of fabric trailing off all about. An almost featureless white facemask on the helmet, with red fins rising on either side. The fabric almost formed into a long, flowing skirt around the legs. Almost attractive, Lucy thought. Tempting.

"That's a matter of opinion"—Lucy licked the tip of her pointiest canine—"and something tells me you didn't get an invitation."

Red and White stood up off the pillar and took a small step to balance themselves square. "Lucy Brightside. I wonder if the humans know why you chose that name."

She ran her hand up through her hair, letting one of the horns glimmer briefly in reflected light from the dance floor. "Seemed fitting." Her voice was calm, but the way her eyes switched from a cool violet to a stormy indigo glow should be all the warning the interloper needed to know that she was on thin ice. "I think the one who's not supposed to be here is you though. I didn't invite you here, and no one gets up here without an invitation. So which of my little munchkins let you up?"

Red and White said nothing, didn't even cross her arms, just stood looking at Lucy as if she could intimidate her into leaving. As she stood there, Lucy noticed her mask wasn't really featureless. Or rather, it wasn't opaque but rather translucent. The face behind the mask was just exceptionally pale.

It was the stern look on that face that decided Lucy. She never could stand smugness on anyone, especially when the smugness had an air of privilege about it.

Lucy stepped forward, and the glow in her eyes flared.

Red and White held up a hand. "The Weaver sends warning."

That froze Lucy in place. If she was her other self, she'd be tempted to laugh with delight, be tempted to dance with the Weaver and put them in their place.

They'd done it before, again and again and again. All the best fun.

She wasn't that other self though. She was just an avatar, a spun-off manifestation. The System managed Mana dictated the rules and the Council's rules, and because of that, she could only be here as a reduced copy of her real self.

That meant she had limitations, so she could fit in with the local environment.

Red and White wasn't the Weaver either. The Weaver had to deal with some of the same limitations, so it was a question of what sort of proxy Red and White was. Not an avatar, because that was something unique. And also the source of the Weaver's hatred of Lucy.

Well, one of the reasons. Still, the Weaver could send some very capable people if they wanted to. Under other circumstances, Lucy would just call it quits and discorporate. The game was usually up when you were found out.

Not this time.

It would be a shame to let the Weaver know the game had changed this early. Nothing for it. It wasn't like a little chaos would be a problem anyway. The game was no fun if you knew how it was going to end.

She smiled at Red and White. "I suppose you have some kind of message, but to be honest? Not in the mood. I'm going dancing. You can just fuck right off."

Rage flashed across Red and White's face, and Lucy felt them sucking in a cold whirlwind of Mana. Powerful. Almost Master Class. The Weaver couldn't afford to send many of those, not yet. So this was likely the only major opponent.

That was all Lucy needed to know.

Her eyes flamed into novas, and Lucy struck a moment before Red and White finished preparing her attack. A telekinetic fist slammed into the armored woman, punching her through the wall, through the hillside outside the wall, up into the air over Vancouver, and far out of sight.

Lucy shook her head and walked down the hall. Red and White wasn't dead—she'd be too tough for that. And she'd be ready for Lucy next time. Which meant Lucy would have to stay put in the Twisted Chapel for a while. And upgrade the security again.

Not for much longer. Things were moving fast now, but it was all working on a timetable that was better rather than worse.

Another few days and Fool would be here.

Then the real shenanigans could start.

Status Screen			
Name	Fool	Class	Priest
Race	Human (Male)	Level (Advanced Class)	1
Titles			
Adept Priest of the (Redacted)			
Health	290	Stamina	290
Mana	620	Mana Regeneration	53/minute
Status			
Normal			
Attributes			
Strength	22	Agility	40
Constitution	29	Perception	116
Intelligence	62	Willpower	63
Charisma	69	Luck	170
Class Skills			
Closseau	1	Have Faith	1
Talent Scout	2	Pants on Fire	1
Transform Object	1	Kiss it Better	2
I know a Shortcut	2	Truth or Dare	1
Dry hair is for Squids	1	Oh god, don't hit me!	2
Mint?	1	Location Scout	1
Face Swap	1	No Fair	2
Geas	2	Feign Death	1
Aura of *	2	Regeneration	1
Hammer of Loki	1		
Spells			
Sparkles			

Status Screen			
Name	Jackal	Class	Bearshirt Warrior of the Claven North
Race	Human (Male)	Level (Advanced)	1
Titles			
(None)			
Health	640	Stamina	640
Mana	670	Mana Regeneration	113 / minute
Status			
Normal			
Attributes			
Strength	69	Agility	65
Constitution	64	Perception	114
Intelligence	67	Willpower	168
Charisma	12	Luck	10
Class Skills			
Pain don't Hurt	2	One Punch	2
INTIMIDATE	1	Mana Steal	1
Knock back	1	Mr. Freeze	1
Only a flesh Wound	2	Death from Above	2
Neo	1	Indomitable Will	2
Maestro	2	Blade Walking	2
Red Rover	2	The Wall	1
Eye of the Tiger	2	Boomstick	1
Spells			
(None)			

Chapter Two

Fool watched the horses fly over the mountain and laughed. A very nervous laugh.

His enthusiasm for going back to his old stomping grounds—Vancouver—had been crushed as soon as his mount had gone airborne.

Flying in planes was one thing. Even the magic carpet they'd stolen from a mark a while back had given them a nice flat surface to sit on. All those were fine.

Sitting on what he could only see as a little brown ribbon of a creature? It was making his insides do very uncomfortable things. It wasn't even a small horse—quite the opposite. But from his point of view, watching the snowy tip of a mountain pass a few hundred feet under? The damned thing was too small.

He hadn't thought of himself as the kind to have a nervous laugh, but he was wrong. When it came to horse galloping in the air *down* the side of the mountain, it was just wrong in more ways than he was able to frame or deal with. So his brain decided to laugh.

Ahead, he saw Jackal turning and watching him with a grin. Probably because he misunderstood the laughter. Probably.

More likely, Jackal was just enjoying himself and assuming that everyone else was as well. Taking pleasure in others' misfortune was more Fool's thing. And he was trying to get past that. Being the only one miserable on this journey had made that difficult.

At least they looked great. The horses galloped on air as if they were on the ground, which gave them a decidedly martial air. Combined with the barding all the horses had, done up in McBride's green, blue, and white, and the riders in a high-tech version of plate armor, all armed to the teeth? As much as Fool hated to admit it, they looked more than just fierce. They looked noble.

And he felt like a court jester in the middle of them.

A good part of that came from being in the middle of a tightly knit group he didn't belong to. The lances of the flying mounted cavalry had all been trained separately and together before this mission by Roger, and Fool and Jackal had only joined them for a single day's familiarization before departing.

Each lance comprised one main rider in heavy armor with an actual lance, two flanking riders armed with their preference of both ranged and close combat weapons, and one support rider who cared for the horses and gear. Yagnar was the one who'd equipped the entire group, somehow.

A lance was intended to operate on its own as a complete unit for extended periods of time, and together as a *lanze spezzate* for massed charges and other unified tactical operations. The entire troop had been training in their roles for over a year, and it gave them a solid sense of *esprit de corps.* Jackal fit in better, being an Advanced Combat Class.

Which Fool was too. Sort of. Now that he was an Adept, he was supposed to be more of a battle priest of the Trickster. Hammer of Loki. When he tapped into his Advanced Class Skill, he had all the strength and durability of a Frost Giant. He could probably wreck half the *lanze spezzate* without much effort, if he wanted to. When he and Jackal had gone out on some hunting trips to try out their new Skills, he'd been truly astonished at what he could do.

It wasn't the same as being a soldier though. Or even a warrior. Those folks had a sense of purpose that was tied into working together, or solo, toward a higher purpose. Fool had that, but he didn't have the confidence in any moment that what he was doing was right.

Then he laughed again, despite the dizzying heights and the icy blasts of high mountain winds. This time it was at himself.

Confidence. Maybe before the System, confidence had been the weaker part of his makeup, but since? If it wasn't confidence that he was doing the right thing, then he didn't know what to call the force that made him leap into stupid decisions. He was still here, still standing. After all those fights he should have lost. Maybe these folks had something else Fool could want, but it wasn't confidence.

Camaraderie, perhaps. But for that, there was Jackal. Always Jackal. Fool knew the fate that had brought them together meant for them to always be by each other's side, no matter what.

Not at the moment though. Jackal had roamed ahead. Fool shook his head at that. The unfairness of it all. Even with Jackal's immense size, they'd still found a mount for him. And he'd turned out to be a natural rider, even with no Skills.

Fool glanced down again and decided he was just going to keep his eyes closed for the entire ride.

They landed in Hope. It wasn't the end of the mountains before the Fraser Valley, the vast expanse of rich farmland that led to Vancouver. It was the start of the navigable river though. And as such, it was where the highway really started toward the city. There was still a highway through the mountains. In some places. A few years of neglect had been enough to remove some of the rougher sections, and the high-level monsters in other areas had taken their own toll.

Fool was grateful for the Air Cavalry giving them the ability to skip all of that. The road from McBride to Clearwater, then to Kamloops, would have taken them a lot of time and effort to cross otherwise. The mountain passes might have ended them completely. There were some serious beasts in the mountains.

They'd stopped a few times for raids. Tearing through packs of lesser creatures, or stronger creatures that just had no tools to deal with the coordinated airborne attacks the *lanze spezzate* could deliver. They'd collected a hefty amount of loot and experience on the journey.

They'd only had to face airborne attacks a few times. Those had been harrowing, especially for Fool, but their tight tactical formations had seen them trounce every monster they'd come across, even the swarms.

Hope was their first official "Lower Mainland" stop. The town itself hadn't survived the arrival of the System, at least not long enough for anyone to notice. That became apparent as Fool looked around before dismounting.

He'd gotten more practice getting off and on his mount. He didn't have a choice. There was no mounting stage for him to use on the trip, and the creature had a bit of an evil streak when it came to "helping" its rider off and on. Fool had taken several falls, to the amusement of everyone else, before he'd gotten the knack of forcefully grabbing the reins to hold the horse in place, then leaping and scrambling up with confidence. The devilish thing seemed to almost appreciate his pushiness, which made no sense to Fool.

The town itself was a wreck. They'd landed at the end of the old main drag, where there'd been a small park next to the Fraser River, the same Sto:lo that flowed past McBride. Every building had been destroyed. Not just destroyed, but splintered, shattered, as if a massive boulder had dropped on them. Nothing had been spared. Even the streetlights, benches, and most of the asphalt had been hammered into scrap.

It had happened long enough ago that the remnants of the town were already covered with fresh growth, mostly moss and lichen.

Jackal dismounted next to Fool, leaping from the mount of his saddle and landing with a graceful demi-crouch. He stood and walked over to Fool, then looked over his shoulder toward the remnants of the town.

"Bit odd," Jackal said.

Fool didn't look at him, keeping his eyes on the town. Something was making his hair stand up. "How so?"

"Moss. Lichen. That stuff takes decades to grow."

"More System fun. I'm not planning on checking it out, that's for sure."

Fool looked for Fran, who was giving brisk orders to the rest of the *lanze spezzate*. She caught his look, gave one last order, and walked over.

"Sup, big guy?"

For a moment, Fool considered not answering and leaving Fran to look awkwardly at Jackal. The moment passed as the itchy feeling on his back got worse. "I'm thinking staying here overnight was a bad idea. Maybe we should push on."

Fran tilted up one corner of her mouth. "Why? Just because of a few rock trolls?"

"The what now?!?"

"Rock trolls." Fran pointed over her shoulder with her long-handled mace, and Fool turned to look.

Looming over the south of the town was a single, imposing mountain. Lush and green at the tail end of summer, with big, swollen sections of granite that rose out of the fir-covered sides. And those firs were swaying in the breeze.

Only there was no breeze. On one of the rock outcroppings, Fool could just see a humanoid figure leaping down the rocks into the trees. Given the distance the mountain was from the town, and relative to the size of the trees, it was a big creature. And judging from the sway of the trees, there were a lot of them.

"Huh," Fool said. "When did you notice those?"

"Saw 'em on the way down." Fran was already heading back to her mount.

Fool noticed that the support riders and their horses were setting up a perimeter around the little park they were in, forming a tiny fort with its back against the river. They were setting up pavise shields to form the walls. All the other riders had unloaded their supply packs and were remounting.

"Figured you and Jackal would be happier fighting them on the ground, and frankly… you'd just get in our way for this batch." She sprang up on her horse and saluted Fool and Jackal. "You boys have fun now."

Then she and her horse sprang up into the air as Fran gave a whoop and swung her mace in circles over her head.

Fool sighed and crossed his arms. "Well. Fuck."

Jackal grinned and bumped his elbow into Fool's shoulder. "Let's have some fun."

"Sergeant's orders, I guess," Fool shook his head at that, then unlimbered his warhammer.

The support crew had already joined the pavises together, and Fool could see they were another high-tech find, probably courtesy of Yagnar. As the shields connected to each other, they extended a glowing crimson field straight up. That same crimson field reached back and down to anchor the shield into the ground. A nice little walled fort, and it looked well-designed to stop a charging enemy.

The fort was almost complete, with the end farthest from the mountain just being formed. Fool took a run at it and leapt over the support crew person and the shield they were setting up. He didn't have to use Hammer of Loki to make the jump. Fool had enough points in strength now to more than match anything a pre-System Olympic high jumper could do.

He landed with a thump and a grin and heard Jackal land next to him. They both turned back to watch the mountain, but the trees weren't moving anymore. Fool remembered from road trips through Hope that there were still more hills and forest between the foot of the mountain and the town. They probably had a moment or two before the rock trolls, if that's what they were, arrived.

He glanced back at Jackal, who had his favorite two swords out and a serene look of peace on his face. "So, charge? Or hang out and wait?"

Jackal cocked his head to the side for a moment. Fool always wound up making the actual plans, but Jackal's advice was always a part of every decision. Mostly.

"Anvil," the giant said.

"Fuck," Fool said.

It was a role Fool hated to play in combat. Neither of them were tanks, so holding their ground fast while the enemy piled on them was a sucky, no fun thing to do. But Jackal had a point. The support troops had built the fort and expected to be charged by the trolls. They were the anvil to the swooping cavalry's hammer… but Fool and Jackal would make a nice hardened face for that anvil. It made sense. It was the right thing, the bright thing, to do.

So Fool tossed that idea away. Jackal was right, but to be honest, Fool wasn't in the mood. He really didn't have any idea just yet what a rock troll was. He'd use his Skills to see what they offered when they showed up, but he really didn't think it was necessary. If they weren't going to act like a stereotypical monster, why did Fran call them rock trolls? Clearly, they'd charge in and be a pain in the ass. Hell, most monsters did. These were probably just tougher and stronger.

If they were a lot tougher and stronger, that would put Fool and Jackal in a terrible spot, and Fool didn't feel like taking that chance. His back was still itching.

They had only a minute until the rock trolls showed up, so Fool played a hunch. "Over the side!"

He grabbed Jackal by the belt, as best he could, and dragged him to the battered fence that used to be a safety barrier to stop tourists from falling into the Fraser River.

The reason that was needed was apparent as Fool looked down. By the time the Fraser reached Hope, it had wound its way down and through almost the entire bottom half of the province and had over two miles of vertical momentum.

He could feel the rumble of the river in his bones. It had a physical presence that reached up and above the banks and sparked its own primal fear in the backbrain.

Fool looked over the bank and found what he hoped for. There was a small bar of gravel at the foot of the bank, with only a few meters to drop. Nothing for two Advanced Classes to drop down and jump back up from.

"Perfect. We'll jump down here and wait till the first clash. Fran's going to hit them as soon as they get committed to their charge. If we jump up just before Fran shows, they'll be torn between hitting the defenses and dealing with us. That pause ought to give Fran a chance to really rip into them." Fool grinned and leapt down.

Jackal didn't follow.

When Fool looked up, he saw the oddest look on Jackal's face. It wasn't quite fear and not quite disgust, but something close to the two. It was gone almost as soon as Fool saw it, replaced with a quick look of resolve followed by Jackal jumping down.

He landed on the gravel bar with a deep squat and his arms spread wide. After a brief pause, Jackal stood and nodded.

Fool couldn't help himself. "What the hell was that? You aren't afraid of water. I've seen you swim before."

A sudden fear ran through Fool at the thought that maybe Jackal had seen something in the water. He spun about but saw nothing.

That made Jackal let out a little snort, almost a chuckle. "No, sorry. Just a memory. Falling in the mud when I was a kid, then I remembered how much I weigh now, and I wasn't sure that this little sand bar would hold my weight."

"Gravel bar." Fool shook his head in disbelief. Jackal was more nervous than he'd let across, otherwise he would have just grunted instead of reciting what was for him an epic. "Whatever. We good?"

Jackal grinned and gave him a raised eyebrow.

"*No.* No Rock impressions. You're terrible at that, and you don't look like him at all."

Jackal didn't reply to that, just turned back to the bank. He kept his swords in hand, which he'd done before jumping down, and climbed a little up the bank until he could see just over the top.

Fool didn't bother to join him. Jackal would let him know when it was time. And while he was waiting, Fool took a quick glance back at the river. Turning his back on it seemed like a bad idea, but he couldn't see anything. And a flicker from above drew his attention.

Fran and the cavalry lances were wheeling about and assembling for a column charge. Fool had seen them practice that in McBride, and it was damned impressive. Once they formed a column, the lances would be lifted out of sockets and pointed straight up. Fool had been slightly disappointed that they'd opted to use nineteenth century lances, closer to spears, instead of the classic medieval lances he'd expected. Fran had pointed out that a flying horse moved a lot faster than a medieval warhorse, which meant that a rider wanted to let go of a lance without delay if it got stuck.

Once the column charged, the lances were lowered in a flowing line aimed at the target. It was a terrifying display of massed power, horses diving out of the sky with gleaming metal points licking the sky ahead of them.

What happened when they hit the target was the real genius. Roger had created the tactic as a modification of a Caracol, a tactic used by the German *Reiter* in the sixteenth century. Cavalry would slow charge in column, fire their handguns, and spin off to the rear of the column while reloading. Roger's idea had been that the flying cavalry would charge in the same column but pull upward once their lance had struck the target.

The net effect was a constant rain of lance strikes at the target. A demonstration Fool had seen had the cavalry putting dozens of lances into a wooden target in seconds. The sound had been a deafening series of cracks, almost like an automatic rifle firing.

From the arc they were taking, Fool figured the rock trolls would not be much longer in arriving. The tumult of the tumbling rocks increased, then changed to a steady drumming thump coming from above them. The trolls seemed to be in full charge.

He scrambled up beside Jackal, unable to wait any longer for the signal.

Just in time to see the trolls burst out from the old highway area, half a kilometer away. Fool was surprised to see how small they were. Part of that impression was that they were running on all fours in a staggering, ape-like gait. They looked about waist-height, but they were all as wide as they were tall. As Fool watched, a brace of larger upright ones came out of the trees, moving in an awkward lumbering roll. They were followed by another wave of the smaller trolls, then a final, larger troll.

"Boss," Jackal said. Fool heard the hunger in his voice.

"Go get 'em." Fool knew he could trust Jackal to choose the right time and place, so he had no problem altering his plan to let Jackal play hero.

With his Blade Walking Skill, Jackal could literally dance his way over the charging trolls, taking a toll on them as he went. Jackal knew the plan, and the two of them were tuned in enough to each other that they could easily alter plans on the fly without worry.

Which meant Fool had to consider his best approach now. He'd stick with his original idea to start. Despite how his brain was now flooding with demanding voices telling him that there was a better way or that he'd made a mistake, he had confidence in what he'd first decided. He wasn't sure if that had come as a result of his higher intelligence or from Jackal's influence. The big man had taken to passing on bits of wisdom from old philosophers, and they were influencing how Fool thought.

One of the Stoics had said that you should stick to your first thought, because it was always the right one. Later thoughts would be your brain lying to itself. Or something. Fool couldn't remember the exact saying, but this was the time to listen to that bit of wisdom.

The troll charge was getting closer, and Fool's combat brain was kicking in. Everything was slowing down just a tick, and his vision was narrowing. He couldn't hear anything anymore, but that didn't bother him. He'd been in this place often enough. Didn't happen every time, or even most of the time, but he always moved at his best when it did.

There was no trigger of movement, nothing that stood out that told him "now." He just found that he was moving forward, his warhammer in hand, and one particular troll was centered in his vision. Just as Fool trusted Jackal to do his job, he had to trust everyone else was doing their job at this point.

Hammer of Loki made Fool's heart sing. A handful of years ago, he'd been on the verge of being a crippled, wasted old man. Now he made a seven-hundred-pound rock troll go crashing headfirst into the ground with a single swat of his warhammer.

Madness. Sweet, intoxicating, joyful madness. A brighter twin to his old madness, a shining joy that took hold of him.

The single battering hit was not without its price, as a pack of rock trolls slammed into him. Even with Fool's increased toughness, his head still rang like a bell when the trolls plowed him into the reinforced shields.

Literal rock fists punched into him over and over. A wave of trolls hit the shields like an avalanche, crushing Fool between them and the shield wall.

The cavalry hit like a lightning bolt out of the sky, a crashing spearpoint of a wave that smashed aside bodies of rock trolls like pebbles before snapping back up into the sky.

The relief of pressure was enough for Fool to fight his way free, and just in time. Hammer of Loki strengthened him, but it was nowhere near Jackal's temporary invulnerability. Fool had been blitzed hard enough—by the sheer weight of the trolls as much as by their fists—that his health was in the red. The travel armor he'd been wearing was a complete wreck, and he could hear the shield behind buzzing and crackling as it failed. The smart part of his brain told him to run.

He'd made a mistake. He'd thought his tactic was perfect, but it had failed because he'd underestimated the sheer power and speed of rock trolls charging downhill. If it hadn't been for Hammer of Loki, he'd be paste.

The pressure didn't come back though. He smashed his now-free hammer into the punching hand of a troll, blasting it right off, and in the brief respite that gained him, Fool glanced up and around.

The air was burning with beams, shots, and other projectiles. The troops behind the shields were letting loose with all their weapons, and at this close of a range, they were decimating the trolls. Every shot was hitting a target, even if it wasn't the one aimed at. The continuing Caracol was ripping into the trolls from the rear at the same time.

And Fool was stuck in the middle. His hammer-swinging arm was pinned against his chest by the crush of the trolls. His ears rang as another fist crashed into the side of his head, and his vision blurred.

Time for the next trick.

"Have Faith!"

The cry was less a prayer and more an admonishment to himself. It worked in both ways. The little babbling voice in the back of his head, the one that was yelling about dying and running and this wasn't where he was supposed to be and it had all gone wrong, petered out into a whimper.

The other way only showed itself at first with a little giggle in his ear, then the calming sense of someone's hand on his back. Time slowed for less than a blink of his eye as he felt the presence of the Trickster.

And then faded. It was enough. In the brief slowdown, he saw the next punch coming and knew what to do.

Just a little lean, a small shuffle of the foot to the same side the punch was coming from. He didn't have room for more, not packed in as he was. Millimeters of movement, the angles changing just enough that the punch just grazed the tip of his nose…

… and slammed into the face of the next troll over. That troll staggered over. The hit was hard enough that its head smashed into the head of the next troll.

And Fool's arm was free. A few inches on either side of him, no more. More than enough. The trolls were so dense around him it was like being buried in a stone well made of faces, shoulders, and backs.

He flipped the hammer around and drove the pick end in between two trolls, who slammed back together and nearly caught the tip. Without hesitation, Fool used all the strength Hammer of Loki gave him and heaved himself straight up, using the pick end as a handhold.

He flew up above the tumult, hammer in hand.

At the apex of his leap, in the moment of rising and falling, he hung in the air, hammer handle in right hand, head in his left, one knee slightly rising as he felt the gentle shift of momentum fading away, the build of potential energy for the fall to come.

Jackal had left a wake of troll bodies of all kinds. He was locked in combat with the boss, slashing swords into its thighs over and over. Incredibly, even though the troll was made of rock, Jackal's blows were causing visible slices to show up. Even as Fool dropped, he saw the boss stumbling.

But not before it used a fist like a piledriver to pound Jackal into the earth.

The boil of trolls under Fool was reducing rapidly under the attacks from the makeshift fort and the cavalry, so he switched tactics. He wasn't needed where he was. Jackal was probably okay. Maybe. He'd likely had his invulnerability Skill active when he got clobbered. Fool had to trust that. And Jackal could probably take out the boss by himself.

The three sub-bosses running toward the boss? Those could complicate matters. Likely not, but Fool didn't see any point in taking chances. Plus, he felt a bit embarrassed by being swarmed, and going and playing hero for a bit with Jackal seemed like a better place to be.

Not that he really enjoyed being a hero at all, but now that he was an Adept of the Trickster? It wouldn't hurt to make a better show of himself. Give the impression that he was a bit more in charge than he felt anyway.

He bounced off the head of a troll as he landed, using the firm skull to springboard himself forward. He aimed for the next troll head as he leapt. It took him about three springs to clear the melee, and his grin grew wider with every leap. He could get used to this.

As he was bouncing off of the last troll, he pulled up his Status screen to see how much mana he had left. Hammer of Loki was a fantastic skill for him, but it was a solid drain on the old batteries. With a glance, he confirmed his suspicion. He had about a minute of juice left. Plenty for straightforward combat, but he'd run dry if anything went wrong. And he always wanted to leave something in the mana battery for a last-minute "Have Faith."

The last leap brought him to about a block away from where the boss was lifting a foot to re-stomp the Jackal-shaped hole in the ground. It was right between the three sub-bosses, who were jostling each other in an eager rush to the big boss. It looked as though the primary tactic of the rock trolls was to jumble together into a pile and slam into their target.

Since they hadn't noticed Fool yet, he knew exactly what to do.

A burst of speed, and a dart to the right. He leapt up and switched his hammer to his left hand. Both legs landed on the right shoulder of the farthest charging sub-boss, and as his feet hit, he torqued his upper body around, hooked the pick end of the hammer around the left ankle of the sub-boss, and yanked up.

Shoved from behind on the shoulder with its left foot hooked up, it windmilled its arms and toppled. Fool snapped his wrist to the side and released the ankle. Instinctively, the monster thrust that leg forward to catch its balance.

Which put that foot in the path of the center sub-boss, who kicked it forward as it tripped over it.

Just as Fool had planned, the three trolls stumbled and crashed into each other, becoming a tumbling pile of rocks. Fool leapt across the scrum, landing precise blows.

There was a roar from ahead, and Fool saw the boss clutching its foot and tumbling backward as Jackal slashed his way out of the ground.

Fool paid for his inattention, with one of the trolls grabbing his ankle and pulling him into the tumbling scrum. He used his hammer to smash the hand grabbing him into shards and tumbled free.

The foursome all spilled apart and groggily stood.

Fool was surrounded by three large rock trolls, who all slowly turned to look at him.

He shut off Hammer of Loki. Activated Clouseau to change the appearance of his skin to stone. Geas to have them believe he was a tiny rock troll. Oh God Don't Hit Me to make them hesitate to attack him.

They froze in confusion at the sudden appearance of an infant amid them. Acting on a hunch, he used Clouseau one more time to change his skin green, for a mere second, then turned off all the other skills, and activated Aziz to flash a bright light at the trolls.

As he'd hoped, they flinched back in confusion.

He grinned and activated Aura of *.

The trolls quaked and shivered so fast it looked as if they were going to sink into the ground. Fool hoped that he had helped their brains believe they were seeing some sort of existential horror and needed to flee in fear. It seemed to be working. Aura of * was a powerful mental attack and setting it up the way he had gave it better odds of working right away.

One of them broke, running back toward the mountain at full speed. Another seemed to just freeze in place. The last one went completely still, then roared and launched a punch at Fool.

Out of reflex, Fool smashed back at the punching hand with his warhammer, intending to smash the fist into pieces.

He'd completely forgotten that he'd disabled Hammer of Loki.

His warhammer still hit with all of his experience and enhanced abilities, but this was no first-level monster. The punch was battered aside and missed Fool, but it didn't slow the troll at all, who continued to flail punches.

Fool nearly re-activated Hammer of Loki until he realized he was dodging all the punches. It wasn't very hard. A small step here, a lean there, a little dip of the head. He wasn't even stepping back, but rather moving continuously at angles. The troll was growing more and more enraged with every punch.

Luck and Agility for an advanced class really added up to an unfair advantage.

Not too much of an advantage though. Fool took every opportunity to reply to the troll's blows with more precise shots, but the damage he did was negligible. And just like the classic trolls, these rock trolls had some regeneration capability. It wasn't much, but the damage Fool was dealing with was minor enough that the regeneration made a difference.

He felt a minor frustration growing stronger inside him. As much as he was enjoying his newfound Advanced Combat Class, his Basic Class was a support class. That meant he had some holes in his build that made straight-up combat a weak spot for him. Fool needed his Skills to balance things out. He still didn't want to activate Hammer of Loki just yet though. He had a hunch he might need the Mana for something else. If he could hold off a little longer, he'd rebuild enough.

The rock troll sub-boss wasn't interested in giving Fool more time. It roared again and seemed to grow a little larger. Another roar, and larger. Fool realized it wasn't growing, it was *expanding*. Some new Skill it was about to launch. He started dodging from side to side, trying to keep the troll off balance as it kept trying to keep Fool centered in front.

The troll split as if it had a seam down the middle.

The seam opened just a little, and a fountain of lava shot out.

Fool dodged, but even a near miss felt like having a telephone-pole-wide branding iron pressed into his side.

He only realized he was screaming when he struggled to take a breath in.

The troll was moving at hyper-speed after its Skill activation, and it punched Fool right into the burned area. He heard bone break, but that wasn't the worst part. As he flew from the force of the blow, he curled in on himself. He saw a spatter of blood and other things he didn't want to recognize trailing out away from him like a bloody comet.

The troll battered Fool again before he even understood what direction he was flying in, up or down.

Something shattered inside him, and he lost all feeling below his chest and his grip on his hammer.

The ground shattered him into a million pieces.

His breath was only a whisper, the last air his lungs would ever hold. "Have Faith."

Time stopped.

DM was sitting on the ground, looking at Fool with her head tilted. She stood on all four legs and padded over. Sniffed at his face delicately, not quite touching him. He felt a tiny whisper of air from her little nose tickling his skin.

She licked his forehead, and it was like a jolt of lightning through him. He would have screamed if he could, but he was just as frozen as reality was.

DM sat back down on her haunches. "Quit whining. It's just a temporary pinch of the C-six nerve. Troll actually punched your shoulder blade almost up into your head. It's already moving back into position. Gonna hurt a lot though."

The little black cat stood up again, stretching her back in a vast arc, looking just like the stereotypical Halloween cat.

Fool still couldn't move, couldn't talk. He shuddered as he felt something else shift in his back, and he realized he hadn't quite finished falling. He was still settling into the ground. Somewhere at the edge of his vision, the troll was approaching.

DM shook herself after her stretch. "This one's going to cost you."

Even frozen in time, Fool felt his guts shuddering in fear.

"I know I told you you should use this Skill more freely, but you shouldn't have let it get this far. You aren't useful to me if you aren't clever, Fool. Be smart. I need you to be smart."

She padded closer to him until all he could see were her eyes.

"Find me. You got in over your head, but you're not alone in that. There's another me here on Earth, and you're heading right for her. She doesn't look like me, she isn't like me, but she is me. You'll figure it out."

Something was twisting inside Fool, and he started to black out, his vision sparkling in dark little spots, filling in from the edges of his vision.

"Not even gods can do everything, Fool. Sometimes we don't even know what's best for us. Sometimes we just need a friend."

Fool's vision faded to black, and the void reached up to claim him.

"Follow the dancers, Fool. Find Lucy."

Blackness.

Chapter Three

Pain.

No pain.

Fool groaned, but it was mostly a confused groan. More of a mutter. Where was the pain? He should be in pain.

His eyes opened slowly. He'd been unconscious, but only for a few moments. There was a boot heel in front of his face, and it was attached to a boot. Jackal's boot.

Next to the boot was the head of the sub-boss that had been attacking him.

Fool had no idea how long he'd been unconscious for, but when he cautiously moved, he seemed to be mostly intact. He pulled up his Status Screen. Health was at about a third and Mana half. Marvelous.

Better than being dead.

He didn't look around but jumped up into a squat.

As he did, his hearing came back with a roar.

Literally.

Fool could now see that Jackal was next to him and still fighting the boss. The boss had let out the roar as Jackal had run it right through the center with both swords.

The boss was still standing. In pain, but standing. Fool had some empathy for that. He was still going to kill the thing though.

His warhammer was somewhere on the field, but there was no time for that.

With nothing left to save the Mana for, he activated Hammer of Loki again and charged past Jackal, who gave a joyful cry.

Fool had a hunch that a Frost Giant was stronger than a rock troll boss, and this seemed like the perfect time to find out. He didn't bother punching, just reached around the ankle of the boss and heaved.

What he expected to happen was that the rock troll would stumble around, maybe trip and fall. He was pretty sure the boss would be surprised by someone as small as Fool being able to lift it and probably wouldn't think to drive all its weight down on its foot until it was too late. That was Fool's hope.

Reality worked out differently, and Fool couldn't help but marvel at how the System broke physics completely once you got to a high enough level.

When he hoisted the troll, it went up. The whole creature. Fool had heaved it up in a semi suplex, and he froze awkwardly when he realized what he'd done. The only thing he could think to do was twist over to his side and drop the boss.

As he moved, the weight shifted, and Fool instantly found the limits of the strength boost the Skill gave him. The boss had been precariously balanced when Fool had done his lift, but as it flailed and twisted about in the air, the rotational forces added up and Fool had to let go as it all became too much.

Even rock trolls could twist an ankle, it turned out. When Fool let go of the boss, it landed squarely on the side of its foot, which folded in half until its ankle cracked into the ground. The troll let out a howl of pain and its leg buckled under it.

Jackal flashed up, not wasting a second of potential, swords slashing into the troll's head and neck. Then Fran and two other riders joined, lances and hooves battering into the beast's head.

A moment later, Fool felt a wave of relief when a notification popped up, rewarding experience for the assist in the boss kill and for ending the attacking wave. It wasn't a bad chunk of experience.

Suddenly he was airborne, what felt like far up in the air, and he couldn't breathe. His waist was being crushed by an enormous force.

"Let. Me. Down," he squeaked.

Jackal immediately relaxed his hug and spun Fool around and squatted, burying his giant head into Fool's chest. "Thought you were dead."

"Might have been. Out good, anyway. I take it you saved me? What happened?"

Jackal let out an enormous sigh and rocked back on his heels. His eyes were still wet, and he wiped them with the back of his hand. "Sorry. Just give me a minute." He took a big breath, then leaned forward and carefully hugged Fool again. "I'm not sure what happened. One moment I was up against the boss, the next the one you were fighting just kind of stumbled in front of me, and I saw you. Things went a little grey after that. What happened to you? I thought you had it all under control?"

Fool felt his face burning and a lie started to bubble up, but he killed it before it could get its legs. Wearily, he sat down and ran his hands through his hair, startled to realize that at some point in the fight, his ponytail had come loose.

"Dammit. That was my last hair elastic." He dug through his pockets for a bit but couldn't find anything. He looked up at a noise from Jackal and took the leather thong he was being offered. A moment later, he had his hair back in order.

"Right," Fool said. "I screwed up. Got cocky, misjudged how strong those things were and how hard they would hit. Wound up getting caught in a kill pocket, had to get out. Then wound up facing the sub-bosses, and just kinda… screwed up?"

Jackal shook his head. "Gonna have to keep a closer eye on you."

Fool grinned back. "I'm still new to this warrior thing. Figured I could just do your scream and leap and I'd be okay."

Jackal rolled his eyes but didn't reply, so Fool turned around to see who was approaching.

Fran sauntered up with a giant grin. "That was awesome! Great plan! Can't believe how well that worked. You guys are great to work with."

Fool looked at her with a cocked eyebrow.

"Seriously! We rolled those trolls up so fast, there has to be a record. And not even a serious injury to show for it. You called it perfectly. The trolls got so caught up trying to figure out who to fight. They didn't know what to do, and when you led them off on a chase? Stupid buggers turned their back on the wall to try to get you! Our support team was able to wipe them from behind in just two volleys. That was the best thing I've seen since we started this crap. We're gonna party tonight! Be talkin' about this for years."

Fool felt the powerful need to sit down again, but he was still sitting, so he just lay down on his back, happy to be able to flop like a fish.

The stars were out and shining brightly. Fran had assigned patrols on foot and in the sky, and Fool and Jackal were free to rest for the evening.

Fool had wandered up and down the bones of the town but hadn't found anything interesting. Just sadness. Broken and desiccated bones. Out of morbid curiosity, he'd examined one. It wasn't just dry and dead; it was slowly turning to stone. And had bits of moss on it already. After looking at it for a moment, he'd tossed it aside. The original owner was long past caring. He assumed the trolls had had some sort of Skill that gradually turned things into stone and moss. Maybe they ate the moss, and the moss only grew on stones? The System was spinning up a hundred mysteries for every one it solved.

Eventually, he settled on a boulder and looked at the stars. The moon was down, but the mountains could still be seen by their silhouette, and he caught the odd sparkle that sometimes came off of minerals or streams when the air played a trick on the light.

It was quiet. Peaceful, if you forgot the history of the place and the day and pretended the air wasn't thick with ghosts.

The mountains sat around as they always had, and Fool thought back to all the trips he'd made through this town in years gone by. It had been a ritual stop for his family, then for his friends. Last place to get gas for a while. Bathroom break. Hit up the restaurants for the all-important "road food" part of the trip.

He remembered once driving through with a girlfriend and deciding to spend the night. He'd imagined them walking through the streets of the town, exploring the river, just enjoying the experience. Instead, they'd crashed into a nap almost right away, then on waking, they had made love most of the night. That memory brought a smile to his face.

Memories were all that were left of that world. Not even a brick was left of that hotel. And that girlfriend had been lost to him for reasons he couldn't even really be certain of.

But the mountains had been there for all of it. He looked at them again, scanning from peak to peak, feeling the latent mass of them in the air all around him. These mountains had witnessed everything. They'd been there long before Fool's ancestors had ever arrived, and they'd been there to see the growth and end of modern civilization. They'd probably still be there after the System was gone, if such a thing was possible.

The mountains would remain, long after Fool ceased to be.

He felt a comfort in that. For a moment, he imagined he was one with the mountains, in an entangled observation. His life was just a flash to them, but they would remain forever. Perhaps because of that, the flash of his life would be entangled with theirs forever. If that was so, maybe it wasn't so bad that he might just fade away at some point.

Jackal sat down next to him, and the two of them sat without words for a time.

Eventually, Jackal nudged him, and Fool sighed. "Problems ahead. I screwed up."

Jackal nodded. "I assumed. Faith issues?"

"Yeah. One of my hunches came true. I figured DM was something like an avatar of the Trickster, not the Trickster itself. Which made me wonder if there was a potential for more than one avatar at a time. Turns out there is another, and it's in Vancouver."

Jackal made an indeterminate noise. Shifted a little. "I kinda thought maybe you were an avatar. Or on the path to becoming one."

That caught Fool off guard. He hadn't considered that. Hadn't considered what the end result of his path might be. Acolyte to Adept was as far as he'd ever bothered to consider. His previous life hadn't really prepared him for any sort of long-term planning. And that part of his status had never really been clear to him, as if it was obscured or hidden by the System or something else. A cloudy and unknown future had always seemed appropriate to him.

"I don't know. I don't think so. Not so sure how it works, but it seems to me that the avatars are like a bit of the Trickster that's been broken off, maybe? Somehow connected to the primary source, but independent? I know sometimes I'm connected through DM, and a few times I've been connected to the Trickster directly. It's the same but different, and I really don't have words to describe it. Make sense?"

A snort was the only response Fool got.

"Doesn't make any sense to me either. Anyway, we've got a problem. Maybe a big one. The other avatar seems to be in some kind of trouble and needs our help."

That made Jackal sit up straight. "That sounds… out of our league. Details?"

"None. Not even a sense of direction. I'm just supposed to keep my head on a swivel and figure it out myself."

"Perfect. Your church is not the most functional, you know."

Fool flung up his hands. "Not a church! You know this!"

Jackal's teeth gleamed in the moonlight. "You keep saying that. Weird words for a priest."

Fool bit back his retort, not being in the mood to let Jackal rile him up tonight. "I'm just saying, be ready for some weirdness, more than we expected."

"Not danger?"

"What, really? Were you not prepared for 'above and beyond' danger anyway?"

Jackal crossed his arms behind his head and stretched until his spine and shoulders popped. "Well, sure. That's part of being your partner. Keeps things interesting."

"You're a strange man, Jackal."

"Takes one to know one."

Chapter Four

Jackal watched Fool neatly vanish, and he smiled.

The older man's face had lit up like the morning sun when someone had mentioned that the mall had reopened the food fair. An enterprising group had figured they could make bank if they tried to recreate some of the previous restaurants, including a Taco Time. That was what had set Fool off. No hesitation, he took off running in the general direction.

Jackal figured the restaurant would make its profits off of Fool's visit alone.

He wasn't so eager himself and figured Fool would be safe enough without him for an hour. He probably wouldn't eat all of their stock in that time. Most of the troops were setting up in the makeshift stables that had been prepared for them in the former above ground parking lots. Jackal and Fool had come in as part of the leadership team for a brief meet-and-greet. The actual negotiations with the Vancouver representatives wouldn't happen until tomorrow. Being a large-ish military group, they hadn't been allowed inside Vancouver proper until they'd been vetted in person.

Festivities and random greeting activities would keep them busy for most of the rest of the day and evening. Jackal was happy the schedule kept him in the background. Vancouver and its environs seemed pretty happy to work their way back into being the center of the province, and delegates from even a tiny village like McBride were being treated like royalty. At least, that was the impression Jackal was getting.

The greeters were cheery and professional, but around them was a swirl of business, and the McBride group wasn't really being noticed. Burnaby had wound up rebuilding itself around the mall, and most of its population found itself in the old mall more often than not. An actual bustle of commerce was springing up.

When the tour came around to showing them the centerpiece of the mall, the Town of Burnaby's Shop, Jackal found himself lingering. The delegation moved on without noticing his absence, and he sat down facing the Shop entrance. His mind was filled with what it used to be.

A giant bookstore. One he'd spent much of his youth in. Most of his allowance had been spent on books, or on the sugary drinks the coffee shop inside had offered. He hadn't had a lot of friends, but sitting on the chairs around those shelves, skimming books and trying to decide which one to read next? It was a special kind of heaven. The nearby library was enormous and had a great selection of the fantasy and science fiction books Jackal preferred, but there was a special joy in choosing a book that would be yours forever. It was a winnowing process, and only the most intriguing books could get through. The library was for lesser books, books he wasn't sure of, or ones to be read for the sake of having something to read.

The bookstore? That was the treasure chest. That was the place where literal dreams came into his head from the crisp and dry pages. He'd first discovered tabletop role-playing games there, and his first group of non-school friends, browsing through the slick rules books. The library gave them a place to game when time permitted, a refuge he kept secret from his parents and their more prosaic demands on his time. And always they would come back to this store afterward, for more sugar and browsing.

Happiness. He'd had enough of it as a child, he thought. But the best of it was here.

Or had been.

He put his hand on his chest as he looked at the former entrance, now a glowing globe marking the entrance to the System Shop. No matter how he pressed, the ache in his chest wouldn't go away.

He was what he'd always dreamed of being, and a Shop much like this one was part of the reason. Still, here, he could only feel the bittersweet loss of what had been.

As he watched, a mother was walking toward the globe with her two children in tow. A young boy, looking surly and bored, and a young girl bustling with excitement. Jackal couldn't quite make out what the girl was saying, but he didn't need to.

She was hoping to purchase dreams.

He sighed and smiled a little. The little girl glanced at him and smiled back, and an unfamiliar ache opened up in him. He knew he wasn't old yet, but he'd still been through so much in life. He couldn't help but wonder what was next, now that his dreams had become real. What was there once the crisis was over, once the bigger mission was done? Was he just going to keep looking for something new to fight for? Or somehow find the right person and settle down? Retire like an old warrior to a monastic life of contemplation?

Rolling his shoulders and looking at the ceiling, Jackal let out a longer sigh. He was dwelling too much on a foolish thought. The universe had opened up for him when the System came, and there'd be no end of things to dream about now. It was up to him to learn to dream in new ways, to open his mind to further potentials.

Perhaps even find another metamorphosis and turn into something he couldn't imagine at the moment. Perhaps, like the last one, he'd have to learn a truth about who he really was first. Clearly, he wasn't ready for that just yet.

Something was nagging at him, something he couldn't put aside, and that had to be dealt with first.

Standing, he went off to find Fool. The food fair was supposed to be in a new location, not the old one. The escalator had been turned on again, and Jackal had to wonder at that. There was no need for such an aid to anyone in a System-powered world. Not really. A small quirk of the new world was a touch of physical equality. Fatigue and effort moderated by Mana and experience meant everyone was a little more physically able than before. Of course, not everyone was a combat specialist, so the top tiers—even the lower tiers—were still vastly separated from each other. But the average human had a more average level of fitness.

As a result, no one really struggled or even noticed stair steps anymore, unless there were a lot of them. But old habits die hard, and that was a lesson for Jackal. It was a habit, or someone's vanity wanting to show off how they could afford the Mana upgrades to the electrical systems in the mall. Walking off the escalator and glancing at himself in a mirror, Jackal had to admit there was a message for him there too.

His body mods, genetic enhancements, and Class Traits had completely transformed him into what he was now. He hadn't actually measured his height, but he had to be somewhere over two meters. He had surpassed his goal of being able to fill a doorframe completely many levels ago. There had been some relief in him when he reached his Advanced Class and the growth stopped. Turning into a veritable giant would have been a bit too much. Being a giant still-human was just fun.

The mirror made him smile even as he chastised himself for the ego. He'd wanted to be huge and strong. Being a walking slab of cheesecake was just a bonus. As was the way his hair had taken to forming thick, strong, tumbling curls.

The escalator rose to the next floor. The mirror had been a feature on the side of the railing, and his moment of ego caught up with him when the escalator reached the top of its ride. One moment he was looking at his grinning face, moving up in tandem, and the next he was looking into the amused face of an absolutely stunning person.

Pale complexion, tousled white-blond hair, with a build on the thin side of athletic. They were wearing a black-and-gold-trimmed bolero jacket over a white bodysuit, and the jacket was closed at the neck with a high, straight collar over the bodysuit's turtleneck. The eyes looking at him were an almost silvered grey, but that wasn't the most eye-catching part of the person. They had the androgynous perfection of a supermodel, which was arresting in and of itself. Not as much as the floating halo of dark, filigreed, and shaped metal shards that surrounded that face though. Combined with the ludicrously long, narrow, two-handed sword scabbarded at their side, the overall impression was alien. Jackal thought he was looking at a Beardsley figure come to life, only somehow more contemporary.

Jackal was struck by the thought that they'd been watching him from above, and he found himself making eye contact.

His heart fluttered. He walked off the escalator and turned toward them. They didn't change their posture at all, only quirking up an eyebrow. As he got closer, they stopped leaning against the railing long enough to cross their arms, then bumped a hip to the side to watch him get closer, with a little tilt of their head.

Jackal grinned. Partly in recognition that he was responding to an enhanced Charisma Skill, and partly because he recognized the look now that he was getting closer. His mind came back to him a little as he resisted the mental effect, but if anything, he was now more intrigued.

The look was a challenge. Maybe an invitation, but Jackal had no illusions about that. The System delivered looks and attraction to those who wanted it, and he'd eschewed that. He didn't lack for lovers, but that was from those who took the time to know him first. That was how he preferred it, but still. Sometimes the bright ones made him wish just a little that he could shine brightly enough to catch their eyes.

Yet somehow he'd caught this one's eyes, and it was time to find out why.

Jackal stopped a few arm's lengths away and leaned against the railing, crossing his arms comfortably. And carefully. The railing only came up to his hip. He didn't want to make the wrong impression by tumbling over.

A moment passed, no rush to speak apparent to either of them.

Jackal broke the ice. "P. Craig Russell?"

That brought a smile to the face of the watcher. "Absolutely an inspiration. You must be a fan. Let me guess… *The Ring?*"

Jackal shook his head slowly. Now that he was up close, he could sense that the watcher was a competent fighter, maybe even at his level. Jackal wasn't going to take a chance. "*Elric.* Friend introduced me."

A nod in response, then the watcher carefully dropped their left hand to their thigh. It had the effect of pushing the overlong hilt of their sword off to the side, making it much harder for them to draw it. At the same time, they extended their right hand forward. "Nicholaus."

"Jackal."

They grasped hands, and Jackal felt the smooth, tight strength of a sword fighter in Nicholaus's grip. No surprise, from the size of the weapon they carried. Using something that large and awkward would require some serious training.

Nicholaus held on for a second, his eyes running over Jackal in apparent appreciation. Jackal just held his smile and grip, happy to the let Nicholaus take the lead in the conversation.

"You're from one of the villages up north, right? With the flying cavalry? Come to be cops?" Nicholaus released his grip with the last word, raising an eyebrow and resting his hand back on his hip.

Jackal nodded, but he didn't say more.

Nicholaus looked him over again, then curled his fingers in a complicated gesture. He extended his hand to Jackal, and there was a card in it.

"An invitation," he said. "You don't look like a cop. Maybe you want to see the other side of the city before you commit. Bring a date, if you like. I don't mind sharing."

As soon as Jackal's fingers touched the card, Nicholaus spun about and walked off, not even waiting to see if the card fell or not.

Jackal held it in the tips of his fingers and watched as Nicholaus walked away. He couldn't help the little smile that crept up or the brief flush of appreciation for the walk.

Then he glanced at the card and resumed his hunt for Fool.

Jackal could see that Fool was in ecstasy.

He didn't even notice Jackal sitting down across from him, so Jackal took a moment to sit back and take it all in.

The food fair had been completely rebuilt in the new location, neon signs and all. Most of the restaurants were new but had only changed the signage, still using the cooking and prep setup of the previous tenants. Some had only paper signs up. The one Fool had chosen still had the original sign up, and it looked as though it had a stash of the previous restaurant's napkins and food wraps in stock, judging by the logo on the massive pile of discarded wrappers in front of Fool.

The clientele were fairly mixed. Mostly human, but a good number of aliens as well. The food seemed to come from all over, and every species seemed to be split amongst the restaurants. It was fairly busy, but not what it would have been in the days before the System. Maybe about as busy as a slow afternoon midweek. Which probably represented a noticeable portion of Burnaby and Vancouver's populations. Jackal figured that meant the food was good.

And he was hungry.

Fool's trays were loaded with round, deep fried tubes that seemed to be filled with meat. He had several small paper cups in front of him, filled with what had to be hot sauce, judging from what Jackal could smell. A number of small, open boxes had what Jackal recognized as tater tots.

It smelled great, so he grabbed one of the tots, half surprised that Fool didn't smack his hand. But Fool stopped him just before Jackal popped the morsel in his mouth.

"Hot sauce! Dip!" Fool gestured at the little paper cups and went back to somehow purring and eating at the same time.

Jackal did as he was told and dipped the potato nugget in the sauce, then ate it.

It wasn't bad. The sauce was smoky, with a peppery zing and touch of sweetness. Not that hot, but it balanced out the greasy salt of the deep-fried potatoes. He tried another, then another.

The heat built, and he sniffled a little. Each bite seemed to taste a little better than the previous, so he took another bite.

Fool was grinning at him. Jackal licked the salty oil off his fingers and pointed at one of the wrapped tubes piled up in front of the older man.

"Crisp meat burrito," Fool said. "Gotta eat 'em just right though. Rip 'em in half, dip 'em in the hot sauce from the inside out, save the crunchy meat for last."

Fool was showing as he was talking, dipping the former middle of one of the meat tubes in the hot sauce, and taking a small bite.

Jackal tried it. The tube, he noted as he removed the wrapper, was still hot. It looked like ground beef inside a deep-fried flour tortilla. Smelled good. He followed the instructions, careful not to let the cup overflow as he dipped the roll into it, then took a bite.

It wasn't great. The tortilla had been deep-fried to a pleasant crunch, but the ground beef filling was a bit bland. It blended well with the hot sauce though. The smoky heat added a much needed bit of flavor. He watched as Fool dipped his roll back in, careful to get the most sauce all over and in the meat, and bit only the bit that was covered. Maximum hot sauce coverage.

"Mm. Yeah. That's okay," he said.

"Damn straight," Fool said. "Best food in the world. I thought this was lost forever. I'm so full I think I'm taking hits on my health, but I can't stop eating."

"We'll be here a bit yet. You can come back later."

Fool snorted and took another bite. "Fuck that. Some things I'll take a chance on, not this."

Jackal didn't nod, but he took another bite. It was growing on him. Not great food, but he could understand how comfort food had a deeper hook than mere flavor. And not that bad.

He glanced around the food fair and didn't see any familiar faces. No one looking at them or paying them attention either. Aside from the usual pull that Fool's Charisma had, and his own size. Neither of which, these days, were all that unusual. There were bigger aliens, and at least two Triunnar elves who seemed to have a monopoly on all the Charisma in the place. They were as private as could be in a public place.

Jackal didn't do anything obvious, like lean forward or whisper, just kept his voice and look as normal as if he was talking about a book he'd just read. "Someone tried to recruit me. Got more than a few factions at play here."

Fool popped the crunchy meat end of his roll into his mouth, made an almost disturbing number of sounds of satisfaction, and finished by slapping his belly a few times. "That was great. I needed that. I'll take the rest back with me and finish them later. Any reason to worry?"

"Not yet. No secret we were coming. No surprise things here aren't as settled as we were expecting."

"No shit. Who needs cops if you haven't got rich people fucking other people over?"

Jackal didn't reply. His upbringing had been pretty good. The only interactions he'd had with cops had been pleasant. But the rest of his family? His cousins had had lots to say about the joy of being brown teenage boys in the middle of a moderate crime area. Fool had even more stories of bad times. Not that he didn't believe them. More that he felt like a nuanced approach was more sensible.

After all, in this case, they were the cops. Or at least, representing the cops.

The cavalry troops from McBride would not be those kinds of cops. From what Jackal had heard, the folks trying to unify and run Vancouver weren't interested in those kinds of cops either. And the Foundation had prepared a contract that would prevent the cavalry from being used in an abusive fashion, or even taking part in any kind of systematic oppression.

That didn't mean anyone local had any reason to trust them. Yet. The contract hadn't been signed yet, so no one outside of the negotiators and the people they represented really knew what was in the contract. And it was always possible that someone in the System galaxy had a loophole, so why trust? It made better sense to be reserved.

Fool covered his mouth and let out a satisfied little burp. "I suppose it's our job to play along then. What's the deal so far?"

"Honeypot, maybe. The tour was being watched by an attractive young man, made himself known to me. Left a card and an invite to attend."

Fool took the card, read it, and flipped it over. Turned it back and forth a few times and spun it through the air back to Jackal. "Twisted Chapel. I'm going to guess that's a nightclub. Goth-looking kid?"

Jackal thought about that for a moment. "Not quite. Strong style, more baroque. Detailed. Like cosplay, but more... I suppose less costume and more clothes, if that makes sense."

"Queer?"

Jackal rolled his eyes. "Gramps." Fool stuck out his tongue, and Jackal grinned at the point scored. "They seemed human, but I wouldn't bet a large amount on that."

Fool ruminated for a bit, but Jackal couldn't tell if he was thinking or trying to get a piece of food out of his teeth. He made a little sucking noise, leaned forward on an elbow, and looked up at Jackal through his eyebrows. "Didn't mean that in any kind of label way, but I'm thinking. Back in my day, before things got all mainstream, we used to have underground nightclubs. A place to be amongst your own people. Let your hair down a little. Take off the masks and not be normal for a few hours. Dressing up was a part of that, but it wasn't for show. It was a way to show who you were. To stand out. Some kickass dancing too. Just got a hunch this might be something like that."

Jackal looked up and thought. "Might be. Tonight?"

"Sure. You get a location?"

Jackal shook his head. "Just the card. I think it might be enough. Nicholaus said it was an invitation."

"Nicholaus, huh? Darling Nikki?"

Fool looked disgusted at the lack of comprehension on Jackal's face. Jackal just screwed his face up in resignation, accepting that he was going to have to sit through another music history lecture from Fool. He didn't really mind. Most of the stuff Fool listened to was pretty good.

Fool muttered something about age. "Anyway. You think the card is some kind of beacon or homing device?"

Jackal nodded. "I get the impression the place can't be found without an invitation."

"Interesting. Because I get a hunch this is related to my small 'q' quest."

That put Jackal back, and he nodded after thinking about it for a bit. "Chapel. Twisted Chapel. That sounds like a Trickster's church. Makes sense."

"Huh. Hadn't made that connection. Just kinda figured that things were gonna get real confused real fast, and this feels like the start of that."

Jackal could only groan in acknowledgment. Fool's pat on his back as the older man walked past him wasn't all that soothing either. He still did his best to shrug off his trepidation as he followed his friend.

Warriors needed to be free of attachments when dancing with Tricksters.

Chapter Five

Fool found he preferred Metrotown the way it was now to the way it had been before. Maybe not before, before—when he'd been young, successful, and happy. It had been the big mall back then, and he'd loved nothing better than spending an afternoon window shopping through it. Taco Time, maybe a cinnamon bun. Ogle the new computers, check out the pet store, spend some hours in the bookstore, buy some borderline goth clothes at Le Château to impress the ladies. That had been okay. He had splendid memories of those times.

In the last few years before the System? He'd taken the chance sometimes to scrounge some food, but the security guards were assholes. It wasn't hard to see why. The place had completely changed. A packed little epicentre of consumerism, with a seedy underbelly of crime. And criminals who weren't too picky about who they preyed on. Hell, just about everyone in there had been happy to get some kicks in on a homeless guy looking for a handout.

He'd gone in once, when he'd scored some money and a cleanup, in a lucid phase. The Taco Time was long gone, replaced by some hipster cali-mex joint. The interesting little restaurants were gone and replaced by more typical chain shops. All with lineups. He'd skipped those and gone to the cheap Indian place, the one with no lineup. The food had been good there. Filling, but not so much that he saved any for later.

After he'd eaten, he had leaned over one of the railings and watched the people walk around. It was the only entertainment he could afford, but it was also something he'd always enjoyed. But all he saw were scuttling consumers, racing from place to place. It had depressed him enough that he'd slid right back into a dark phase. He'd never enjoyed watching people reduce themselves to creatures of enforced habit, especially not when that habit took over what should have been an act of casual pleasure.

The pleasure was back in the mall now. It was a safe place, a System Shop, and a place for artisans to make and trade goods. It had a cheerful buzz, better than what he recalled. Fool wasn't ready to move down from McBride, but he could see the appeal for big city survivors. This had all the makings of being something magical in time. More like the dream of a village square or a farmers' market on steroids.

Jackal caught the smile. "Should I be worried?"

"Probably. But no, that's not why I'm smiling. Just thinking about change. Always sucks in the short term. Even the good changes. But if you're lucky, the change makes everything better. Even with that, you still have to embrace the change before you can really grow into it. Have to accept that the world and you are different, and you're making a new world. It looks like that's happening around here."

Jackal said nothing, so Fool glanced at him. The big man was looking around with a thoughtful expression, so Fool let him keep to his thoughts. If Jackal had anything to add, he would say something, and Fool was content to see what the seed sprouted later.

For now, Fool had to figure out what to do next. They had to find this Twisted Chapel place to start. Or was it the start? He wasn't really sure, but something had made him get up and walk. A tiny hunch that made his feet itch. Not the hunch that came from an outside source, but something in his subconscious that was prying at him.

Whatever it was, he figured it was better to go along with it instead of trying to figure out what the hell it was. Get up and follow his feet. That was what his brain told him to do.

And then it hit Fool. His feet were taking him toward the far end of the mall. An old habit. If they walked the way, they'd exit out toward where the Skytrain was. Or used to be. The rapid-transit light rail would have had them downtown in less than half an hour.

He couldn't imagine the Skytrain would be running anymore. Getting that thing running required a massive investment in infrastructure. It was a complex network of power and timing that likely would not be rebuilt anytime soon.

But his feet still said it was the way to go, so he kept walking. The little voice in the back of his head was getting clearer. They had to get downtown. There was something he was remembering from downtown.

There was another food fair there, and another Taco Time, but he didn't think that was it. It was something else. Something underground.

He hadn't even realized he'd tapped a local on their shoulder. But they turned and looked at him with a quizzical eyebrow, so he blurted out the first thing that came to his mind. "What's the best way to get downtown from here?"

"Skytrain," the local replied.

Fool nodded his thanks and picked up the pace, continuing in the same direction. Apparently the locals had put the work in.

"Downtown?" Jackal asked.

"Yeah. Hunch. Not sure why."

"Fran would fly us." Jackal's tone had that weary tone that came out when he knew Fool would not accept any advice.

"Yeah. No. Gotta go this way. Dunno why."

Fool sped up a little more, not from a sense of urgency, but to clear the block in his head with action. Something downtown, but he couldn't pull the memory. It wasn't really blocked, but his mind seemed to distract him with other thoughts when he tried to focus on it. He bit the end of his tongue gently in frustration and let out a little puff of exasperation. The direction felt right. He was confident that the back of his brain knew the best place to go to find the Twisted Chapel. That part was fine.

It was more like something was buried, some memory associated with wherever his feet were taking him, and his brain was reluctant to free that memory while it still had the chance to keep it buried.

While he was struggling with his brain, his feet carried him all the way to the outside of the mall. The Skytrain line was still intact, if rough-looking. The same sweeping concrete pillars and bridges, unchanged since the eighties, but now with System-altered moss and vines working their way up the sides. A brief wave of déjà vu struck him, and he recalled seeing this same view from a different angle decades ago.

He'd been having tea with his great-grandmother in a cafe. They hadn't been talking about much in general, just family and health—the things you talked about with older relatives. He'd caught her looking up at the SkyTrain, just a glance, and he turned to look over his shoulder to see what had caught her eye.

Nothing was going on. It was just the SkyTrain passing overhead. A rolling rumble that he'd long since ignored. Then he saw what she saw, which was the same thing but from a different perspective. She'd been born in pre-war Paris, and her earliest memories were of that city.

He'd found himself looking through her eyes. The SkyTrain was just another part of the infrastructure to him, but to her, it was a science-fiction future become reality in her lifetime. It had humbled him to think that, and it had given him a new appreciation for how far the world had come and how lucky he was to be alive at this time.

And now that same structure looked to be on the edge of failure and less like something out of a sci-fi movie than like something out of a post-apocalyptic movie. Which was, he had to admit, accurate.

He was thinking of finding another way downtown when he noticed a small lineup at the foot of the stairs going up to the main platform. Just a few people, but they looked as if they were paying someone and heading up.

Jackal followed Fool across the road, and Fool silently laughed at how the two of them glanced both ways first. That was a trained reflex that wasn't so useful anymore.

They got in line behind the last three people. No one in front of them said anything. Just walked up, waved their hands over what was clearly some sort of payment device, and went in and up the stairs.

When Fool walked up, he noticed that the gatekeeper wasn't exactly human. Mostly, but they had what looked like a short, fine, and dense fur covering their skin. And faceted eyes, almost like an insect, but more like a princess-cut diamond.

Fool wasn't really sure what his great-grandmother would think of this. It might even remind her of Paris.

"Downtown?" he asked.

The gatekeeper nodded and held up two fingers. A notification popped up telling Fool that the fee would be a reasonable twenty credits, so he imitated everyone else and waved his hand over the device the gatekeeper held up. His savings went down by twenty credits, and a green arrow popped up at the edge of his vision.

Jackal paid without comment, and they walked up the stairs to the right, following the arrow. When they got to the top of the platform, the arrow faded. Fool noticed that most of the folk he'd seen lined up were waiting at the side of the platform, and the rest were on the other side of the rails.

Except, instead of two rails, there was now a single rail, and it was unusually shiny. Fool glanced up and down the tracks and didn't see anything coming. Or going. At least the tracks looked in much better shape than they had from the ground. The concrete sidings didn't look exactly clean, but the track itself and the trackway looked pristine.

A moment later, something that looked like a single SkyTrain car pulled up. Instead of being automated, there was a driver of the same species as the gatekeeper. As the vehicle pulled up, stopped, and opened the doors, Fool saw that it was actually an old SkyTrain car. Same crumbly old seats and everything. He figured the driver and his friends must have refitted them to run on whatever System-powered setup was currently in place.

It felt just like old times, stepping in and sitting down in an empty bench seat, facing into the center of the car. Most of the other folk grabbed the forward- or backward-facing seats, but Fool always got motion sick if he read while facing forward. And he always read on transit. He had nothing to read now, but the habit stuck anyway. Jackal took a seat opposite him, but turned to look out the window as the train car moved the second the doors closed.

Fool gulped a little. The car was faster than a SkyTrain. A lot faster.

The next station blurred by, and the car kept accelerating. He turned to look out the window, but they were whipping by at breakneck speed. The only real scenery he could see were the mountains and the more distant parts of the city.

No time for reading on this trip.

He realized he hadn't asked where downtown the ride would stop. The old Skytrain line had had a ton of stops along the way and nearly a half-dozen downtown.

It looked as though he'd learn pretty quickly though. With a wrench, the high acceleration stopped, and the train decelerated. Judging from the stations still whipping past, he figured they'd be stopping at the old Stadium-Chinatown station. He'd planned to get off at the Granville station, but they could do the short walk to wherever it was his feet wanted to go.

A moment later, they were slowing down into the Stadium-Chinatown station.

The reason the train car wasn't going any farther was clear.

The tunnel leading under the city was nothing but a pile of rubble.

As was the portion of the city on the other side. Some of the office towers were down, and from what Fool could tell, the rubble was from them. He couldn't imagine what would cause that, but it looked as if the entire area had selectively dropped into a bit of a sinkhole and the towers had crumbled down. It might take them longer to get to where they were going than he'd thought.

In any case, nothing was to be done about it, so he followed everyone else off the train and up the stairs.

When they got up to the top, he saw that the rubble was covering most of the area, but the roads had all been cleared. It wasn't close to as busy as it used to be, but for post-System Earth, it was almost bustling.

He paused to get his bearings, and Jackal stopped next to him. Fool looked over and found himself glancing at Jackal's twin swords. He'd settled on them as his personal blades since hitting Advanced Class and had some kind of bond to them. Fool hadn't really asked, but if nothing else, the way Jackal's hands kept touching the handles unconsciously reinforced his belief.

For some reason, seeing that right now gave him some comfort.

And then he knew exactly where they were going.

He must have broadcast that, because Jackal turned to look at him. "Figured it out?"

"Yeah. Dancing. We're going dancing."

They weren't actually going dancing, Fool had to explain. They were going to watch dancers. He didn't explain more. It would make more sense when they got there, and Jackal was patient enough to wait.

The city had seen better days. From what Fool had been told, the Thirteen Moon Sect had started a fair bit of rebuilding, taking advantage of their near-slave-labor grip on the population. If Fool, Jackal, and crew hadn't tripped up one of their main plans for the region, the Sect would still be in charge of the city.

Instead, it was now owned by some Adventurer dude who was off causing all kinds of havoc in other places. Apparently, he'd nearly single-handedly wiped out the rest of the Sect and freed Vancouver. Had scarpered off shortly after. It sounded as though he'd set up the current ruling system before leaving, and part of what Fool and Jackal were in the city for was to evaluate the impact of what was going on. Things had moved fast, and the Foundation had concerns.

So far, the impact had been aligned with their plans, but had screwed their timetable all to hell and back. The Professor had declined to share the specifics of that timetable with Fool, but he was clearly pretty miffed. That struck Fool as petty, but also typical for the Foundation. They planned to do things, but they weren't so good at planning for things to happen.

Regardless, the current management seemed to be working hard to build the place back up into a major population center. The area near the SkyTrain station was wrecked, but once they got past that, things cleaned up rapidly. The skyscrapers were a mixed bag. Many of them had windows blown out and looked wrecked, but there were signs of life everywhere.

The population looked to be booming from the amount of construction and rebuilding happening. As they got closer to Granville Street, there were more and more signs of commerce and little neighborhood communities shooting up. Mixed species too. Mostly clustered in their own little areas, but Fool wasn't surprised to see kids of many species running around in packs, causing trouble. That made him smile. Hope for the future, there. Troublemakers.

Granville Street itself was a better version of what it used to be. It had always aimed to be the heart of the city, but much like Vancouver itself, it really had no idea what that actually meant. Or what it really was. It had been the "Theatre Row" of the city, then a pedestrian mall, then an "Entertainment District." It had always tried to present itself as being more than it was, but the seedy underbelly always grew out into daylight.

Now it was vibrant, and the vibrancy came from a chaotic blend of shops and beings making a living and just coexisting. It was the good parts of commerce all come together in one cheerful buzz. There was no order or design to the place, aside from the sidewalks and street itself, mostly being respected as a place where travel happened. No concession was made for any kind of vehicle priority though. A car would never be able to make it through the tangled weave of pedestrians and single-stall shops. Scooters and motorbikes and a few riders mounted on smaller beasts were visible. And one guy on a ten-speed bike, happily eating something that looked like an ice-cream cone, if the cone was a tentacle.

Jackal was gawking, and Fool had to grab him to nudge him back on the trail. Now that his hunch had solidified somewhat, he was eager to get to his destination. It wasn't the hideaway thought that was still in the back of his head, but it was the next step. The sooner they got there, the sooner he'd figure out what the next step might be. Besides, if things were still going the way he had a hunch they were, Jackal was really going to enjoy the destination more than Granville Street.

Robson Street was just ahead and turned west. One more block.

Robson Street was, outwardly, just as Fool remembered. To the right was the Art Gallery, with its expansive concrete plaza, which continued across Robson to the Law Courts. The juxtaposition of the theoretical artistic center of the city with its legal heart had been an intentional design choice by someone. Fool had heard that it was supposed to represent a balance of the two, but in his experience, it had reinforced that the law and the arts were for rich people, and they loved to have monuments to how wonderful they were. Especially if those monuments were inaccessible in every way to the poors.

To really hit the point home, they'd built a below-ground ice rink between the two locations. That wasn't normally too bad of a thing, because Vancouver was still Canada. But the placement made it rarely used by the general public, and as a result, the open space got used for other purposes for most of the year.

Being a weird, somewhat hidden part of the city, but still centrally located, meant it was ripe for a takeover. While Fool had still been living in the city, a pretty unique group had managed that takeover.

At any part of the day, you could head to the rink, or look down on it from any of the many open vantage points, and see street dancers of various types hard at work, practicing and drilling endlessly. They had made the place their own by constant use.

Fool took the path to the left, toward the Law Courts. There were quicker ways to get to the underground ice rink, but in a System world, he wasn't a fan of going down unknown, snug, winding staircases if he could avoid it. Besides, the view had always been better this way.

It still was. They crossed over into the Law Court plaza, with the defunct waterfall (Fool couldn't remember the thing ever working, it was always under maintenance) on one side and the stairs on the other. The stairs were a work of art. They stretched the entire width of the plaza and down into the underground space. They were intercut with a winding ramp that went from side to side. The small offices and ticket booth off to the right looked as decrepit as ever, but on the left the lights were still on, and that interested Fool. The other part of the ice rink was the entrance to a surprisingly large downtown annex to UBC.

The dancers were the best part. Still were.

The tiny *thud-thud, tish-tish* of the music hadn't changed at all. Just loud enough to dance to, but not so loud as to drown out other dancer's choices. The moves though? Those had changed.

A small group was practicing at the moment, all human and young-looking. At first, it looked to Fool as though they were still dancing the old dances.

One b-boy was working his six-step, shuffling about in a circle, and flipping from face down to face up as he circled. He moved into his power-move set, spinning about on his shoulders, and bounced up to single hand and double hand spins.

Fool was impressed. That took tons of strength to pull off, and tons of time training. It warmed his heart to see the old school stuff, and he was wondering if the street dancers were kin in spirit to the Mountaineers Guild, choosing to eschew System enhancements to keep the purity of the art form.

The b-boy broke that illusion pretty quickly though. He dropped back from his hands to his shoulders, still spinning… then he rose in the air. Fool thought he could almost make out a transparent silverish disc under the dancer's shoulders, giving him some sort of support as he rose.

Regardless, the illusion of a floating, spinning human was amazing, whether the dancer was supported by a flying platform or not. Then it got better. The dancer kicked his feet and bounced off of some invisible surface, then ricocheted around what looked like an invisible cube. It was like watching a mime do the lame box trick. Only in this case, it looked as if the trick was being done in three dimensions by a traceur—a parkour expert. And all in perfect time to the music.

The faint silver disc had disappeared, and Fool was struggling to figure out how the dancer was doing this trick. He thought maybe it was some sort of force-field box, but then the dancer made a mistake. When they kicked out to bounce off of the surface, their foot went right through. They let out an awkward squawk and thumped down on the smooth concrete to the joyful laugher of their fellow dancers.

Fool sat on the steps to watch the action for a while. This was where he wanted to be, but he still didn't really know why. Aside from a vague sense that if it was a nightclub they were looking for, then the dance community was the place to do some research.

For the next half an hour, they watched the trio practice more. Fool was impressed by how they incorporated System Skills into their dance routines, and more than once he heard a grunt from Jackal. He'd only had to glance at the warrior to see that he was taking mental notes on things to integrate into his fighting style.

Fool was doing the same thing. Now that he had some actual fighting skills, he was paying more attention to how different people practiced.

Some folk just sparred. Some people found a sturdy something to hit over and over. Some people did old-school martial arts forms.

These kids? These dancers? They were doing something a little different. They were dancing and fighting all at the same time. It had taken Fool a bit to see it, but once he did, he couldn't see it any other way. They were fighting imaginary foes, but also somehow cooperating with them. It was almost like a rehearsal for fight choreography, but without acting out injuries.

And always to the beats and rhythm of the music. More than once, Fool found himself swaying along with the action, reacting not just to the music, but to the imaginary foe the dancer was up against. It was almost as though he could feel the blows coming.

Eventually, the group stopped, flopping about the concrete, chatting, laughing, and opening their bags to share food and drink with each other. While they'd been finishing up, other dancers had arrived. Some of the other groups were warming up, some were doing solo or group dance moves, and Fool got up. It seemed like the right time to head down and start some conversations.

That was when the vampires showed up.

Chapter Six

Maybe not actual vampires, but to Fool, they looked the part.

Five men, tall, lean, and severe to a fault, all of them. Three of them had prominent white, full beards. Of those three, one was bald and had a fur of some animal draped across his shoulders. Another had matching white hair to the beard, but in a ponytail. The last of the three beards had shoulder-length white hair, but skin that was a vibrant slate grey. Fool figured him for one of the dark elves he'd heard were common up north. The other two figures were both bald, one with a short and business-like mustache, the other free of any hair that could be seen. All wore perfectly tailored black suits. The two without beards sported short red ribbons with a large cross-shaped medal instead of ties.

When they stepped down from the stairs on the far side, all the dancers went silent, stood, and moved to the sides. Fool felt Jackal tensing beside him.

The quintet didn't stop to look at anyone. They just walked to the center of the space.

They'd come down the stairs with an arrogant stride, but the closer they got to the center, the more their steps synced. By the time they reached the middle of the space, they were in military lockstep.

When they stopped, they were in perfect formation, and almost seemed to stare right at Fool.

The bald figure without a beard was in the center. His eyes were stern—severe, to match the sharp axe of a nose. The suit jacket he wore was cut with a simple band collar, and his lips formed a thin frown. After a brief pause, he nodded.

The music started. Not from any source Fool could see, so he chalked it up to some System Skill.

The vampires danced. Just a slow sway to start, to match the eastern-tinged goth music. Nothing more than that, but Fool couldn't look away. It was like being a bird hypnotized by a snake. No Skill though. Just old-fashioned skill and dance training.

A new beat started, something electronic with a drone in the background, and now some footwork was added to the sway. A slight shuffle, a brief movement of the feet. They added a little roll to the shoulder.

It was otherworldly. Any one of the five would have fit in standing in the lobby of the fanciest hotel you could imagine. Or standing at the side of royalty. They gave off an impression of wealth and extreme danger. You could imagine them moving through a crowd of enemies like John Wick. You could imagine all of that. But not them dancing. And yet, there they were.

The dance picked up in tempo and energy. They moved, stepped, swayed, stomped in perfect unison. There was a powerful sensuality to their movements that was rooted firmly in the concept of masculinity. They stripped all the rigidity, the restraint, the reserve, out of what that would normally mean, and instead tapped into the older parts. In their proud head movements, they brought out echoes of warriors past, and in the hands, the tender touch of lovers. As the music picked up in tempo, the legs and feet exploded into motion, carrying them back and forth across the space in an ecstasy of motion that echoed of playful pride and explosive preening display.

All without changing one eyelash of the stern facial expression.

When the music came to a crashing stop, the quintet crashed their feet into the ground with a stunning clap that shook the entire area. A wave of power came off of them, and Fool could almost taste the Mana charge of the Skill in use. It echoed down into the pit of his stomach.

They froze in place in dead silence.

Then all the watching dancers erupted in applause, and Fool was not at all surprised to see Jackal start forward. That display of masculinity could not have been tailored better to attract him. He'd either be trying to find one of the members to bed or to teach him how to move like that. Probably both.

Everyone froze though, as the central figure held up his hand.

"If you think you are worthy, the next round starts tomorrow. The winning crew will be offered a unique, one-time favour from the divine Ms. Brightside."

He looked across the gathered dancers, then looked right at Fool.

And vanished. All of them did. Like a frame cut out of a film, one moment there, the next gone.

The dancers exploded into action, yelling and grabbing each other, everyone talking over everyone else, and other dancers came pouring out from the old university side to share in the news.

Jackal turned to look at Fool and shrugged. He looked almost hurt, but still too hungry for more to really let it get a hold of him.

Fool grinned at him. "C'mon. I bet that was an invite to the Twisted Chapel."

Jackal raised an eyebrow in agreement, and they started down the steps, walking up to the first group they'd seen when they arrived.

Fool didn't waste any time with introductions. "You guys are pretty good. Gonna go for it?"

The group didn't quite freeze, but the chatter slowed a little, and they all turned slightly toward each other and away from Fool and Jackal. Nothing obvious, but still a clear sign they'd rather not talk to strangers. One of them took the lead and shuffled forward a bit, making himself a block in front of his group.

He gave the interlopers a quick once-over. "Thanks. You guys movers? Haven't seen you before."

Fool shook his head. "Just fans. Heard about the chapel, figured we'd check out some of the local scene before heading there tonight."

One of the other dancers leaned forward to interject. "No fans allowed there. Movers and dancers only. If you ain't got an invite, you're S.O.L., buddy."

That ended the conversation completely. The group turned their backs on the two of them and kept chatting away.

Fool decided to try the direct approach. He walked up to another group and just flat-out asked them where the Twisted Chapel could be found. They didn't even say no, just repeated the turning of their backs.

A young woman walked up to them after that. "Ain't no one gonna tell yah, boomer. Move on." She walked away after that, heading off to the underground university entrance.

Fool took the hint and nudged Jackal. They walked across the space and up the steps on the far side, up to the plaza by the Art Gallery. He found a bench and sat down, and Jackal joined him.

"Any kind of luck with that card yet? A pull or anything?"

Jackal shook his head in the negative, pulling it out to look at it for a bit, then passed it over to Fool. "Challenge as well as an invitation, I'm thinking."

Fool took the card. Smelled it, tossed it from hand to hand, looked up at it while blocking the sun with it to see if it had any sort of hidden features. Finally, he sighed and gave it back to Jackal. "Yeah, I think you're right. Something weird about all of this. I took a chance and ran 'Talent Scout' on some of the dancers. Some weird shit going on there. All of their Skills seem performance based… no fighting skills, no crafting skills. But somehow, they've got some decent levels. It's almost like there's a second System that applies to them or something."

"Not likely," Jackal said. "But the System is complex, and from what I gather, the Galactic Council seems to have a hand in making some of the rules. I might be wrong about that, but if it's true, then it's entirely likely there are some loopholes in the setup."

Fool grinned. "Yeah, that makes sense. I like it. Hack the System. Figured some little buggers would find an exploit or two and work it to their advantage. Ha…" He stopped and looked around, then grunted and turned back to Jackal. "Figures. It wasn't far from here, when I was working in IT, that I hung out with a group of hacker folks. Kinda cool to see that same energy showing up again in the same place."

One side of Fool's mouth lifted in happiness as he reminisced about the old days. Maybe that was why he had been driven back here. Maybe some part of his brain remembered not just the dancers but the hackers too. And it made sense that he would come down here, because this was the area where the community had come together for him, because this was where…

The memories came back to him in a flood, and the wave rolled over him long enough that Jackal eventually set his hand on Fool's shoulder.

"You okay?" he asked.

Fool took in a deep, near-sobbing breath, then let it out in a long sigh. He looked up, and for a moment, he thought he saw a figure watching them. A wraith, a woman wrapped in a cloak, strawberry-blond curls whipped by the wind to cover to her face… and then gone.

Fool looked a moment longer, just long enough to realize it was only his own mind that made that image appear. The real woman was long, long gone.

But his heart had never let go.

"Memories," he said.

Jackal gently squeezed his shoulder, then took his hand back, letting Fool sit with his thoughts for a bit.

Fool let his mind blank out. He couldn't bury the memories, but he wasn't ready to let them all out yet. Instead, he stood and let the world flow around him, and his thoughts drifted off to emptiness.

Breathe in, the soft wind, the sounds of people walking about and getting on with their lives, and the constant, sure presence of Jackal.

It stopped eventually. He stood up then. Best thing was to keep moving. Besides, they had a job to do. Fool wasn't sure what the job was just yet, but he felt some momentum building. Ever since his little sidestep with death in Hope, he'd felt a crackling buildup of something growing, like a storm brewing just over the horizon.

"Good to go?" Jackal asked, concern tinging his voice.

"For now. Either way, it's just a thing from the past. I'll deal with it later. For now, let's head back to Granville Street and ask around, see if anyone has heard of this place and can point us in the right direction. I don't think there's a rush on this. I'm curious now."

"Fran should be okay without us for the day."

"Good point. Today was supposed to be checking out Vancouver. Negotiations start tomorrow, so I guess we've got the night. Let's see what we can find."

Fool couldn't help a slight sense of frustration as they walked back to Granville. He'd been so sure they were going in the right direction. That feeling in his gut had driven him all the way down here with overriding purpose, and in the end? All it had amounted to was a fun show and the re-opening of something he'd rather forget all over again.

He'd trusted his gut. Apparently, his gut had been craving a whole lot of grief over an ex, and he was, he had to admit to himself, feeling more than ashamed by that. Jackal probably had an inkling of what was up, but without the details, he'd keep it to himself. The two of them had had more than a few late night talks about the bad stuff in their past, and Jackal wouldn't pry. Fool knew that part of the reason was that Jackal trusted Fool to share when the time was right.

And he would. Part of keeping his brain working well was having someone to share the dark stuff with. The ugly things, the shameful things… the hurtful things. The reboot he'd taken advantage of when the System, and the Trickster, had offered it had helped a lot, but the maintenance was on him. He'd been given enough sanity to understand how to manage his brain, but understanding didn't replace hard work.

Which meant later, he and Jackal would have a good long sit-down over a drink or ten, and Fool would share all about the first time his heart got broken.

It was only two blocks to get back to Granville, and they were out of sight of the Art Gallery in minutes.

Neither of them had lingered long enough to watch the woman in the cloak come down the steps of the Art Gallery, her ringleted grey hair all that was left of a bright strawberry-blond.

Kantele walked up out of the ocean like a dreadnought of old. Not in size—even in her red and white armor, she was only barely topping what was normal height for females on this planet. And it wasn't rage either. There was rage in her, but she'd learned long ago to bury that deep inside, compact it into a fuel that charged up the engine that drove her on.

It was that engine that drove off the few hardy fisherfolk when she emerged from the waters. The aura of indomitable will and dedicated purpose rolled off of her, clear as a storm cloud on the horizon.

Her armor had repaired itself, and she'd healed up from Lucy's blow on the first day. The problem she'd run into was that the Mana-fueled punch had blown her not just clean across the city, but nearly across the entire Salish Sea. She'd plummeted down into the depths and sunk into the mud at the bottom. She'd never learned to swim, and even if she had, it would have been pointless. Her mass was much too high to give her any kind of flotation. She'd been forced to walk across the bottom of the sea back to Vancouver.

The soft, deep, sticky, muddy bottom of the sea. Which was also filled with more than its share of System-mutated creatures.

The only benefit of her two-day walk was that she'd leveled up, thanks to a nest of some kind of gigantic octopi. The hideous things had actually built an underwater village, complete with an immense nursery. If she hadn't crushed every one of those boulder-sized eggs, the city of Vancouver would have been cephalopod food before another year had passed. The System had rewarded her discovery of the cephalopod village with a quest to destroy it, and the completion bonus had been enough to push her up one more level. Her luck that they were all sentient creatures and worth more.

Two days underwater had pushed the limits of even her armor's ability to keep her alive though. She took a moment to crack her helmet loose and breathe in the musty rot smell of the seashore. Better than the stale and thickening air in the helmet, but not a place she'd care to be in for long. A quick cleanse spell cleaned all the dreck off of her armor, even drying the remaining water.

With a sigh, she pulled off her gauntlets and stuffed them into her helmet. There was a convenient log high on the shore, and she let herself have the luxury of sitting down for a moment.

Time passed.

The sun wasn't high in the sky anymore, but it was the warm season for this part of the world, so she had plenty of time before the night. And she had the beach to herself. She'd walked up on what appeared to be a gigantic spit, splitting the sea off from a large river that the city lay on the other side of. The side of the spit she was on faced a small bay, and across the bay was some sort of spaceport. Probably an airport, given the primitive nature of the inhabitants. They'd clearly been doing their best, but without the benefits of the System, that wasn't very good at all.

Still, it was oddly pretty. And soothing. Aside from the stench.

There was no point in putting it off anymore. She scrubbed her eyes with her palms, then ran her hands through her hair. She had a wild moment of rage, of wanting to bury her face in her hands and scream, but she held it off. A strong deep breath, then holding her hands out in front of her to make sure they were steady. Strong. Strong enough. She was ready.

Time to call the boss.

All it took was a little click on a ring. A small notification popped up, and she was in the queue for attention. Kantele didn't think she had long to wait. The Weaver had an uncountable number of projects on the go, but anything to do with the Trickster was usually high on his priority list. She took a moment to confirm that no locals were left in the area, then took a breath and composed herself.

The glowing blue face of the Weaver popped up only a few minutes later. He didn't speak, just looked expectantly toward Kantele. She only paused for a moment, taking in the Legendary member of the Galactic Council. He had no tolerance for dissembling or excess politeness. Only information as accurate as Kantele could give it. But even with that in mind, experience had taught Kantele it paid to determine his mood first, so she could prioritize the information order she presented him.

His main eyes were staring at her with a passive, emotionless regard. The seven eyes that ringed his face were darting around, and she could see the slightest glow of reflected information screens flickering in them. From that, she inferred he was in the middle of a working session. It was likely that a large part of his attention was elsewhere. That was good. With her emotions in turmoil, his full attention would be unwanted. He might decide that she wasn't up to the task. She'd invested too much in her position to risk that.

"I've found the avatar. You were correct. The Trickster has manifested here on the new Dungeon World. There were two avatars, but I cannot sense or find a trace of the other anymore. I believe it has chosen to be assimilated by the primary avatar in order to increase their Skill and Ability pool."

The Weaver didn't respond, aside from a slight flicker in his eyes. Kantele bit back the urge to rush forward. Concise information. That had been grilled and even beaten into her once.

"I attempted, as you instructed, to warn them off, but was struck hard enough that it has taken me some time to recover and contact you. They are extremely powerful."

That got a slight shake of the head and a dismissive noise from the Weaver. "Are you going to need more help? Do I have to remind you that I can't be there directly? The System, in its divine wisdom, keeps those at my level of power from attending such new worlds. Our Mana needs are not in balance. That's why I've sent you, and that's why the cursed Trickster is using his twisted clones to work around that limitation. There can't be many of Master Class there yet. You should be able to beat them all. Even the Trickster's avatars can't be up to Heroic yet."

Kantele kept her face calm with no outward reaction. She knew all this information already, and to have her master explain it to her was a condescension that was supposed to sting. Showing it had would only make it worse. "Master Class only. But the avatar is a very high Master Class. They are stronger than me by many levels. I cannot reliably deal with that on my own."

The Weaver let out a snort but didn't otherwise reply. Kantele waited patiently while the Galactic Council member ruminated. After a few moments, he made an impatient noise and flicked away an unseen screen with his fingers.

"Very well," he said. "I'll send the Twins and the Spear to assist you. Expect them sometime tomorrow. They will contact you when they arrive."

The connection blinked out without even a flash.

Kantele let a satisfied smile curl up the edges of her lips. Of her Holy Order of the System knights, the Twins and the Spear were almost as strong as she was.

She turned away from the ocean and started the long walk back toward the lights of the city. There was no one on this world who could stop the four of them.

No one.

Chapter Seven

The smell of deep-frying food was still bringing a lazy sort of happiness to Fool. As soon as they'd gotten back to the mall, he'd dragged Jackal to the food fair again. Word of the crisp meat burritos had spread, and a bunch of McBride folk were partaking of the treat.

He found himself only half paying attention to the food though. A brief, blasphemous thought had crossed his mind that maybe the snack wasn't as good as he remembered. It wasn't that though. Fool was just preoccupied.

He wasn't all that worried about finding the Twisted Chapel. Worst case, he could probably use some of the Foundation's funds to pay for the information. Unless it was too expensive. He expected that to be the case, so he hadn't even bothered to try. Thinking about it, though… that bit of pressure relief potential kept his thoughts from getting locked up and running in circles.

He was still convinced this was the right path to follow, and the events at the street dance gathering had only reenforced that. The weirdness of the whole thing, and especially the Mana use. Fool was still trying to figure out his new Mana Sense Skill, but he'd become familiar enough with the usual flow of Mana in combat and otherwise. The dancers were doing something different. It felt almost like a cheat, and that intrigued him. The sheer amount of Mana being used, especially by the vampire-looking dudes, had been impressive. Equal to that being pulled for combat.

How had they managed to level up with those Skills? None of the big Mana-draw Skills he'd noticed had looked to have any real combat application, but to draw that much Mana would have meant a whole ton of grinding. Or crafting actual things. This was a way of doing things that Fool hadn't heard of before. The System, or at least Mana, was turning out to be more complex than he'd thought.

It was possible that the dancers were out hunting monsters with weapons, but the Mana cost of Levelling up to where they were was significant. It should have prevented them from having whatever dance Skills they were using that drew in so much Mana.

Fool was mentally kicking himself for not using Talent Scout to see what the actual Skills' descriptions were, but he had been too caught up in watching the performance. Whatever else, he had to admit they were damned good dancers.

Still, it was time to do something. Olivia looked up at Fool as he pushed his chair back from the table and stood. Jackal was still eating, and Fool could tell his mind was elsewhere.

"Just gonna go check in with Fran," Fool mumbled, wandering away.

He'd been happy to see that Olivia had arrived while they were downtown. She'd stopped in Valemount for something first, along with a small second group of cavalry. The Professor had thought it best to send a large group down south first, then a smaller but strong group second. The route south wasn't anything close to settled yet. Being a Dungeon World, it likely never would be. The Professor wasn't much for tactics, but he had the whole "grand strategy" thing down pretty good.

Instead of light scouts, the right process in this new world was to send a mighty fist to clear the way, and a smaller, but still powerful, rearguard to come along behind as a reserve. Close enough to react if needed in an actual emergency, but far enough back that anyone triggering a trap would feel safe in thinking they had the entire force.

And of course, being a professor, he was using the staggered group to collect data on how quickly, and to what extent, the monster spawns on the road regenerated.

Fool had wanted to object to Olivia being in the second group. They rarely talked. Oliva wasn't much for talking at the best of times, and since they'd realized the relationship between them, a sort of shyness had come between them. Fool had been hoping the journey down would give them a chance to break the ice a little.

He wasn't worried about her being in any danger. She'd been fairly low level when they met in Prince George, but since then, she'd been power-leveling, mostly with Alex. The two of them had an affinity. Alex's Hedge Witch with Olivia's Chaos Mage Class. Both seemed to tap into a new kind of wildness as their Skills grew, and they'd been an absolute terror on the local monster spawns. They'd even made a few trips back into Wells Gray park. The two of them were getting close to Advanced Class.

Fran was looking at Fool as he got close to her table, her usual expectant eyebrow already in action. He didn't acknowledge that verbally, just sat down with a distracted huff.

The cavalry lead leaned forward and looked at him over crossed arms, elbows rested on the table. "Rough day?"

Fool shook his head. "Not so much. Minor mystery on my mind, but I'll get it settled. How are negotiations going?"

"Not hardly negotiations at all. Most of it was worked out before we arrived, and kinda the last thing that needed to be settled was us getting here. They agreed to all our conditions so far, and all that's left is the week we asked for as a 'hand's on' before the contract is settled. We'll start doing some patrols tomorrow to get a better sense of what the job's gonna be like, but I don't see anything coming up. Gotta admit, kinda looking forward to the job."

Fool had to smile. Fran was in a younger age bracket that him, but only by a hair. Far enough along the path of life that she'd really enjoyed the full benefit of the System rejuvenation effects. She'd embraced the very real physical rebirth and thrown herself into the combative elements of the world with an almost intimidating glee. Getting the chance to turn that sense of fun into a sort of community service would suit her well.

She'd also been instrumental in making some key parts of the contract. Policing in a System world was by its nature a paramilitary job, but Fran had insisted that the primary focus of any policing done would be to stop repeat offenses. The most obvious application of this would be stomping flat any real bad guys and harvesting the experience. That was the reality of policing in a System universe. Beyond that though, it meant that police intervention for anything that didn't require stomps had to be focused on long-term solutions for every issue that came up.

The city council hadn't really paid much attention to that when it had first been brought up, but when they saw the budget layout for healers and counselors to be provided by Vancouver, there had been some squawking. The Foundation had been able to use the modeling capabilities of the Machine to show the long-term benefits to the city, with reduced overall costs and an increase in economy over time.

It had been a tough sell from the beginning, when the concept of providing a force for Vancouver had come up. But Fran had insisted, and the Professor and Jackal had found a way to make it work. And that work had, in turn, made it possible to sell the idea to the city council. Which meant Fran and her troops were going to get the fun of being authority figures while actually being a concrete benefit to the people of the city instead of just the people that ran the city.

Fool nodded to cover up his brief distraction. "Glad it's working out. Got a question for you though. Ran into something interesting today, and I want to follow up. It's something a bit… underground. Have you run across anyone that might be a resource on that?"

"Maybe. This a dangerous thing, or you just being curious again?"

Fool had to think about that for a moment. He wanted to default to saying it was nothing, but Fran had a job to do, and they were all supposed to be working together. Even if Fool and Jackal had a sub rosa second job.

"Maybe dangerous. Personal though. I suppose you could call it a matter of faith."

"You're the closest thing I know to a preacher these days, at least in the System sense. Is that what you're looking for?"

"Hadn't thought of that. I don't think so though. Not really. Maybe? I figured we were looking for a dance club. I might have been jumping to conclusions though. It's something called the 'Twisted Chapel.'"

Fran let out a single laugh and leaned forward. "Sounds like a goth club to me!"

"That's what I thought. That might just be our age though. But I can't discount that it's an actual church of some kind. I hadn't really thought of the System too much that way. Makes sense though. We already came across the Thirteen Moon Sect. Gotta be other religions out there, even if I haven't run across any other kind of priest Class folk yet. Bound to happen."

"As long as they aren't like you." Fran took the sting out of that with a grin, and Fool shook his head with a slight smile.

"Big universe. We'll see. I think I was right though. I remembered there being a group of street dancers downtown, so Jackal and I went down there. Still there. And some real heavy-hitters in the area too. But no one would talk to us about where this chapel might be. So I'm still thinking night club, but open to other areas. Got any ideas where we could look next?"

"Yeah, I think so. One of the Vancouver negotiators used to be a local cop. I'll go ask him, let you know later what comes up. That good?"

"Thanks." Fool nodded and got up. Wasn't much else he could do.

He glanced back at Jackal. The big man was still stuck in thought. Olivia looked busy as well, chatting with a few of the younger cavalry riders who had wandered over. She'd made friends fast when she'd arrived in McBride.

With his companions busy and no one else around he felt like sharing his thoughts with, Fool went for a walk. Nothing really worked as well as putting one foot in front of the other to get his thoughts organized. And there was still something nagging at the back of his mind, no doubt about it.

He found a fire exit door leading to a stairwell, and a few floors later, he was down and out walking the street. They'd been put up in one of the hotels that had been attached to a part of the mall, sort of an extension of the whole place, and he found himself wandering over to Kingsway.

The street wasn't anything like it used to be. Back in the day, Kingsway was part of his cruising strip. A strange road. It sliced through Vancouver like a knife cut, a diagonal slash chopping through the otherwise regular grid of the city. It connected New Westminster to Vancouver, with Burnaby in the middle. As such, anywhere you wanted to go, you usually started by driving up to Kingsway.

So many nights, when things had been going well, he'd head out on the road in his car or a friend's, full of excitement, heading downtown for whatever excitement they could find. And later, when things had started to go crazy, he'd drive up and down, sometimes all night. Always with the music cranked, trying to make sense of the riot of emotions that were taking over his life. Even before the really bad hallucinations had started, he'd lost control of his emotions.

Relationships were the hard part. He'd had a hell of a time sticking with one partner. It had felt as if there was a yawning emptiness inside him, and he'd interpreted it as a need. A need for love. He'd only been able to snatch comfort when he had someone to hold on to, and when his need got to be too much for his partner… well, there was always someone else.

That memory still hurt him. He hadn't been a good person. He'd developed a flirtatious personality, and no matter how serious the relationship he was in was, he couldn't feel comfortable unless there was someone else on the side. A safety net to fall into. That approach has lasted him for years until…

He shook his head to stop thinking about that. It didn't help. He'd been an ass, breaking hearts and playing loose, and he'd finally gotten caught. Like a stereotype right out of a bad romance movie, he'd fallen hard for someone he shouldn't have.

They'd had an affair, and he'd found he didn't want anyone else. He'd even been open about it with his partner, an experiment in having an open relationship.

That had not gone well. At first, the open communication had been great, but then he'd discovered what jealousy was. It had been a vicious fire, and the spark had been a fear of loss. He'd realized too late that the woman he was having an affair with was as close as he'd ever imagined to having a soulmate, and she'd been open about wanting a life partner, not a lover once or twice a week.

He'd tried to balance it but had wound up breaking two other hearts. In a panic, he'd done the absolute wrong thing and decided that he had to be with the other woman and told his partner he was leaving her.

It was too late. The other woman had done the right thing and decided to cut him out absolutely. And she'd explained it in terse words, with no exception possible.

It wasn't the final straw that broke his sanity. He'd already been down that path and there was no stopping it, but it was one of the main events that accelerated it. He'd made an art out of self-destruction.

Fool stopped to sit on a bench. The wind was picking up a bit, and the moon was peeking out through scudding clouds.

For the first time, he admitted to himself that his broken brain wasn't entirely at fault for what had happened. He'd been more than sane enough to make good choices back then, and he hadn't. For sure, his childhood and all the fun of that had put him in a bad spot to be an adult. In the cold light of decades of context to reflect on, it was easy to see that he'd made willful and poor decisions. A broken brain was just icing on the cake.

It wasn't a big revelation. It was knowledge that had been in his head all along, and the re-wiring the System had done to his brain just made it easier to see.

And it made it easier to cope with his current realization as well.

It wasn't as if he could go back in time and smack the crap out of himself for being an ass. And as far as he knew, all the involved parties, aside from him, were long dead. He'd confirmed part of that with Olivia. Her grandmother had died in the first days of the System. She'd at least found some happiness before that, a life of success.

Becs? Rebecca though? He hadn't thought about her in years, not consciously. But some part of him had always held on to the memory of her. He hadn't looked up her fate in the Shop. He didn't want to know. The only reason he hadn't thought of her was because his subconscious mind had shied away from the memory. The pain was almost as bad as if she had died, but a part of that pain was the knowledge that she was still out there, and maybe someday, somehow, there would be a chance for them again. A fresh start. But once he looked in the Shop, that hope would die for good.

And avoiding that thought was a small kindness he gave himself. He figured he'd grown enough, done enough good, in the last few years to make up for some of the wreckage he'd done to others when he was younger. Not enough to truly make up for it, but enough that he could give himself a brief break.

He took a deep breath and shook himself to rid the melancholy. It was a beautiful night, and he wasn't doing anyone any good by digging up thoughts to mope about.

Besides, one of the first things he'd done when the System gave him his mind back was swear to himself that he would do his damndest to make the world a better place and be only of support to the people around him. Selfish whining and being all dramatic about his past was no way to follow his goal.

He forced himself up and walked down the road toward Central Park. If he remembered correctly, there was a stretch of open field where you could get a bit of a view of the mountains of the North Shore and the lights of the city.

There was still a minor ache in his chest as he walked, and he found himself surprised to realize it was a little heartache, and a little longing to feel the touch of Rebecca one more time.

Something wasn't right.

His walk slowed. He'd been a melancholic person when he was younger—that had been one of the first signs of his deteriorating mind. Being back in his old stomping grounds, he'd expected some of those old feelings to come back.

And he'd felt an almost comfortable nostalgia at first. But looking out over the city and its lights, it just felt wrong. He wasn't just reminiscing anymore, especially not thinking about Rebecca. This felt more like when his brain was veering into madness, the lingering thoughts on things that were out of his control.

All damned day. He'd been sinking more and more into it, but that wasn't how he worked anymore. The more he realized that, the more the way he'd been thinking all day stood out to him.

He'd acquired the Mana Sense Skill on his last level up, but he hadn't really paid much attention to it. It was, for the most part, a passive skill. Everything looked somewhat the same, but when he put his mind to it, he could see almost a field around things. The kind you see around magnets when you put them under paper, and scattered iron filings on the paper. A gentle halo. When he concentrated, he could see that it connected to other things, and people like Jackal had a somehow stronger field. With Jackal, he could sense the big man's Mana more like gravity, a kind of pull that attracted things around him.

He'd been meaning to mention that to Jackal. They'd talked enough before about what Mana might be, what would need to exist for an energy field to somehow allow all the laws of physics to be broken. He hadn't gotten around to it, but from the little they'd spoken of, Fool assumed Mana would work something like gravity. Permeating everything, but at the right scale, you could see its uneven distribution. Instead of being universal, you could see its ebb and flow. Fool figured that was what his Mana Sense did.

He leaned into it now, using the Skill to perceive the surrounding Mana.

Everything looked much the same, only a little brighter than the nighttime light would allow for. No one else was walking around, but in some of the nearby buildings, he saw a slight warping in the Mana field as people moved around. The warping was a little stronger for some than others, and he assumed that represented different Skill levels. Or maybe some activity they were doing? Something that required Mana, so it was drawing it in at different rates?

He held his right hand up in front of him, and he saw the faint ripples haloing around his fingers. Faint ripples all around. Some of them... leading off. To his left.

He turned and looked into the woods of the park he was walking by. He had to squint a little and move his head slightly side to side to make sure he wasn't imagining things, but there was indeed a kind of rippling divot... a stream... running from him into the woods. A connection of some kind.

And that connection led to a little dark spot in the woods where Fool could almost make out the faint outline of a human.

He didn't think about it, just walked toward the woods. There wasn't enough of a thread of Mana to make him think anything nefarious was afoot. And the pulsing waves of Mana in human form didn't seem to be all that strong, at least not up to his level. But there was clearly a connection between them.

So he walked closer.

It was a bit of a walk, maybe half a kilometer, but the figure never moved. The closer he got, the clearer the outline became. He still couldn't make out anything, but there was no feeling of threat.

He stopped just before he got to the woods. Who, or whatever, was in the dark patch didn't come out, didn't move, but he felt their attention on him. He peered deeper into the woods, but it was pitch black. Maybe… maybe an outline. A hood?

He was about to open his mouth and say something when the figure shifted and moved closer. He could see an outline now. And then a little more.

A woman in a cloak. Somehow… familiar.

He cleared his throat, surprised to find that it was dry. "Have you been following me? All day? Or just thinking about me?"

"I had to know." The soft voice came out of the woods, and Fool didn't doubt at all anymore. "I saw you earlier and asked around. I wasn't sure it was you, James."

Everything went a little numb for Fool, but his voice seemed to continue without his feedback. "Haven't heard that name in a long time."

"Fool. That's what you call yourself now? Or is that what they call you?"

"I think I earned it. Long ago." He stopped, the next words choked in his throat. He started to talk again, then just dropped his shoulders. Despite all the daydreams, there was really nothing right he could say. "How ya been, Becs?"

A soft little sigh was all the confirmation he got it was her. "As good as anyone, I suppose. Didn't mean to follow you. Didn't want to, but as damned as it makes me, you're the only person left I know from… from before. I had to know."

"I'm not the same. I am, I guess. I'm sorry."

A sharp snort, enough to let him know that the hurt was there, even if it was only a memory. "Who is? Lot of changes."

She walked the rest of the way out of the woods, and the moon and starlight lit her face up just enough. She still looked the same. Older. So much older. Once, he'd dreamed of growing old with her and watching her face change along with his. That old vision was still there, but there was a lot else. Some softness where he wouldn't have expected, and a lot more hardness.

"You look good, Becs."

A flicker in the eyes, bright enough to be a moonbeam. "Don't."

He sighed. "The old us is still inside, but we aren't those people anymore. Neither of us. Good or bad."

She stared into his eyes and said nothing. He met her eyes and didn't look away. He owed her his attention, at the least. And he owed her the right to control the conversation. It wasn't his to fix or guide. He realized he hadn't said nearly enough, but he'd said all he could. Now all he could do was listen and accept whatever she said.

The light was just bright enough that he could see her hair had greyed, just like his. Her eyes were still that deep forest green though. He wasn't just imagining that. He'd fallen into those eyes enough times to recognize them. And to recognize that he could fall all the way back in, as if he had never stopped.

He pulled back from that line of thought, but he could see that she recognized the thought in his eyes anyway.

No secrets between old lovers. Not when some part of them still remembered the love.

Rebecca shook her head. Short, sharp, side to side, twice. In denial. And then looked up at him. "Coffee shop still open two blocks away. Let's talk."

Chapter Eight

Jackal put his finger on the page so he didn't lose his place. He didn't look up. Not yet. He sensed someone looking at him, but this scene was really great.

The hotel they'd been put up in was serving a double purpose. Keeping out-of-town guests in was one. The other was as a library. Before the System, the Bob Prittie Metrotown library had been next door. It was a lovely, many-floored, modern library with an excellent selection. When the System arrived, it had been alternately looted and hosted a nest of smaller monsters. The librarians had all been killed off, but once Vancouver had been taken over by its new owner and Burnaby had been amalgamated into its safe zone, librarians from other locations had started a drive to recover what they could.

There wasn't a big call for library books anymore. The System Shop provided more information, and a wider variety of information, than any pre-System library could. But some folks still loved physical books, and Jackal was amongst that number.

He'd grabbed a paperback copy of a book by one of his favorite authors and retired to his room to read it. But for some reason, he'd been too restless to sit in the room. He wasn't in the mood to be completely isolated. In the old world, he'd have put on some background music or TV to provide the sense of community around him. Tonight, he'd felt like something a little more than that, so he'd wandered back out of his room down to the lobby to find a quiet corner to read in. It had worked pretty well. It wasn't busy, but there was enough traffic from the McBride cavalry walking in and out to keep his monkey brain satisfied enough to let him read.

Until a moment ago, when he'd noticed the watcher.

With a sigh, Jackal resigned himself to having to finish the scene later. With a small wince, he folded the corner of the page he was reading and closed the book, putting it down on the table next to him.

The woman had been leaning against a doorframe near the reception desk. When he put the book down, she didn't hesitate to walk toward him.

She was fairly tall, on the slim side, but with a dancer's curves and muscles. Slightly more muscles than curves. Black hair in a pixie cut, black leather pants with an oversized zipper that would have split the hips of the pants in two—which probably explained how she'd squeezed into them. They were beyond skin tight, almost into compression sport-wear land. Big black combat boots, but her steps were anything but clunky. A ripped hoodie, the arms torn half-way off, mucky and paint-splattered enough that Jackal couldn't tell what the original color would have been. The only other thing she was wearing on her torso was some sort of latex bandeau.

He could swear she had horns just barely peeking up through her hair.

And somehow, he felt as if he knew her.

She stopped next to his chair, just far enough away that he found himself looking into her eyes, which were a startling shade of violet. She managed to imply that she was popping a piece of chewing gum while she looked at him, hips cocked.

Jackal found himself at a loss for words, so he cocked his head a little to the side.

The woman imitated his gesture and looked right back at him.

He tilted his head the other way, then crossed his arms and leaned back.

She crossed her arms and stuck her foot on the arm of Jackal's chair, then leaned into his face. He found himself getting strangely flustered and leaning back away from the sharp cut of her eyes.

"Where," she said, "the fuck is Fool?"

"What?"

"Jackal. Keep up. Where the hell is Fool? You two idiots were supposed to be at the Twisted Chapel by now. What the hell kept you?"

She was still leaning into his face, and Jackal was becoming uncomfortably aware of her scent. Sweaty, musky, and—something more. His face flushed deeper.

"Uh… do we know you?"

The muddled state of his head cleared suddenly, and Jackal realized it had been some kind of Charisma effect. With his Willpower, he hadn't been affected by such things in a long, long time. And his Perception was almost as high.

"Better?" she said.

He nodded and looked at her again. He'd swear he'd never seen her before, but there was something… the way she carried herself, but deeper. Like an aura. A familiar aura. Then it hit him, as crazy as it seemed. "DM?"

The woman snorted as she pulled her foot off of his chair and stood up. She was still well within his personal space, and even with whatever effect she'd turned off, he was flustered by that.

"Close," she said. "Not quite. Think of DM as a shadow of me."

The attraction evaporated, and Jackal's belly went cold and hollow. "Are… you…?"

That made her grin, a wild, crazy grin. "Not quite, but as close as you'll get on this world. The big guy is out there, but the System isn't going to let someone that strong come cruising by your raw little dungeon world. He'd suck it clean of Mana in no time, so instead…" She leaned forward, her exceedingly cute little button nose just brushing Jackal's, and he was suddenly very aware that she did indeed have two sharp little horns peeking out from under her bangs. "You get me."

This time, Jackal resisted the shudder that twisted in his belly and looked right into her eyes. A hint of a smile crossed her lips, and she stood up straight and took a few steps back to a more normal distance.

"All right," she said, "now that we've got that settled… Where. The. Fuck. Is. Fool?"

"Went for a walk. He won't be far though."

"Let's get him. C'mon." She didn't wait, just spun and started walking, her boots slamming a crisp percussion on the floor. "And call me Lucy."

Jackal took advantage of his height and was walking next to her in only a few steps. "May I ask what's going on?"

"That's my line. What took you assholes so long? You got the card. I expected you right away. Instead, I gotta blow my cover, leave the Twisted Chapel alone, and come and get you assholes? Explain yourselves."

Jackal didn't bother to hide the irritation in his voice. "We spent the day looking. Fool was following a hunch, looking for clues. If you wanted a quicker response, you should have been more direct."

Lucy stopped and turned to look up at Jackal. "Are you fucking kidding me? I had the card given to you. It was in your fucking hands! What the hell did you think you were supposed to do with that?"

"There was no address. It seemed obvious that we were supposed to try to find the place on our own?"

Lucy trembled, her hands shaking in a steady tremor. "And it never occurred to you that you were standing right next to a fucking SHOP when you got that? You never thought to *BUY* the information? The goddamn card was a fucking KEY that the SHOP would have unlocked for you."

Jackal didn't have a response. It was, in hindsight, the first thing they should have tried.

Lucy shook out her hands and let out a short, screaming growl. "It was Fool, wasn't it? Fuck, living up to that goddamn name of his. Probably thought he was being clever. I'm gonna wring his neck, but later. No time now."

She picked up her pace, and even with her smaller frame, Jackal struggled to keep up.

"Are we going the right direction?" she asked.

"Maybe. He's probably walking along the road, westbound. He does that."

"Fine. Hurry the fuck up."

"Why?"

"If we don't hurry up, I might not need to explain it, so pick it up, big guy. Don't want to miss the fight."

She didn't say anything more, but somehow doubled her pace.

Before they got to the coffee shop, Rebecca stopped Fool with a sudden grab at his elbow. He stopped and turned to look at her. She was glancing over her shoulder and chewing the corner of her lip.

"You okay?" he asked.

"Wait. Just wait." She looked down, then closed her eyes and let out a deep breath. "I need to know something."

She opened her eyes, and when he looked into them, he saw the entire history of what they had been, and he knew what she wanted to know. There was something else there though. Something almost a bit frantic.

Time for some overdue truth then. Something told Fool there wasn't any time to work his way up to it. "I was wrong. About everything. And I treated you badly. Worse than that. I used you to fill my own needs and made it seem like it was all about you. I was a pretty fucked up person back then. I'm sorry. If it helps, I've been doing my best to be a better person. At least, for as long as I've known what it meant to be a better person."

She shook her head, but not quick enough for Fool to miss the hint of a tear. No way for him to tell if it was for anger or sadness. She held up a hand, looking down at the ground. "Just one question, James. Was it real? To you?"

He didn't even hesitate to answer. "Never stopped loving you, never stopped regretting… well. I guess I'm sorry. Can we talk? Do you want to talk about this?"

She shook her head, still looking down, then she looked up and darted a glance from side to side. A startling stream of profanity came out of her mouth. She grabbed Fool by the collar and dragged him—not toward the road and the coffee shop, but back toward the trees.

"No fucking time," she said. "Just run."

Fool wanted to ask why, but there was an urgency in her voice and actions that compelled him to move.

Her hand slipped off of his collar. He had no idea what her Class was or her experience, but she was no match for even his neglected Strength stat. She spun to look back at him. He saw her eyes widen as she looked down the road, over his shoulder.

"You go. Don't worry about me. We'll catch up later," he said.

All he really needed to know about what was going on was revealed by the flashes of guilt and fear in her eyes, just before she turned and bolted for the trees.

Someone had gone to great lengths to set him up. He didn't waste time wondering who it might be. He'd made more than a few enemies over the last few years.

Still, he didn't recognize who was waiting for him in the middle of the road, a block away. An imposing figure, clad in red and white armor, with a white helmet that covered their face. Red fins rose on either side of the helmet, almost like fox ears.

Fool felt the power emanating off of them. He didn't bother with Talent Scout—they were way over his level, so he wasn't going to try to fight them. Not fairly anyway.

And he wasn't going to run either. Rebecca had meant a lot to him, and he owed her for how their relationship had gone. That someone had used her to get to him? That was something they were going to pay for, one way or the other.

With a flick of his wrist, he activated Hammer of Loki. The satisfying weight of the weapon settled into his hand. And his new Mana Sense Skill was showing him something as well. The enemy was a glowing pillar of Mana, as expected, but something was streaming off of that Mana pillar. Two streams, reaching back out, beyond sight.

He snorted and spun the hammer once. Some kind of trick or trap, no doubt. He couldn't think of any reason for that. They clearly over-matched him in every way. Maybe they were just overly cautious.

Only one way to find out.

As he walked toward the figure, he wondered if it was a person at all. The armor was intricate, with an elaborate mechanism at all the joints. It looked almost robotic. Except the ribbons of fabric hanging off of the hips, looking somewhere halfway between a cloak and skirt. And what he had first taken for more fabric hanging off the back of the helm looked more like an oddly flat red hair. If it was a robot, it had a lot of creature trappings. Like a narrow waist, wide hips, and a muscular, feminine bust. No weapons were visible, so Fool assumed they'd rely on Skills to overpower him.

Half a block away, and the enemy hadn't moved as Fool approached. They just maintained a loose, open stance, hands held down at their sides.

Fool could almost feel the theme music starting. Standard bad guy versus good guy fight. The script was all written in advance. He'd get closer, they'd say something, he'd reply, they'd get tenser and closer to the fight, and with a sudden explosive movement, it would be on.

He wasn't in the mood to play that out.

Hammer of Loki, while active, gave him immense speed and strength, so he used it.

Half a block away, he exploded into motion. In a heartbeat, he was in their face. The savage burst of speed and strength made him grin. Moving like this, at his age? Too much of a miracle not to enjoy, no matter the outcome.

He didn't really have a plan. That was good, because as he got close to the opponent, he realized just how big she was. Not quite Jackal's size, but bigger than he'd expected.

The sweet adrenaline of combat took over. Even with all the Skills and abilities the System brought, moments of mindless combat perfection were rare for Fool. It was almost like he was a step back from himself, observing in slow motion, yet somehow still more tightly one with his body than he'd ever been before. He knew exactly what to do, and his body was doing it almost before he realized it.

Straight charge, and all the terrible momentum built up. He slammed it right into the ground, snapped the hammer back behind him, and used all that rotational energy to vault himself up and over his opponent, narrowly dodging her reactive punch.

Fool grinned as he floated through the air, his senses ramped up enough that he could see the minute shifts in his enemy's posture as she realized she had missed and shifted weight to counter his sudden move.

Too late for them, Fool thought as he gathered the hammer in both hands and swung toward the sweet spot at his opponent's back, right between the shoulder blades.

He was really starting to enjoy this whole "Adept Priest" Advanced Class thing. He hadn't been a big fan of combat before, but this?

This was fun.

He was completely upside down when he smashed the hammer into the enemy's back, all his Skill-boosted strength and speed going into the blow for an epic amount of damage.

As tough as she was, she was still blasted away from the blow.

The red and white figure, arms thrown wide, was flung forward by the force of it, arms akimbo.

Fool used the last of his speed burst to do a half rotation through the air and land nimbly on his feet, just in time to watch his foe crash into the ground.

Or that's what he expected to happen.

Some of the fun of the game dropped away as he saw the armored figure spin in the air with a balletic pirouette and land facing him in an extended stance.

"Shit," he said.

All he could do after that was cringe. The worst part was he could see the attacks coming, but they were faster than he could deal with.

Fist, elbows, knees, kicks… all crashed into him, one after the other, with no pause between. He struggled to block them at first, but after the first few landed, everything turned to a ringing judder and he wasn't really aware of anything. He felt as though his feet were slipping under him on ice.

And then he fell, a hard slam, but somehow more gentle than the barrage he'd just been blasted with. The assailant paused, then she yanked her knee up to stomp him into the pavement.

It was crazy. It was unfair. She still wasn't using any Skills that he could tell, but the difference in levels, gear, experience, training, whatever it was, was more than he could cope with. His vision started to fade to black, and all he felt was his hand scrambling for purchase.

And finding the Hammer of Loki.

He stole a single breath in, rich with the iron reek of his blood, and tried to snap his body over the hammer, lifting it as much as he could. The speed and strength boost was still there, and it was just enough.

It didn't stop the stomp. The armored boot still crushed into him, but the hammer blow knocked it just to the side. Just enough for it to pile drive into his left hip instead of his belly.

He couldn't help but scream as he felt the pelvic arc snap, the bone driving into his belly with an electric burn.

His scream was cut off as he was yanked up in the air. Not even the dignity of being lifted by his collar, instead by an iron-cold grip on his upper arm, leaving him dangling like a broken toy.

The armored helm that faced him wasn't featureless. It was eggshell white, and like an eggshell in texture, with faint whorls across the surface.

He couldn't help but smile through the pain as he looked at it. That egg would crack, and somehow, he'd make it happen.

"That was too easy." The voice came from the helmet, and Fool saw the surface vibrating as the voice spoke. "You live up to your name, it seems."

This was, Fool thought, the point where he was supposed to heroically cough up a wad of blood and spit it in her face. If he were Jackal, that's what he'd do. Fit into the image. He wasn't though, so he just looked at where he figured her eyes would be.

He'd gotten his butt kicked, but he still didn't feel as though he was losing. Sometimes luck just went the other way, but he'd learned to trust his Luck. Something would happen, and it would all work out in his favor. It was likely to suck until it did, but that was the price of being an Adept of the Trickster.

Still, best to keep up appearances. He tried to think of something witty to say.

"Who…" was all he managed to get out. And he got a hard shake for his efforts, ragdolled hard.

His head spun, and his shoulder seemed to pop out of its socket and back in again, in a flurry of pain. His brain went away for a bit, and it came back with only the thought that at least he wasn't being hit again.

The helm in front of him started to clear. The face that looked at him seemed mostly human, from what he could see. Except the eyes. The pupils were a bright yellow and vertically barred, with radiant lines coming out inside a slate-grey iris. Cute little snub nose though. Fool had been assuming it was a she, and that feeling was reinforced a moment later when the voice that came, via some kind of System translator, was a stereotypical honeyed villain voice of the vixen kind.

"I am Kantele," she said, "and I wouldn't count on your 'luck' to save you this time. I've shut that down. Do you think you are the first of the Trickster's ilk we've hunted?"

"There's more than one of us?" That was news to Fool.

"Not that many. Not anymore. Your kind, your false god, is an abomination against the System. We will cleanse all of you."

"Huh. What'd we do to piss you off?"

"The System is purity, and you are a taint."

He would have shaken his head if he was able. It was starting to make sense. "Let me guess, this is a religion thing?"

It was really weird to watch the twisted goat's eyes narrow in a glare. Effective though. Fool was recovering enough to feel like adding a quip, but Kantele's look was enough to give him pause.

"Have you not prospered from the System? Has it not cleansed your world of the weak and shown you the path to attaining your ultimate self? Can you not see that it is the source of everything in the universe and the only thing worthy of your worship?" Kantele leaned in closer, and he felt a lazy scorch of heat coming from some vent somewhere on her armor. "Instead, you worship the false idol, the Trickster, the one who would bring it all down. For that alone, you deserve death."

Fool managed to shake his head, and the fact that the motion only caused a slight stabbing pain let him know he was healing even more. "News to me. I admit I'm not a fan of rules, but I'm okay getting the System to work for me. It's made my life better."

She looked startled and leaned back a little away while lowering Fool until his feet touched the ground. The pain relief in his shoulder was almost orgasmic, but she still held on to his upper arm like a vise. Fool dived into the opening before she could get back on track.

"Hell, I wasn't even able to think right before the System, and the Acolyte Class looked like my only good choice at the time. In case you didn't notice, this is a dungeon world. It's not like we had a lot of time to make our choices. Or any real idea what we were doing." He kept talking, but something was really off about this. Each second that passed, he was more able to get his brain back, and the odd sense was growing. "But I'm no stranger to bigots or fanatics, so I'm not going to try to change your mind. I just want to know one thing."

Kantele's face had gone what he could only describe as an icy shade, but she hesitated. "Ask, before I remove your tainted soul."

"Why Rebecca?"

A sound like a soft snort. "Some of you humans understand the truth of the System."

Fool suddenly realized what was bothering him. She was a Master Class. She could clearly have killed him almost instantly.

Why was he still alive?

It made no sense. Falling into some sort of twisted religious war made as much sense as anything else, but sending a high Advanced Class to kill him, even if he was low Advanced? Seemed like overkill. Something else was up, but there was no time to try to work it out.

There was a slight slack on his upper arm, and activating Clouseau to shrink his upper arm down to a quarter of its current thickness gave him all the extra wiggle room he needed to slip out of her grip.

As soon as he dropped out, something felt slightly different. Something in Kantele's armor or gauntlet must have been damping some of his attributes. Whatever the cause, he did the smartest thing he could do.

Kantele was expecting Fool to run, and she had already shifted her weight to sprint and reach him in whatever direction he went.

Instead, he dropped straight down into a squat and swung his hammer with all his might into her ankle. It was a good blow and caught Kantele just right, smacking her foot to the side as she was about to shuffle her weight on to it. She lost her balance and stumbled. Fool hooked the end of his hammer around her other ankle and yanked as hard as he could.

Kantele was falling, but she was an experienced warrior, and she spun as she fell, aiming to land like a cat. With a last burst of speed, Fool jumped up and springboarded off of her head as she landed. As he landed, he swung the hammer behind him without looking.

The meaty *thunk* was very satisfying. For a moment.

Until everything went black.

Chapter Nine

Jackal saw Fool's backhand blow land, and he was proud of his friend. The old man had really been upping his combat game since acquiring his Advanced Class. He still had the bad habit of ignoring all of his Skills and relying on his Luck attribute more than was healthy, but…

It was hard to argue with results. And since Lucy had filled Jackal in over the last few blocks, he knew what Fool was facing. A strong Advanced Class fighter. Fool was hopelessly outclassed, but he was still landing shots.

And now it was Jackal's turn. The disparity in levels didn't bother him at all. This was what he'd built himself for, right from the beginning. The lone hero, the last stand, fighting win or lose against all odds.

Jackal didn't even try to stop his grin from splitting open into a feral smile.

He started to stack all of his Skills and pulled the Plasma Spear out from his new storage. The only thing he held back on was his Mana Damage Skill. It worked better in range, and thanks to his Gugnir Skill, he could now attack from a distance.

The spear almost leapt from his hand, striking across the distance like a bolt from a sci-fi blaster.

It hammered right into Kantele's chest, burning through her chest plate.

Her scream almost deafened him, even a block away.

She wasn't down, but she was hurt. Jackal couldn't tell how much she was hurt, but her frozen stance, arms at her side, fists clenched, with a burning spear sticking out of her chest spoke volumes.

By the time she managed to recover and rip out the spear, Jackal was ten steps away. Fool was behind him now, and Jackal had only been able to spare his companion a single glance before leaping into the battle.

His favored twin swords sliced down, one after the other. They didn't break through her armor, but the damage to the armor was visible. Another scream came from Kantele as his newly stacked mana drain Skills notched her mana down. He didn't pause to enjoy that. It wasn't that much of a drain, and her scream was from anger.

That was what he wanted. Make her angry. Out of control. If he could keep her off-kilter with his speed and toughness, Jackal could wear her down. At the moment, all he had to do was keep her focused on him long enough for Fool to recover. Once Fool was back in the game and using his Skills, they had a solid chance.

Jackal landed to the side of Kantele and spun to face her, pulling his right sword up to block the descending cut from Kantele. She was strong and hadn't let go of the Plasma Spear. He felt his face tingling from the heat of the blade.

The left blade lashed out, striking into the exposed armpit. He stepped to the right as he threw the cut, letting the spear blow slide off of his sword, and followed up the left cut with one from the right sword into the same spot. The left sword was in just the right place to follow-up. Its cut battered the spear even farther off to the side, and Jackal used the momentum to pull the sword up above the follow-through of the right-handed cut.

He completed the rehearsed form by driving a thrust home into the now-weakened armpit armor, and the tip of the blade punched through. Kantele took the hit, and this time, she didn't even flinch. She let the force of the blow on the spear spin the tip all the way around behind her, and even as Jackal thrust home with his sword, she slammed the butt of the spear into his face.

The blow was strong enough to rock his head back and made Jackal take a few steps back.

The two warriors stopped for a moment, each just out of the other's range, and locked eyes.

Kantele smiled, and the still-transparent visor of her helm slid up. "Jackal. As planned. I like your spear. Thank you for the gift."

"It will mark your grave."

"Lovely." With no warning, she leapt backward.

Fool had been trying to sneak off to the side of her while she was distracted talking to Jackal, but she'd apparently picked up that. She laughed at the look on Fool's face.

Fool shook his head and walked over to stand next to Jackal. "I tried. I guess we just take her down the old-fashioned way, huh?"

Jackal grinned and flicked his swords in a tight arc. Kantele's blood flicked off of the blades, making a brief glittering arc in the streetlights.

The look on Kantele's face showed no fear or concern. Jackal was happy to let her keep her confidence. It would be a close fight, but he knew they could take her. Even if Lucy did as she'd warned and left the fight mostly to them.

Apparently, she'd changed her mind though. Jackal didn't see Lucy, but Kantele's next words left no doubt.

"And the pawn master appears. You were warned, Lucy Brightside. Now you end, by the hand of the System Knights." Kantele pressed a button on her wrist.

There was a brief flicker of static, then three beings appeared next to her.

Two were nearly identical, clad head to toe in shiny grey modern armor. The face masks of both were molded to look like human faces, the eyes glowing a molten yellow. Matching yellow lights flickered on and off all along the armor, never repeating a pattern or location. The only difference between the two was that the armor of each showed a binary representation—one with a more sculpted feminine breast, and the other with a more sculpted masculine codpiece. Otherwise, they were identical twins.

The third was an androgynous figure clad in iron and gold armor, capped with an open-faced helm with large wings on either side. Their eyes were the same yellow shade as the twins, but in this case appeared to be truly molten, with lazy waves of heat rising from the glow. In their left arm was an oval tower shield that ran from ankle to neck. In their right hand was an enormous glowing spear with a wicked-looking spearhead that was about three hand-spans wide and thin as a razor, glowing almost as bright as the Plasma Spear, but with etched runes. Jackal could just make out that the armor had normal-sized bird wings on the ankles.

All the newcomers gave off the aura of Master Class warriors.

Jackal's impression seemed to be backed up by Lucy, as Jackal could hear a muttered stream of profanity coming from behind him.

With another burst of static, a fourth newcomer appeared.

A giant.

A gaunt, skeletal figure, as armored as the rest except for its waist, which was only a stretch of spine jutting out from the visible curve of lower ribs.

Four arms, the lower two with scimitars, the upper set holding a titanic longsword across its shoulders.

The longsword spanned the entire street. The giant itself topped the two-story shop next to it.

Words came out of Jackal's mouth without thought. "'From the nunnery of thy chaste breast and quiet mind, to war and arms I fly…'"

"Lovelace!" Lucy chuckled. "My kinda poetry. You boys ready for a fight?"

Jackal nodded. Fool had no words, but he seemed content to continue the profane mutterings Lucy had abandoned.

Kantele gave no order to attack, but her visor slid back down and turned a smooth, opaque white.

There was no time to think, but time dropped to a frozen crawl, regardless. It felt like the first time Jackal had ever been in a fight. A stillness, a tension, like a high-wire thrumming just before it snapped. A moment where he didn't know whether he could even take another breath, and his body felt empty and as hollow as if it was made of straw.

Then, as now, he'd felt the inevitable weight of a decision bearing down on him. Only there was no decision. It felt as if he was deciding whether to run, curl up in a ball… or fight. That wasn't real though. What was real was that the decision had already been made, and some demon inside him was building in power and momentum and choosing its right moment.

The first fight? He'd blacked out. Come to awareness a moment later to find himself sitting on his opponent's chest, raining down blows.

There was no blacking out this time, but also no conscious control of his body. A pulse arose from inside him, but he was already moving as it breached the surface like a leviathan.

Everything inside him swelled, and he exploded across the distance between him and the giant in a flash.

There wasn't any specific target to strike. He was too close to even make out where he really was in relation to his enemy. A flash of white bone and a black hollow? He was on the thigh of the giant, looking across its midsection and down into the space where its hips should be. He didn't know where to cut to have an effect, but his blades sliced in, regardless.

Things slowed down again.

His left-hand blade was hitting the thigh-thick spinal column, and when the blade made contact, it was like pushing a sharp knife edge against a thick piece of tire rubber. The spinal column bent, and where it bent, an oily liquid oozed out. A tiny fleck of it clung to his blade as the white bone spun and shrank.

He crashed into the side of the building.

The other side.

He could see a hole in front of him, almost like a cartoon cutout of himself.

Through the hole was another hole and flickers of motion.

He'd been knocked all the way through the building, and at least one internal wall. A third of his health was gone, and he couldn't even recall being hit, couldn't feel any pain.

He had to get up.

Something cracked when he started up, and he howled as something in his leg snapped back after being bent the wrong way. Snapped back to where it should have been, his regeneration and healing already taking effect. Just a stumble. But then he was moving again, leaving that endless lifetime of pain to disappear into memory.

Through the hole in the wall, fighting to get back to the big hole, to get back into the fight.

Fool.

He had to protect Fool. He couldn't leave him out there with those monsters. The old man wouldn't last a second. Lucy was strong, really strong, but Jackal didn't think even she could handle five enemies of that level. On the way over, she'd explained how she wasn't much of a combat classer, but she'd acquired a number of artifacts that let her surprise opponents. She'd used one on Kantele but didn't think she'd be able to pull the same trick on her again. And that was when they'd thought they only had one enemy.

Jackal's only real hope was to use his Mana Damage Skill and give the other two a chance of escape. He'd ramped up his Thrown Weapons Skill as well. Now was the time to use it to full effect.

He activated Ramstal Skill, and the storage locker loaded with weapons, and he emptied them all out. A literal heap of spears, swords, axes, maces, and knives piled out onto the ground. A dragon's hoard of weaponry. He'd collected many of them from defeated enemies, and others he'd bought with the considerable funds he and Fool had collected. He'd always wanted to have the perfect weapon for every situation ready, as a just-in-case. Most were tier three, but many were tier two and even a few cherished tier one weapons. He'd planned to use those if they ever had to take down another Master Class opponent. His last aces in the hole.

Fool had told him a story once. He'd been drinking with a friend, and the friend had gone to the liquor cabinet and brought back an expensive bottle of whisky. Fool had complained, because it seemed a waste to open that bottle when there wasn't an occasion for it. The friend had laughed and said that the greatest shame would be to die and leave the bottle behind undrunk.

A few years later, that friend had died from an illness, and Fool had found the same half-empty bottle left in his possession. He said that had been when he'd really started to grieve his friend, and for all the things they hadn't done.

Jackal didn't want to add to Fool's grief, so he vowed to use all of his hoarded weapons before he died.

He'd dumped the pile of weapons just next to the hole he'd gone through. He didn't harbor any illusions that the giant thought he was dead. The lack of experience notification forbade any lies along those lines. It was likely that the giant, and the rest of the System Knights, assumed he wasn't strong enough to be a threat, so they hadn't bothered to follow up on the giant's swatting.

Time to show them the error of their ways.

He took a quick glance out the hole, and the fight, somehow, was still going on in earnest. He could barely make out the forms of Lucy and Fool. They moved from blurred shapes to what almost seemed like duplicates of themselves, then another one of them would appear out of nowhere and land a shot on one of the attackers. Clearly, Lucy had some powerful skills at hand.

She was also using, of all things, some sort of scythe-rifle, alternating between cuts and beam-powered blasts. Whatever the weapon was, it was knocking the enemy around like bowling pins.

The brief flare of hope he had was dashed when the giant just batted the scythe-rifle away. And the System Knight with the glowing spear used a skill to freeze Fool in place, setting him up for a shattering punch from one of the twins that knocked him ass over teakettle. It was a strong enough blow to kill the older man.

And it would have, if Fool hadn't used one of his newer Advanced Class Skills.

Jackal almost regretted the flash of pain that hit him and the aching loss of over half of the health he'd regenerated and healed. Friendly Fire was the name of the Skill, and it let Fool transfer damage to his allies. Lucy caught some of it too, judging from her scream.

Now was the time, and Jackal moved through the pain. Gugnir's Wrath was the name of the Skill. It gave him the ability to throw any weapon. He'd leveled it up three times, gaining a seeking trait as well as the ability to throw multiple weapons. There was also a minor party modifier that boosted everyone's resistance a small amount.

He didn't look to see what weapon he was throwing, just reached into the pile with both hands and tossed them like rocks, a pair aimed at each System Knight, cycling through all of the weapons as fast as he could gather and throw. There was no stopping to see what effect they were having, no time but to throw as fast as he could.

Jackal was losing the cumulative effect he might have enjoyed by using the weapons in hand for repeated blows. The tradeoff was that he got an almost guaranteed hit with each weapon thrown.

In the end, it was almost enough. The rain of steely damage, and the extra stacked effects that each weapon offered, not only stopped the System Knights from finishing off Fool and Lucy, it also drove them back, forcing them to regroup and shelter each other.

The damage was satisfying to see. Great bleeding wounds affected all of them. Burns, dripping acid, limbs covered in ice, vines, and other things writhing through open wounds, chains pinning legs to ground and slowing movement... an army of System-enhanced weapons was enough to slow even a Master Classer.

Slow, but not stop.

He'd done better than he'd hoped, but it was never a tactic to win the day.

Down to his last weapons. His favored twin swords.

Jackal leapt down and charged the System Knights. The death he'd always hoped to have, overpowered and outnumbered, dying to give his friends one last chance.

He'd thought he'd die with a poem on his lips, but now that he was in the face of it, all he felt was an ache at the back of his throat and a bitter taste. It didn't stop him from moving, charging in, but all he could see now were the strange eyes of Kantele. Those eyes were filled with rage and indignation, but all Jackal felt was a slight sadness. This was no way to die. There was no choice though.

Jackal could almost see himself, as if he was suddenly floating above and slightly behind his body. A powerful figure charging, screaming, swords out to the sides, starting to coil himself into a striking pattern that would put him between his enemies.

Something was wrong.

The System Knights were slowing, freezing into place, eyes dulling over.

And someone other than him was yelling.

It was Lucy.

"Stop! I can only hold them for a moment, and I can't if you hit them."

Jackal snapped back into his body and slammed to a halt.

Five statues in front of him, frozen perfectly, as if somehow time had stopped, but just for them.

He turned to look at Lucy and Fool.

Fool was running away… or toward something? Lucy was gesturing at Jackal and pointing back over her shoulder.

Toward rescue.

Diving out of the sky were Fran and the entire McBride Flying Cavalry.

Chapter Ten

Fool leaned back against the leather-backed booth and took another sip of the cold drink. There wasn't any reason for it, but the headache wouldn't go away.

Things hadn't exactly wrapped up neatly, but they'd gotten away by the skin of their teeth. Fran's cavalry had swooped in in the nick of time and hauled them away like eagles before Lucy's altered-reality illusion skill either wore off or was overpowered by the System Knights.

He'd come too damned close to being dead too many times since leaving McBride for this stupid mission, and he was thoroughly sick of it. The headache was just a manifestation of that, he was sure. Another sip of the drink, and he slurped a little extra around the ice cube that had, annoyingly, insisted it belonged in his mouth. At least it was small enough that he could spit it back into the drink.

He glanced up again, trying to make eye contact with Jackal, but the big man was still sitting slump-shouldered, staring into his drink. If Fool had to guess, he'd say that Jackal was somewhere between depressed, furious, and confused. Clearly, they'd need to have a sit-down alone after all of this and help sort each other out. Nothing he could do about that now. With a sigh, he turned and looked at their new companion. His new boss? He was going to figure that out, as well as everything else.

"You're sure they can't find us here?"

Lucy gave a little shake of her head. "No more than we can find out where they are. A lot of the normal rules of things are getting twisted right now, but this is one way that benefits us."

Jackal snorted. "Legendaries." All he added to that was a slow shake of his head.

Fool could only nod in agreement. This had all gotten way too big, way too soon. "What's this Weaver dude's thing again? He just hates the Trickster. And what the hell is the Trickster? Not you, but kind of you? Feel free to go slow and use small words."

Lucy grinned and gestured with one hand to the server to get them another round of drinks. They were in Lucy's lair, the Twisted Chapel they'd been looking for. Fool was at least right that it was a nightclub of sorts and that dance competitions took place in it. He was wrong about everything else, as Lucy had beat into him on the flight over.

It had at least been a short flight. The nightclub had been built into what had once been a water reservoir for the City of Vancouver, located at the top of one of the highest points in the city. It had been fairly well-hidden even before the System, and heavy lifting had been done to transform it.

If you drove to Queen Elizabeth Park, you'd find a lovely geodesic dome conservatory and a quarry that had been turned into a showpiece garden—both of which acted as a small dungeon complex currently. To service those attractions, a large parking lot had been built. All around the parking lot was lovely park space on a little mountain. Rose gardens, trees, a golf course, and tons of little picnic spots.

If you walked down from the parking lot toward the rose garden and kept going, you'd eventually run out of path and wind up at a little patio, somewhat hidden in trees, with a small access road. Where that patio met the edge of the little mountain, an immense square concrete arch surrounded a large metal sliding door. Behind that was the reservoir.

Or what had been the reservoir. Lucy, with significant funds and aid from some heavy-hitters, had transformed the entire thing into an epic underground dungeon of a nightclub.

Invite only, reinforced by the strays from the dungeon they abutted and a ton of purchased protections. Fool still wasn't sure what it was all in service of, aside from fulfilling the whims of a Master Class/Avatar of a Legendary/God/whatever Lucy was. Hopefully she'd get to that as part of the explanations.

Lucy waited for the server—who was something like a Kobold, a small, bipedal, red-skinned lizard in jeans and a T-shirt—to drop off their drinks before she answered.

"Might as well start with the Weaver." Lucy took a drink and stared off into the distance for a moment.

It gave Fool time to confirm that those were, indeed, tiny horns poking up through her hair. He'd always figured he'd sell his soul to the devil, but he'd never figured that would be literal.

"The Weaver is a member of the Galactic Council. One of the folks who decided to make Earth a Dungeon World."

Jackal jerked back. "You mean we're in conflict with a member of the rulers of the universe?"

Lucy shrugged. "Sorta. Hang tight, got some background to fill you in on here. Weaver's been around forever, like the Trickster. Weaver's one of those folk who see the System as a religion, as a divine power that shapes the universe into its true path or some crap. He's the head of a faction of people who feel like him, and they're a voice to be reckoned with on the Galactic Council. They shape the way the System spreads, how it takes form, all that fun stuff—at least as much as they can. Not sure how they do it, but they do."

"Religious fanatics," Fool cut in. "Great."

Lucy nodded. "Pretty much. It gets worse obviously. The System religion they worship is a bit weird, because of course there are all kinds of Priest and Cleric classes. Mostly, they accept… encourage that, and see them all as products of the System. If the individuals don't understand, that's from their ignorance, and it's part of the grand plan."

"Except for you?" Jackal said with a raised eyebrow.

"Me-ish. And DM. And the Big Guy, but I'll get into that in a bit. But yeah, we're the enemy as far as the Weaver is concerned. The devil in the flesh. Fair, because that's how we like things. It's what we are. The universe is vast and unending, but it's still too small for sanctimonious assholes to think they can get away with controlling everything. We've been a thorn in his side since he first hit Master Class millennia ago. Started out just twitting the asshole to get a rise out of him, make him look like a fool—nothing personal there, Fool—in front of everyone. Somewhere along the line, he took it real serious, and he's spent the last thousand years or so crushing everything connected with us and hunting us down. Which ain't easy to do, not with the Avatar Skill, but yeah. Here we are."

That brought them a small moment of silence. A few weeks ago, Jackal and Fool had been feeling relatively on top of the world. They weren't just Advanced Class, but they'd leveled repeatedly. They'd always had an underdog spirit, but a big part of that had come from their enemies underestimating them. It had felt pretty good to actually be capable of handling most issues without having to hide themselves all that much.

The rock troll had knocked the wind out of Fool's sails, but he'd known he'd recover from that in time. Being bounced without effort by a Master Class? That had not been something Fool enjoyed.

And now learning they were the enemies of a Legendary? That didn't feel fair at all. Not that any of this was fair, but it had been nice to feel as though they had their own angle that was working.

It was too much to think about. With a muttered profanity, Fool let his head drop onto the table, and he slowly banged his forehead against the hard surface. He stopped after a bit, because the rattling shake was starting to feel good, and he didn't think that was a habit he wanted to pick up. He'd already had enough experience with bad habits.

When Fool pulled his head back up, Lucy and Jackal were looking at him with patient expressions. At least Jackal looked patient. Lucy looked bored. Everything was shitty enough that Fool figured he should just start with the more personal stuff. Might as well be selfish. Couldn't hurt.

"So you're the cat? Or the Trickster? I'm still trying to wrap my head around that."

Lucy sighed and leaned back in the booth. "Both. And neither. DM was an Avatar of the Trickster, and so am I. It's a Legendary Skill. The Trickster can duplicate himself, but since he's been around a long time, his Skills are more than a little affected by chaos. Another reason the Weaver hates us. This shows up in the duplicate process by having each duplicate be a little different. 'Conditional' is what the Trickster calls us. Truthfully, he's more than capable of making an absolute clone of himself, but he really can't stand the thought of that. And the best he can do is Heroic for Avatar classes. And even at that, he has to be cautious. Mana gets *strange* at those intensities."

Jackal was leaning forward, clearly interested in the direction this was going. Fool was following so far, but he hoped he wasn't going to wish for a notebook soon. Lucy took another sip of her drink and continued.

"That's one of the reasons you don't have to worry about direct intervention from the Weaver, by the way. Dungeon worlds are pretty strong with the Mana flow, but a Legendary can almost suck that dry just by being in the area. Skills at that level need a lot of Mana. It's also why the Trickster shouldn't be able to help you directly. Not with Skills anyway. And he'd also been hoping not to draw too much attention from the Weaver to Earth, not until he was able to get his plans rolling a little better. That's why the avatar for Earth was DM, your little black cat. Just strong enough to give you local support for your 'Have Faith' skill by channeling some of the Trickster to support you."

Fool leaned forward and held up a hand. "So what happened to DM?" He hated to admit that he missed the cat, but he was missing that cat. It had been a pain in the ass for the most part, but that was part of the charm of cats. "Is she really gone?"

Lucy shook her head. "I'm DM. Or I guess we are. I got sent down here around the same time, for another reason, but then something big enough happened to get the Weaver's attention, and we needed more ability to influence things. So... hm. Kinda hard to explain. DM and I come from the same source, so we just kind of blended our potential together. Not like becoming one person or anything, but more like you giving all your Mana pool, Skills, and Experience to Jackal so he could do whatever he wanted with them. And when that happened, you would go and live inside him. Make sense?"

"No." Fool shook his head, held up a finger, and drained his drink. "Fuck no. But I guess. Is it reversible?"

"Maybe. Don't know. This is new. Welcome to the real joy of the Trickster, Fool. We're all making it up as we go along."

Fool slammed his empty glass onto the tabletop. "But what the hell for? There a point to all of this, or is it just survival at higher and higher levels? What's the fucking reason for all of this?"

Jackal was staring at him. That made sense to Fool, because he'd rarely let the other man see his angry side. But seeing Rebecca used for this had pissed him off. Pissed him off enough that he was feeling a level of rage that echoed back to the range of emotion he used to feel before the System had fixed his broken brain.

Dammit, Fool still loved Rebecca. And now he had to grapple with not only seeing her again and feeling a very old wall torn open in his heart, but also feeling the flare of hope he'd thought he'd long buried soar back up. And then get crushed back down by not only uncertainty but also worry. Was she safe? Had she just been using him? When he'd escaped, how had Kantele reacted to that?

Whatever was going on, having Rebecca used like that, having him used like that, made him taste blood in the back of his throat. And he didn't think the taste of that would go away until he could replace it with someone's hot red blood. Preferably Kantele's. Or the Weaver.

Or maybe the Trickster.

He looked at Lucy and didn't try to hide what he was feeling at all. She met his eyes and didn't flinch. He saw her violet eyes flicking back and forth, tiny motions, like she was scanning deep into the backs of his eyes.

"Freedom, Fool. What it's always been about. What the Trickster means, what you mean, what you've always wanted in the world. Freedom. Not a false freedom of gluttony and tyranny in the pursuit of desire, self at the expense of all, but a real freedom. An open universe to explore, to play in, to find the limits of yourself… open and accessible to everyone without any barriers at all."

"That's not possible," Jackal said in a quiet voice.

Fool glanced at him, but the big man was just looking into his drink. Lucy put a hand on Jackal's shoulder.

"Possibility is the greatest tyrant of all, Jackal. The first thing in the world that breaks our heart is learning that there are limits to ourselves. Every philosophy you humans ever came up with is just a way to reconcile yourself to a life limited in every sense. Caged by possibility. And the System is the greatest lie of possibility ever. It's a clapped-on cage that shapes and forces Mana into something that can be understood. Something that can be grasped. And that means controlled, and through that, everyone can be controlled. Forced into a fucking atavistic machine of levelling up, dying, or settling for a shorter life at the whims of those with the will to push harder and kill more. Possibility is the chain that shape Mana into what cages us all, Jackal."

Then she turned and looked Fool in the eyes, and this time her gaze locked into him like a magnet. All he could see was the swirling depth of hidden motion, a universe-sized black hole pulling him in.

"The Trickster wants to break those chains and set the Mana free. And you two are the hammer and chisel to do that." Then she laughed, and that broke the frozen tableau of the moment. "At least, if you think you're up to it."

Fool shook his head. This was a stupid level of grandiose. Which obviously appealed to him. But even so, words were just words without something concrete to back them up. He supposed that a Legendary, with world-breaking powers, would be capable of just about anything. That was far too much for his mind to comprehend, and he really didn't even want to try. Jackal was the theoretical physicist, not him. Fool was intrigued, but there had to be more earth element to this.

"We might be. Fairly sure you don't mean for us to find this Weaver person and punch them in the face though. What's the plan?"

The grin on Lucy's face could only be described as predatory. "The plan, my dear Fool, is complex, fraught with risk, and has a tight deadline. And, of course, almost no chance of success. Still interested?"

Jackal laughed, and Fool tried not to break his neck with his exaggerated eye roll.

"Obviously," Fool said. "Sounds like our kind of thing. So there is an actual plan then?"

"Yup. I suppose the short version of it is that the Trickster has been analyzing the flow of Mana and the expansion of the System over a few millennia and found some patterns. These patterns represent a very remote possibility. In order to make this even remotely possible, certain alliances had to be made. Ever heard of the Technocrats?"

Fool shook his head, and Jackal tilted his head.

"You don't mean the twentieth-century political movement, do you?" Jackal said. "The one that wanted the world to be run by scientists and engineers?"

Lucy's eyes went wide. "Holy Pauper's Horns. You people seriously had something like that? Humans. Damn. One of something everywhere, I guess. No. Not that. And I might have translated the name wrong. Technomancers might be better. A group of crazy folk who either try to use pre-System science to understand the System, or have tried to work around the System by stretching technology to its limits. As a result of this, they spend more time outside of the influence of the System, staying ahead of its advance throughout the universe and trying to develop new tech to deal with it."

Lucy stopped, because Jackal had frozen in place.

"You okay?" she asked.

"Can… can you put me in touch with these people?"

Fool burst out laughing. "Dude! You look like the biggest fan boy in the world right now!"

Jackal's lips thinned out and his eyebrows drew down, and he gave Fool the meanest glare he could.

Lucy tsked and waved at the server for more drinks. Fool squawked when she nabbed his neglected drink and downed it, but she ignored him and continued on with her exposition.

"Anyway. Technomancers have access to space travel and tech without access to Mana or the System, so they've been building outposts and colonies across the universe. Trickster's been helping them from time to time, and they finally found the opportunity we've been looking for. A world a few decades ahead of the encroaching System wave, but already experiencing the effects of a far-reaching eddy of enhanced Mana. We've found a few of these before, but there's always been the same problem—travel time."

Jackal nodded. "FTL? Faster than light travel?"

"Right. Not a problem in the System universe, and the techies have a drive that works, but the physics-warping effects of Mana and the System make a kind of wave front that's been expanding across the universe unevenly. That wave front can fuck with their drive in unexpected ways. But this new world is lying in a goldilocks location. Just right for access… but."

Fool shook his head and looked at the ceiling. "This should be good."

There was no way something that relied on that much complexity would be easy. And Lucy had been soft-selling the hard sell all along, so this was probably the real nasty bit.

The server arrived with the next round, but Fool passed on his. The alcohol wasn't doing much anyway, and he'd lost his taste for chemical distortion past a certain degree a long time ago. Lucy seemed to chew on her next words, so he took a moment to look around the club while he waited for her to jump ahead.

It was spacious, but it clearly showed its legacy of being a reservoir. Concrete predominated, though it was mostly covered up. The vast space had been broken up into multiple platforms that all connected into a staggered set of floors and a plaza, short steps connecting them all. There was a central dance pit of considerable size, with a stage at one end of it. On every wall except the one behind the stage, an extended gallery had been built. There were a few different bars around the place, scattered at prime locations. The overall impression that Fool got was an eighties-era goth nightclub blended with a cyberpunk elf aesthetic. He kinda liked it. Felt like a cozy new home.

Lucy cleared her throat a little, and Fool realized he'd been woolgathering.

"The 'but' in this case is that the window to access this world is only open for a short time. That's good and bad. Good, because it means once we get a team there, the window closes pretty much until the main wave front arrives. So not only will there be time to prepare, but we'll also be uninterrupted until then. Bad news is it's a one-way trip. So we have an escape hatch from the System, and an opportunity to build up a more solid resistance force than we've ever had before. We'll have decades to level everyone up."

Jackal held up his hand, for a moment looking enough like an eager school child that Fool had to resist the urge to pat his head. Lucy glanced at

Jackal and brushed the hair away from one of her horns, nodding at him to share.

"How is your army supposed to level up without the System? How does that work?"

"Strangely. Poorly, for the most part. And we also have no real idea. We've done some testing on Forbidden Zone worlds, but the theory is that they're different. The key element is that it's not going to work the same way though." She smiled at Jackal and Fool, and the smile was bright. "No limits. No structure, no patterns to fall into."

"How is that supposed to work?" Fool asked. "No classes? No skills? That doesn't make any sense."

"You already know the answer to that. Those eddies of Mana started long ago, drifting in and around Earth. You've got the written legacy of all of that, but when the Mana passed on again, you lost the context for it."

"Magic." Jackal was nodding and grinning. "Magic. Ritual and incantations, a way to shape the wild Mana, turning into the will of the practitioner."

"Got it in one, big guy. The folk who make this trip will have to embrace and develop their own systems of magic. From scratch. That's why Earth is so important to us. The Mana power of a Dungeon World, but fresh and raw enough that it's still possible to find people who haven't become locked in to the System."

Fool tapped his fingers on the edge of the table. He was realizing where this was going. "That's why the nightclub. Pull in the outsiders, those who can't fit into the mold. Give them a safe place, give them a way to prosper, and guide them into getting ready for your little mission. This is a recruiting office for your army of rebels, isn't it?"

"Testing lab, more than that. It's not going to be easy, and every day that passes, the System ingrains itself more into everyone. At a certain point, they won't be able to really break free and take advantage the way we need them to. By the time anyone finds this place, they've already got the mindset and willingness to fight against the System, but once they're here, it's training and testing them."

"The contest," Jackal said. "The dance we saw, something strange going on with the Mana. That's who you've been training, and that's your test, isn't it?"

"The contest is the final test. We've finished everything else and finally built the engine to transport a team. We've got a few hundred people for support, and some other candidates, but the final crew will come from here. The dance contest is designed to filter and test for the candidates with the highest potential. When the winning crew is chosen, they'll be transported to the new world immediately. And that will be the last chance to ever reach that world. They all know this, and they've all volunteered."

Fool had learned a little too much about the world to take that at face value. "A few decades away from the world, away from leveling up and gaining power, wealth, making family or friends or connections, on a whim of a chance? You found that many true believers willing to sacrifice it all?"

Lucy didn't wince at his tone, just reached up and flicked a finger against one of her horns. It made a bright ping, like a tuning fork or a bell. Or a hammer striking an anvil. "You already saw some of the competitors, didn't you?"

Fool and Jackal nodded. The vampire gang had made an impression, and the other street dancers had also seemed to fall into distinct groups.

"Whoever wins gets to put their approach to power on top of the pack. If our calculations are correct, when the System arrives, they'll be the equivalent of Heroics, maybe even Legendaries themselves. Not quite strong enough to take on the Galactic Council, but they'll be more than strong enough to attract armies… worlds to their sides. They can forge empires, if they wish. It's a journey that might turn them into gods. Some of them want to go from pure ambition. Some are going to make sure the ambitious ones don't get the chance to shape the future. Some of them are true believers even. We've got a lot of crews ready to do this, and they make up all kinds of humans. That's your world. These are your people, good or bad. And they are going to find out what absolute power does to them."

Fool stood and walked away. Not far. His head was swimming, and a lot of pieces were falling together for him. What he was realizing was not making him feel good at all. He looked at his hands, and they were shaking.

He wasn't feeling rage, and that surprised him. If he was right, a lot of people had been used without their knowledge, including him and Jackal. That should be pissing him off royally.

The only reason it wasn't was because… maybe… it was for a good cause.

Either way, he had to know.

He turned around and walked back to the table. "The Foundation, the Machine, you used that, didn't you? That's how you recruited your teams, isn't it?"

"The Foundation shares our goal. Professor Xi knew about this from the first day. He was recruited in almost the same way you were. You didn't think they could afford that huge damned base all on their own, did you? The weapons and Skills that let you advance much faster than you should have been able to? Trickster can't come here, can't interfere too much, but moving Credits is one of his oldest games. He's damned good at it. It was never enough to tip the balance too much, but more than enough to ensure that his Adept had the support to keep ahead of the game."

"Christ," Fool said, "I've been an actual priest in an actual church this whole fucking time, haven't I? It was never just a Class, was it?"

"Not really. But also yes. You knew none of this was ever going to be easy or make sense. You knew that from the start. You've been a good priest. You've recruited some stand-out followers who will keep the faith going."

"Alex. Olivia."

"Yup. They'll be offered a shot at the trip. No need to compete."

"Trickster's not a god though. Just a Legendary." Fool's voice sounded odd to himself.

A whole part of his mind had split off and was raging about unfairness and lies and cheating and wrongness. That split-off part felt as if it was slowly being locked away in the back of his head, but that wasn't true.

His own internal Trickster was finally waking up. That was the truth. Fool's entire view of the world, of himself, was being shaken. And somehow, he was able to just let go and let it flow. He'd been carrying a lot of cynicism around with him, and it had really shaped how he felt about things. Maybe, just maybe, he could let himself scale up a little bigger. Maybe... be a little bigger. Maybe let himself hope and let go of hurt.

Lucy smiled at Fool. "What's a god if not a Legendary? And you already know how the System imprints things and shapes a common understanding—orcs and elves, dwarves, goblins, trolls, dragons. You didn't think the same thing applied to all of your myths and tales? To your religions? Tricksters been around a long time. So that makes you as much of a priest as most others." She leaned back and let out a laugh. "I suppose that makes me an angel!"

"Fallen angel," Jackal said. "Lucy Brightside. You chose that name for a reason."

Lucy just grinned, and her horns twinkled like dark stars.

Chapter Eleven

"So who we looking at?"

The Twisted Chapel was packed, which led Fool to wonder just how exclusive the place was… until he saw a group of ball-shaped aliens appear on one of the floors. The wall had briefly turned transparent with a purple sheen, and the aliens had just walked through. Clearly, Lucy had set the place up with some sort of teleportation access. Or set it up to allow easier teleportation access? He had no idea how that worked, but he figured there had to be some kind of expense involved.

Actually, the whole damned place looked incredibly expensive. They'd spent the night in a quite pleasant guest room, then stayed inside for the day. Lucy had been pretty clear that the Twisted Chapel was the safest place for them, with a group of Master Class opponents out hunting them. She confessed Kantele had found her way in once before through a weakness that had since been patched, so there was no longer any way for anyone to access the place without an invite. And while they were in there, their location was hidden as well.

The kitchen was more than serviceable, so they'd been happy to spend the day there. Especially after Lucy had set them up with a temporary communications method that had let them inform Fran and the team that they were okay, but incognito for a bit. Fool had even chatted with Olivia for a bit, confirming that she already knew where the Twisted Chapel was and would make her way over after some more shopping in Vancouver.

No one had heard anything more from Kantele and the System Knights, and part of that was the Vancouver City Council's doing. The McBride Flying Cavalry had been hired to be auxiliary police for the city, but not the usual kind of police. Most law enforcement was handled by System contracts that enforced a certain standard of behavior in the city, keeping most crime to a minimum. The auxiliary were here to prevent any abuse of power that occurred in unpredicted ways. And a group of Master Class attackers materializing in the city and laying into folks was pretty much what the city had imagined as the worst-case scenario, so they'd thrown in some upgrades and new restrictions to make things harder for Kantele to rampage at a whim. It was only a temporary fix. Partially due to expense, but mostly because the fledgling City Council wasn't keen to piss off not just a team of high-level Advanced Classers, but also what appeared to be a highly connected team. So the Trickster's team had at most a day or two free of potential attack. Probably.

Which would almost be enough time. The dance competition, and the resulting jump to a new world, was only a few days away. Should be plenty of time to get that wrapped up and figure out a solution to Kantele and the System Knights.

Privately, Fool hoped that the dance comp would go off without a hitch and Kantele would just decide there was nothing more she could do and bugger off.

He was always happy to hope.

In the meantime, they were guests of the Twisted Chapel and getting a guided tour of how the underground dance competitions had been running, and a who's who of the best dance crews.

The current crew performing for the crowd comprised six striking humanoids. Lucy had assured him that all the competitors were human, but the System allowed for a ton of customization on that basic profile.

Lucy was watching them from the same elevated walkway as Fool, and she was leaning over the railing. "House Ember, current champions and heavy favorites to win the whole thing."

Fool could believe it. They had a physical presence that alone must have put them near the top.

The lead dancer was currently in the spotlight. She was a tall, trim woman, currently standing stock still with her left hand raised to her chin, her index finger resting on her lower lip. Lips parted, she stared off into the audience, and it was hard not to stare at her. It was the intensity of her pose. Not even moving, she stood upright with just the slightest s-curve to her stance. The effect was as if she was frozen between one step and the next, about to do… something.

She wore a long black robe, open in the front, and a translucent black body suit underneath. Barefoot, but the body suit covered her feet as well.

Her irises were a bloody ruby red, and instead of hair, there was a crown of sharp-pointed horns all around her head with two larger bull-shaped horns rising from just above and behind her ears. The epitome of a demon. As were the rest of the members of House Ember.

A young man squatted at one end of the stage, clad in red and orange silky robes, with elven ears and flowing curling locks of golden yellow hair, with two black curling onyx horns.

A giant slab of slate-grey muscle, nearly Jackal's size, with a serpentine tail weaving behind him nearly twice as long as he was tall. He wore no clothes other than a rough fur loincloth but was covered with horny spikes and projections. Bison horns sprouted from his head.

A woman with an absolutely flat face and the mouth of a serpent, wearing a long red dress slit so deeply on the sides that it looked more like a rectangle of red hanging from her breasts. A shimmering halo of ice-like spines glowed around the perimeter of her skull.

A small waif, barely five feet tall, no horns, but eyes and hair of white flame.

The final member was an almost classic demon, eyes of pink fire, purple skinned with two large pink horns projecting from her forehead. Her fingers ended in long and narrow points, evil claws that glimmered in the light. Completely nude, she capered almost nonstop in the background, her motions contorting between seductive and menacing from one heartbeat to the next.

The music started. It was a heavy and fast disco beat, which surprised the hell out of Fool. He'd expected metal or maybe opera, but when the dancer moved, it all made sense.

Her dance was a blend of stillness and sharp, staccato motion. She stepped forward languidly, a leg settling to its place on the stage with ownership. Her hands jerked and flicked faster than he could follow, then her elbows. She added in shoulder shrugs in staccato counterpoint, the entirety of her arms moving in explosive confidence.

"Holy shit," Fool couldn't stop himself from saying, leaning forward to watch more. It was mesmerizing.

"Surprised you haven't seen this before."

Fool glanced at Lucy, but she was pointedly looking at the stage and ignoring him. He'd been familiar with street dance, just from being the kind of person who was never seen by others and spent a lot of time watching. That wasn't what she was talking about though.

It looked familiar. The dancer was doing her own thing and it was different, but he could see parts of it that were a throwback to an older style, to an older world he'd been peripheral to.

"That where you got the 'house' context from?"

Lucy was still looking at the stage, but the lights highlighted her toothy grin. "You could say so, yeah. Trickster was right. Some of you humans were pretty damned cool."

"Sometimes. Some of us. So 'Trickster.' You kind of skipped past that before. Just how related are you?"

For a moment, Fool thought a shrug was all he was going to get, but Lucy took a moment to chew her lip before answering.

"I'm, like, a part. A hologram, I guess? Maybe a facet of a gem, if I'm feeling shiny. All his memories are there. At least as far as I can tell. Imagine you split off a part of yourself right now. Just took a snapshot of your mind and all its thoughts. Then you dumped those thoughts into a robot that thought it was human. The thoughts that the robot would have would be shaped from the moment it got turned on, but because your thoughts assume you have a past, then the robot would too, right? And all its thoughts going forward, even into the next millisecond, would be shaped by what it thought it had just experienced. It would be you, but every single thought from that point on would diverge, especially when it realized it was a robot that had just had memories put into it. So I'm like that, with an echo or selection of chosen Skills. Make sense?"

Fool nodded, and it brought back a memory. "I read a comic book a long time ago, can't remember what it was, but one character said a line that stuck with me. 'Am I a butterfly dreaming I am a man, or a man dreaming I am a butterfly?'"

Lucy laughed and leaned back from the railing, holding on with one hand. "You screwed that quote up, Fool, but yeah, something like that. Am I the Trickster dreaming? Or… yeah. Something like that. Bit more complex because of quantum mechanics or Mana or something. And a lot of what makes a Legendary capable of the things they can do is that the System has deeply and profoundly changed them. I'm only a Master Class, so about ninety-nine percent of what makes the Trickster who he is is just inaccessible or beyond comprehension for me. But that one percent is enough. Plus, everything I'm made myself into from that seed is pretty kick-ass. That answer your question?"

"I suppose. Don't mean to pry. It's just… personality is a complex thing for me. Sense of self and all that. Mine was pretty damaged, but the Trickster and the System guidance and rebuild put me back together. I'm more me than I was ever able to be before. If that makes sense. So I'm just curious…"

"If you're actually you? Or if the Trickster snuck you in as some sort of Avatar?"

Fool went a little numb. That was exactly what he was afraid of, but he hadn't actually let that thought rise to the top of his mind. But apparently it had been driving his subconscious.

Lucy punched his shoulder then bumped her head into him. It was the sort of thing DM might have done, and Fool had to resist the urge to scritch Lucy behind an ear.

"You're you, Fool. I suppose that doesn't help, because I'm me. And I will confess that the Trickster has far more history with this world that you might imagine. But nah, that's not the kind of thing he would do. He can for sure be a dick, but some things he'd never fuck with. And that's one of them."

"So what about DM? What happened to the cat?"

"Ever have a daydream that felt real? Or a dream that felt so real that you woke up feeling like you'd lost something? She's like that inside me right now, only she doesn't fade with time. Same'll happen to me if the Trickster ever recalls me. It's not an end, just kind of a pause. As long as he's around, he can always call us back up. But that's all I want to talk about that, 'kay?"

The first dancer had stepped back to let their opponent take a turn. The competition was running as a head-to-head, single elimination tournament, team against team. Or House against House. Each House was free to put up as many dancers as they wanted, and the dancers competed against each other in some kind of complex one-on-one/group-versus-group flow that didn't really make too much sense to Fool. Somehow, it was still easy to tell when one group was better than the other, even if it felt like it all came down to style in the end.

The experience gain was weird too. Lucy had explained it, but the whole thing had gone over Fool's head, especially when she'd started talking about how the whole dance floor setup was akin to a really strong dungeon in how much Mana it pulled out of the environment—something to do with crazy powerful but useless prizes that were awarded. One example was boots that would allow you to leap to any location you could see, instantly, with no Mana cost. Only you needed both boots and only one boot was available. Craziness like that, but somehow it allowed level ups, and the System supported it all. It was clearly the kind of loophole that would drive the Weaver insane, Fool figured.

House Ember easily won their match, and the next few teams weren't nearly up to their quality. They all put on good shows, but they had a heavy reliance on showy Skills. The extra drama was cool and sometimes jaw-dropping, but Fool saw what Lucy, and the Trickster, were looking for. The lesser houses were more tied to the System as it was. They leaned into big, showy uses of Skill to pull off tricks. They were showing off.

The stronger dancers were warping Mana to suit them, just touching on Skill to stretch physics and human limits enough for them to reach extra levels of artistic expression. They used less Mana, but they used it much better.

It really showed up when combat fit into the dances.

Earth was a Dungeon World now, and it made sense that dance would include a level of violence that wouldn't have been imagined in a pre-System world. It was frowned upon to kill or seriously injure an opponent, but as long as it was done in the spirit of the dance, and to the rhythm, attacking your opponent was part of the dance.

The less skilled dancers? Attacked when they saw an opening. Relied on power, speed, aggression, surprise. The things that worked when you were fighting monsters. The kind of Skill use the System rewarded.

House Ember had shown why they were the top contenders. In the bout Fool had watched, the other team had countered with dance moves for a bit, but knowing they were out-matched, they'd tried a surprise attack. Three dancers had advanced in a line, getting right up to the side of the Embers, then exploded into complex power moves, backed by an explosive display of pyrotechnic and gravity-defying skills. It was a muscular and eye-catching display.

Of course, it was a cover for the two other dancers who crept behind the showing line, then leapt up and over and delivered perfectly synchronized spears of flame right into the waiting and watching Embers.

Fool had been impressed. It was a good, sneaky tactic, and they were clearly leveled up enough to be more of a threat than Fool would be happy facing.

The Embers, who'd never stopped dancing when they yielded the center stage, didn't even bother to counterattack. They seemed to somehow dance around and through the firestorm until the flames looked as though they were dancing with the Embers. The flames solidified into a spiral almost-snake, that settled down to ground level and spiraled in and around the feet of the Embers, who used the glowing fire as footlights, dramatically showing them off as they marched forward in a line. They moved in a coordinated wave of powered stomps that visibly shook the footwork of the other side, and the Embers' rapid hand gestures leaned into a shaming display. Throwing no attacks of their own, they'd not just turned their opponents' attack against them, they'd made it a centerpiece of their own performance.

The crowd had erupted into applause, and the System-backed judges had awarded House Ember the win.

That had impressed Fool, but mostly he'd been impressed by how quickly and smoothly they'd turned the tables. They'd made it look easy, as if it was part of their plan from the beginning.

Fool had caught the truth of it though. Perception was one of the chief attributes of his class, so he'd seen how the Embers had been caught off guard. The surprise had worked, but they'd reacted as a well-trained combat team. One of them had made the first move to deal with the fire, using some Skill, and the others hadn't moved in a planned response to that… they'd reacted. Fluidly, naturally, but still reactively. To Fool, that showed a level of skill that left him in awe. He was positive that he was a higher level than House Ember and could probably beat them in a standup fight. That didn't mean he wasn't envious of the skill shown though. He wanted to watch them again with Jackal and see if the two of them couldn't pick up some clues on how they could improve their own teamwork.

If they could add those skills to their own Skills, they'd be able to walk over much stronger opponents.

He glanced around to see if he could spot Jackal and found the big man down by the side of the stage. Jackal was talking to a pale young man in a black-and-gold bolero with a floating halo of black shards around his face. Fool grinned. That had to be the "Darling Nikki" Jackal had been talking about the other day.

Wouldn't hurt to confirm, so Fool nudged Lucy and pointed toward the two with his chin. "That your way of trying to reach us when we got to town?"

Lucy shrugged. "Just a little nudge. Nicholaus volunteered for the job. Said something about a 'tasty bear,' if I recall."

"Ha! I don't think Jackal would object too much to that label. So… no issues I should know about? Safe for Jackal?"

"Look at you! Quarter the size of Jackal, but you gotta look out for him? That's cute!"

"I don't have to anything. He can look out for himself. I just haven't seen him get involved with anything serious before, and if I'm not mistaken, Nikki there is looking a little smitten."

Lucy watched the two for a bit. Nicholaus said something that made Jackal laugh, and while he was laughing, Nicholaus touched Jackal's elbow. It was a brief touch, a fingertip and nothing more, and Jackal didn't seem to react at all… aside from moving just a little closer as their conversation continued. Something jumped in Fool when he saw that. Jackal was never short of lovers, but the truth hadn't been hidden from Fool. There was a loneliness in Jackal that bodies, or even friendship, couldn't answer. Nicholaus was bringing out something different in Jackal, and Fool found himself hoping it was what his friend really needed.

She nodded. "Want to learn a bit more about the earnest suitor?" When Fool nodded, she continued. "He's good people. Been through a bit of rough times, came out rougher, but he's learned to put a shine on things. Part of House Masque. They're expected to get to the semifinals, along with House Magus. Both underdogs, but they've got a chance."

"Other than Ember, who's the other house you think will final?"

"House Dark. Creepy elegant dudes."

"Vampire vibe? I think I saw them downtown yesterday."

"That's the ones. Great dancers, real strong vibe. Probably not great if they win. That kind of aristocratic vibe isn't really ideal, but rules are rules. Everyone gets a chance to play for the prize."

She looked out across the crowd for a moment, then seemed to make up her mind. She gestured to someone, then turned back to Fool. "Dark and Masque won't meet until the semis, but the tradition when we've run previous comps is to whet the crowd's appetite for the coming days with some one-on-one dance-offs. I've seen these two before, but you might like this. Get a sense of what young master Nicholaus is like."

Fool raised his eyebrows but turned to watch the stage. Sure enough, helpers had nudged Nicholaus and drawn him to the stage. Jackal glanced up at Fool, and Fool just shrugged. It wasn't like they didn't expect Lucy to play games.

The young man strode up on the stage, and Fool noted that he had a slim rapier strapped to his side.

Another figure was making his way through the crowd toward the stage. A tall, powerfully built man. He vaulted onto the stage from a distance away, and it was obvious right away that he was a member of House Dark. He didn't have the same goth/business vampire style as the others, but the whole silver cuirass, helm topped with a flowing red tassel, elbow length white gloves, and big ass cavalry boots somehow echoed the same feeling. Tainted nobility was certainly a look.

The trooper had a matching cavalry sabre, but neither he nor Nicholaus drew their swords. Instead, they stared at each other as the music started.

The trooper started first. He didn't move his hands at all, just his feet. Fool recognized the rapid steps and angled feet as coming from Irish step dancing, with some added stomps to accent the dramatic look of the cavalry boots. After a quick burst of that, the trooper slowed the steps until he was doing a slow-motion step dance. It was captivating, and it took Fool a moment to realize that it wasn't an optical illusion that made the trooper look like he was floating. He was using a Skill to warp gravity around his feet, on and off, to add a bizarre strobing effect. It was a captivating performance, but then it was Nicholaus's turn.

The halo of black shards never changed around his face, no matter what motions he did, like a mask that never touched his face. Fool couldn't quite tell if they were solid or some kind of hologram, because when Nicholaus danced, sometimes it looked as though his hands passed through the shards. Or they moved aside.

The dance was an eye-catching opposite of the trooper's, flashing arms and still feet. Nicholaus hardly moved his feet at all for the first bit, instead making complex geometric shapes with his arms and somehow weaving his body around those shapes to the beat. Just before his turn ended, he moved his feet, pivoting and sliding about, adding to the complex body weaves. It was beyond hypnotic, and the audience roared its approval. Round one to darling Nikki, Fool guessed.

In the comps Fool had seen, the two dancers would go through a few rounds of taking turns dancing until a clear winner emerged. That this was different became apparent when Nicholaus and the trooper drew their swords on the same beat and advanced on each other.

Just out of reach, they circled each other, throwing cuts at lightning speed.

Nicholaus was the first to attack, slipping just into range of the trooper and slicing a cut at his head. The cut was fast, deadly… and right on tempo, with Nicholaus somehow still maintaining his unique dance style while throwing the cut.

Trooper dodged with a series of rapid pattering dance steps and prodigious leaning backward, then he jerked back upward and responded with a series of hammer-blow cuts from his sabre.

Nicholaus parried all of them at the last minute, letting the ring of blades add a subtle counterpoint to the beat of the music. Somehow, each parry lit a glowing spark on his rapier that left a trail in the air to the next parry. By the time the trooper finished his attacks, Nicholaus had traced a complex, arcane symbol in the air.

Nicholaus backed up a pace, moving his blade through the pattern, re-shaping it from a rectangular outline to a square one. With a single forceful cut, he smashed the pattern down through the air toward the trooper's feet. The pattern lanced into the floor, becoming a bigger, burning outline on the dance floor.

Trooper dodged away from the sigil, and Nicholaus chased him with another series of blistering razor cuts from his viciously adept rapier.

The combat continued back and forth, Skills blending seamlessly into dance and sword work.

It was engaging. Rapturous. It didn't take long to become clear that the sword blows weren't quite intended to land, at least not in a damaging way. Both participants had hair-fine cuts on them, but Fool saw them pass up lethal or disabling blows again and again.

It was a showcase of skill and passion, almost an exercise in a mutual display of braggadocio more than competition. Fool didn't need to see the grin on Nicholaus's face to know he'd won. The young man had put on one hell of a show, consistently out-pacing what was otherwise an amazingly capable opponent.

Lucy shoulder-checked Fool, and when Fool turned to look at her, she had a grin to match his. The devil was absolutely in her eyes, and her words a moment later confirmed Fool's impression. "Like what you see?"

"That… that looks like *so* much fun." He surprised himself with his own enthusiasm. Watching those two perform? It had filled him with a burst of energy, and he was buzzing with the need to release it somehow.

Her eyes just about swallowed him. "So, wanna try it?"

Chapter Twelve

"I'm too fucking old for this."

Jackal laughed, and Nicholaus leaned forward so Fool could hear him over the pounding bass. "You'll be fine. Just fight like you always do. Except do it for fun. All you have to do is listen to the music. The rest will just happen."

Fool looked up at the stage. His hammer felt oddly cold and slippery in his hand, almost too heavy. As if he'd never held the thing before almost. The damned stage looked huge from down on the floor. Not like the small and almost intimate space it had looked like from above.

It felt open and exposed from down here.

And Lucy, waiting on the stage, looked as big as Jackal.

The big man leaned in, and Fool felt Jackal's beard tickling his cheek. "Just have fun. Or kick some ass." Then he hugged Fool and shoved him toward the stairs.

Nicholaus wrapped his arm as much around Jackal's waist as he could and shouted, "Your partner awaits! Dance, Fool. Dance!"

The goddamned stairs, Fool thought, had been sized for giants. What the hell was he doing?

When he got to the top of the stairs, the stage didn't look so big anymore. It looked like a postage stamp surrounded by surging crowds.

It only took a moment for all that to fade though. The lights were all pointed down at the stage, but thankfully, due to some kind of System magic, there wasn't any heat associated with them. All the brightness was there though, and the audience faded out to blurs.

Fool was floating in space on a white square, and opposite him was the avatar of his god, the Trickster. Carrying a hammer to match his and a grin that didn't leave him feeling too happy at all.

A hammer fight with a Master Class opponent, even if it wasn't supposed to be more than the equivalent of a friendly sparring session, didn't strike him as a fun idea.

He didn't think there was any point in cursing ten-minute-ago him for agreeing to this stupid idea.

Hell. The only way forward was through.

Lucy snapped her fingers, and a microphone appeared in front of her, floating by itself in the air. The music stopped, and Fool felt the weight of the gaze of the crowd on him.

"Good afternoon, mortals, masters, gods, and all those in between! You are in for a treat. Y'all know that you're here due to the evil machinations of the Trickster, the darkest lord of all creation…" She had to pause to let the roar of approval, mockery, and catcalls roll to a peak and recede. "So! Now! For your pleasure, you get to watch two minions of the old bastard batter the hell out of each other!"

The roar this time was ear-popping, and Fool was not amused to see Jackal and his new beau stomping their feet and roaring along with all the others.

Lucy grinned at Fool and flicked an eyebrow up. He was disliking her almost as much as DM.

"In my corner… me! Scion of the God of Lies, black-clad stomper of pure hearts, lover, and corrupter of innocents of all races and persuasions, owner of your beloved Twisted Chapel, let's hear it for me, Lucy Brightside!"

Fool was pretty sure his ears were bleeding from the noise, and he'd probably lost some health or something. The roar went on for quite a while, and Fool found no reason to doubt his impression that he was facing the reigning champion of this sort of shindig. Or at least the crowd's favorite.

He was way too fucking old to be spontaneous. He reminded himself to never do this again.

Lucy made a patting motion in the air, and the wall of sounds tumbled down back into cheering mob territory. She pointed at Fool, and the crowd went silent.

"In *that* corner, the newest Adept of the Trickster, an aging has-been, a wreck of a human being, a rescuer of princesses, wooer of ladies of shining power, friend of spiders, slayer of wizards, a liar, a cheat, and a backyard sneak, let's hear it for Fool the God-Slayer!"

Fool put the hammer into his left hand so he could give the finger to Lucy. The invisible audience roared, this time with boos and catcalls and shouts.

That made Fool grin, and he had to nod at Lucy. She'd read him pretty well. The essence of the competition was dance, but Fool hadn't danced seriously a day in his life. And that was the smallest of the storm of insecurities that had been raging through his heart as the start of this nonsense show. Lucy had named and exaggerated enough about him, playing him up to be the villain until he couldn't keep taking himself seriously.

And hell, mugging it up as the bad guy just seemed like fun.

He turned and leered at the audience, lolling his tongue out and hunching his body in a contorted twist. It took some effort to avoid throwing in a "Mwahaha," but he managed.

Lucy swung her hammer in a lazy arc, catching the head in her other hand, and strutted toward Fool. When she was no more than a step away, she leaned in and whispered in his ear, "Don't overthink it. Just have fun."

That sounded easier to say than to do, as far as Fool was concerned. He had to admit though… he'd chosen to do this because it looked like fun. So why was he doing his best to make it something angsty?

This time, the grin that crossed his face was more natural and maybe a bit more wicked. Doubt and anxiety were part of his old brain. The System had fixed him, but the old habits still sneaked through once in a while. But now that he had a normal brain, he knew what to do when those feelings cropped up.

Embrace them, acknowledge, and move on.

It was time to have some fun.

Lucy had returned to her side of the ring, and Fool took a moment to evaluate her again. Aside from the sometimes-visible horns, she looked like a normal human woman, if on the very athletic end of things. Tough chick, for sure. Based just off of that, he expected her to move fast, hit hard, and generally be all over the place.

Based on the fact that she was also a Master Class and an avatar of basically a freaking god, he had to expect that she had more experience than him. More raw talent, stronger attribute scores across the board, and probably a hell of a lot more deceitful than he could manage.

His whole fighting style was based on doing the unexpected, but Lucy was probably better at that than he was.

Then he again, he wasn't supposed to win.

Just have fun.

That meant that all of his usual expectations and ways of fighting could go by the wayside. There was nothing to lose. Hell, he'd been set up as the bad guy, so the crowd would probably be happier to see him lose. All that meant that there wasn't any risk for him, so this was a chance to try things he would never do in an actual fight.

Crazy things.

Stupid things.

Fool things.

The grin on Lucy's face faltered a bit when she saw the look in his eyes. Then the music started, and they stepped in to battle.

Fool didn't rush. He stopped for a moment out of range, half-closed his eyes, and let the beat wash over him. Again, Lucy had made a good guess. It was some sort of modern metal tune. Fast, hard beat, but not crazy fast. Screaming drama queen vocals. That made him happy, and he slowly headbanged to the beat.

He glanced at Lucy, and she was banging along with him. Her horns had grown, rising out of her hair, ebony flashes as her hair whipped back and forth. He had to laugh.

She was air-guitaring with her hammer.

He let the laugh carry him forward, the biggest, strongest, one-armed overhead swing he could manage, aimed right between her horns.

The hammer smashed into the stage. Lucy had kept up the air guitar and spun like a matador out of the way of the strike. She didn't counter, so Fool followed up by grabbing the hilt of his hammer in both hands and spun himself in a circle with his arms outstretched.

He could just glance at Lucy ducking under the blow at the last second… but he didn't stop. Kept spinning, faster and faster, stepping quicker with his feet in smaller and smaller arcs.

Pushing the limits of his Agility to keep on his feet. And using his maxed Perception to keep an eye on Lucy, who was continuing to play at being a rock god, bouncing around him and mocking him with her guitar-hammer.

Just as Fool had figured she would. He pulled his arms in, and even his massive perception could barely keep up as the world spun faster and faster, a blistering human tornado spinning faster than any Olympic figure skater could have ever dreamed of.

Then he stopped.

Lunged and snapped out a blow so fast and hard that it actually cracked the air as the head of the hammer broke the sound barrier. The only reason his arm wasn't ripped right out of the socket was that he had activated Hammer of Loki at the last second. As it was, he felt tearing, and there was an actual loss of HP.

He'd never thrown such a powerful attack, and the force of it surprised him. He didn't think he'd be able to pull this off in a real fight, but he was going to try. The damage would be off the charts.

A jolt of pain went up his arms as the blow was stopped solidly.

Lucy has cross-blocked it, catching the blow in the middle of her hammer. Fool was shocked by that, but some of the sting was taken out by the surprised look on Lucy's face.

One side of her lips curled up in amusement. "All right. Let's play."

Fool couldn't even finish the internal "Oh shit" before she rained blows down on him.

It was all he could do to dodge, duck, dip, dive, and parry as many blows as he could, but even so, almost a quarter of them got through. Each one made him wince, but they were landing with perfect control. Painful, but not really injuring.

He wondered why he was still standing, but then he realized what was going on.

The blows were landing perfectly timed to the blast beat of the music.

She was playing him like a literal drum.

He bit back the flash of rage that kicked up. This was supposed to be more performance than fight, and Lucy was just playing her part. He'd have to do the same.

Rhythm was predictable. He knew when the next blow was going to land, even if he didn't know where. One way to beat that.

Limit the options of where Lucy could hit him. Standing up and blocking and moving, she could hit him anywhere she wanted to.

He dropped into a low squat.

That gave him all the time he needed. In order to hit him, she'd have to strike down. That didn't limit her potential targets all that much, but it meant that the next shot would be coming down on him. All he had to do was figure out which side it was coming from and…

He whipped up the back end of his hammer, the long horn catching on the back end of Lucy's hammer as her blow came down from the right. He gave it a swift yank, trying for a disarm, but she was ready for that, and her grip solidified.

She wasn't ready for him to let go of his own hammer, drop onto his left side, and kick out with his right foot. He connected solidly with her left ankle and sent it flying.

It was a beautiful attack, but she wasn't just a Master Class. She was a master of this game.

She didn't try to catch her balance. Her left ankle went flying back, but instead of trying to bring it down, she kicked it even farther back, spinning in place into a picture-perfect flip…

And landed in a perfect superhero three-point pose, her face inches from Fool's.

"That's more like it. You gotta use your Skills if you want a chance though."

His hammer dropped out of her grip, landing right on his crotch, and she somersaulted over him.

Fool winced the pain away, grabbed his hammer, and spun back around and onto his feet. Lucy wasn't doing the air guitar bit anymore. Instead, she was doing a tap-dance number and using her hammer as a cane. Adding in some hip sways to keep up with the driving tone of the music.

Fool paid more attention to his Mana Sense, watching the subtle signs of the ebb and flow of the energy moving around Lucy. He hefted his hammer and stepped forward.

And stopped.

Big spike of Mana, somehow connecting him to Lucy. That made sense to Fool. She had some way to predict his movements. If not predict them, at least get a sense of what they were going to be. That hunch was confirmed when he saw Lucy had moved in response to his steps.

Time to test that out a little more. He thought about throwing a chop to her shoulder, but she didn't react. Same thought in mind, he stepped forward. This time she shifted again, keeping up her tap dance, but moving her hammer so that it would just about be in the right place to intercept his blow.

That was interesting and got him thinking. She wasn't as fast as he'd thought; she was just able to tell what he was going to do and making sure she was ready to deal with it.

That sent Fool's brain into overdrive, and he stomped and moved his feet in time to the music, circling around Lucy. He threw careful shots, watching to see how she reacted and trying to determine what she reacted to.

It took a few careful circuits—and a fair bit of catcalling from the crowd—but he figured out exactly what triggered whatever Skill she was using. It wasn't something that looked into the future, so he reasoned it wasn't a Master Class Skill, but probably a device. Maybe even the hammer. What it was doing wasn't predicting as much as reading his intentions and communicating them to Lucy.

What he thought or planned didn't make a difference, and any really obvious feints were ignored too. But if he shifted his weight just right, moved his eyes a certain way, and transferred the hammer just so in his hands while moving it toward a target, Lucy would react to block that.

At least, that was what he hoped was happening. It was entirely possible the entire thing was some sort of elaborate trap.

He tested out his theory by setting up two shots in a row. Each shot made Lucy parry and dance off to the left, then he quickly set up an attack to the other side… and she moved just a hair before he did.

This time he was able to keep the smile off of his face. He'd made her move to his command, as if she was a puppet and he had the strings. He knew better than to play with this too much. She was far too experienced not to understand that something was going on, and he wanted to make a good show while he still had a chance.

Fool had picked up a few tricks from watching Jackal, so he paid attention to the music in earnest. He let the beat drive him. It was pretty easy. The music went right to his spine. All he had to do was relax, pull his secret uptight stick out of his ass, and let himself move.

He was having fun. Lucy was a talented dancer. Far better than Fool, but she was also good enough to move in a way that made him look better.

The dance turned into a playful back and forth, both of them darting back and forth, taking easy shots at each other and exaggerating their motions. Before he knew it, Fool went from having fun to actually playing and giggling. This was a hoot, and he felt himself breaking a sweat as he tried to dance out of the way of a slow, lazy backhand swing from Lucy.

It was time though. Time to show that he was more capable than she knew.

A quick spin of his hammer. A fancy pass behind his back, and a little jig step he remembered from somewhere, and as he came out of that, he spun himself about, transferring the hammer from one hand to the other. He stepped out of the spin, dropped his shoulder, and started a sudden full-power forehand shot.

Lucy's hammer was there, snapping like a serpent to put a stop to his shenanigans.

Her hammer was there, but his wasn't.

He'd passed the wrist forward but let the tip of the hammer lag slightly behind. Just enough so that Lucy's hammer went slightly past where his was supposed to be, and suddenly there was nothing between his hammer and her body.

It was the perfect setup to land a shot on her, but he wasn't done yet. While the hammer was still slinging its way toward Lucy, he set up a second follow-up shot. To do that, he had to start the process of pulling the hammer back, cranking his body forcibly on a new line to get the angle he needed. The net effect slowed the hammer down, taking away a little of its impact in order to land the second shot just as hard if not harder.

Lucy twisted to block that shot.

That was when Fool knew he had her, and he set off his trap.

Instead of slowing his hammer down, he snapped it back fast enough to make the muscles of his back and thighs creak. Just as he'd planned, the head of his hammer snagged Lucy's hammer on the way out, and her twisting posture meant that the force of his pull twisted the hammer in her grip…

And pulled it right out of her hand.

Fool spun again, his left hand darting out and grabbing the handle of Lucy's hammer. He dropped to the ground, spinning again, then jumped up in the air, both hammers swinging behind and above him.

Lucy grinned up at him as he swung down with both hammers. He didn't want to really hurt her, so he was aiming to land a hammer blow on each collarbone, doing enough damage to slow her down at least.

She didn't even wince as the hammers came down.

They didn't pass through her. She just wasn't quite there.

The Mana flareup this time was more what Fool would have expected from a Master Class Skill, and he regretted he hadn't actually had a chance to see her Skills in play when they were fighting the System Knights. He'd been too busy trying to minimize his own ass being kicked. Now he recalled that the Knights had had really terrible aim near the end of the engagement. Lucy clearly had some sort of combat Skill that had a displacement effect.

The hammers crashed into the dance floor, and Fool let out a grunt as Lucy's combat-boot-clad feet slammed into his back, between his shoulder blades.

He had to admit that maybe she was just flat-out fast.

Still, he wasn't ready to give up on the contest yet.

Fool had landed in a squat, and Lucy hadn't quite knocked him into a sprawl, so he was able to spin back up and face her again.

Somewhere in the exchange she'd managed to steal her hammer back.

He let the frustration pass out of him. He wasn't here to win. That wasn't an outcome he expected, even if it was one he would enjoy. Losing would be fine. Losing badly though? Not gonna happen. He wasn't going to allow himself to get stomped on, and he wanted Lucy to know she'd been in a real fight. Or dance. Whatever this was.

Dance. The answer was in there somewhere. He had to stop thinking about the fight and focus on the dance. He let himself open up to the music again, closed his eyes partway, and dumped all his self-consciousness out the window. Swayed his hips, let his waist follow. Let the head keep banging, let the shoulders roll a little. Pick the feet up and move.

It was feeling pretty good, and he had to admit he was enjoying himself. He could also sense a bit more Mana swirling in toward Lucy, and he knew she was about to do something else.

He let the world slow. Mana was the underlying structure of everything, and his Talent Scout Skill had already been upgraded a few times. If he combined that with his Mana Sense Skill, he might be able to figure out exactly how Lucy's predictive and displacing skills worked.

She was back to dancing, throwing quick and hard shots at him, but whatever trick she had up her sleeve was being held in reserve. He wanted more information, so he kept throwing good hard shots at her, and the air was shivering with the ring of the two hammer heads blocking and smashing against each other.

Fool couldn't stop grinning. This was too damned much fun.

Finally, he saw it. Just as the music was building to a climax and the song ending, the pattern of Mana swirling and pulsing, combined with her actions, all clicked in his head.

Everything was Mana. Every time they used their abilities, as well as Skills, Mana was working. He couldn't see it in great detail, but there was a regular pattern to it, like a heartbeat, or…

Music.

A beat under the beat of the actual music.

A steady thrum of power driven by Lucy's whims. It was subtle, but it was there. And somehow it was echoing with his own strumming of the Mana chords.

And that meant he didn't have to stop or even manipulate Lucy's timing or Skills at all. All he had to do was change the tempo of his own Mana use at just the right time.

The music hit its rising crescendo, and Lucy became a whirlwind of power, seemingly splitting into multiple versions of herself, all spinning and throwing a series of crashing overhead blows right into Fool. The blows wouldn't kill him, but they would paste him right into the dance floor and leave Lucy the clear winner.

And there was nothing he could do as the hammer crashed down.

Except not be there.

Lucy froze as her hammers hit the floor.

Fool, standing next to her, reached out just as the music stopped and tapped her on the head with his hammer. "Boop."

The crowd went nuts. Some were cheering and ecstatic, but most were still enjoying a mocking chorus of boos and catcalls.

Lucy slung her hammer back over her shoulder and hugged Fool. She whispered into his ear before letting him go, then turned to the crowd, hammer up in the air again.

"And that's the show, folks! The miracle of an old dog learning a new trick! You saw it here. Enjoy the band, next competitor up in twenty minutes!"

Chapter Thirteen

Fool wasn't surprised at all that Olivia had found her way in. She'd greeted him with a big high five, and Lucy had led them both to a more secluded booth.

"I really didn't think you had it in you, Fool."

Fool cocked an eyebrow at Lucy, then glared at Olivia, who had snorted into her drink at the comment. Jackal had disappeared with his new beau, so Fool was left alone in the company of the two *belle dames* sans mercy.

"What, to kick your ass?"

"Pfff, hardly. No, you found a way to break out of the Mana structure that the System imposed. I mean, not by much, but still. Impressive."

Fool tipped his glass a little to the side, watching the cherry bounce around, chasing the ice cube remnants around the whisky. "Wasn't quite that. Just combined a few things I already knew how to do. Don't get me wrong, I'm happy with the result, but… wasn't a big deal."

Lucy and Olivia glanced at each other, and Olivia shrugged. Lucy responded to that with a long sigh, and Fool resigned himself to a lecture.

"No, it's not a big deal, and it was a pretty shitty attempt, honestly."

Fool stuck his tongue out at Lucy and sulked into his drink.

"But it's a great start!" she said, patting his shoulder. "Honestly, the theory we've been most closely tracking is that it's related to age. Not physical age, but time from exposure to the System. One of the reasons Earth was our chosen planet for this, even if the Dungeon World thing didn't come to pass. Figured the best chance of finding people with the right adaptability would be in the first few years here."

Olivia rapidly waved her hand in confusion. "Wait wait wait. What? You mean there was a plan for us to be a Dungeon World? I thought it was kind of an accident. Some ass in the States made it happen, right?"

"Uhm. You know, let's go with that for now. I mean, we kinda figured the Weaver had something planned, but honestly, that was a little out of my pay grade. Or interest. Doesn't matter. Anyway, good job, Fool. That's the important part. I know it didn't seem like much, but it was a big step."

"Didn't seem like that much, but glad it was cool." Fool took another sip of his drink. It really had felt like little, but he had to admit the bit of playing with how Mana worked had kicked his brain open. He'd never been a fan of the whole Skills thing, and he was getting an idea of how truly amazing things might be if he could just go from willpower and imagination. Somehow. He couldn't really imagine what the next step might be though.

"Olivia, how did you work all this out?"

She shrugged and glanced at Lucy. "Dunno. Just kinda made sense. Figured the Skills were kinda suggestions. Like school, you know? Never paid that much attention, but once in a while, the teacher might say something interesting."

Fool didn't say anything for a moment, just looked at the young lady.

"What?"

"I suppose that's my genetics. I don't know if I should apologize or not."

Lucy nearly fell off her stool. She'd been balancing it on two legs until her sudden burst of laughter. "Apologize! Ha! Yes, do it!"

Fool looked at her for a moment. Lucy was in a great mood and on her way to being a happy drunk. That was fine, but he wasn't in the mood for that just yet. He had something more important to discuss. He glanced at Olivia and found his granddaughter looking back at him. Looked as though she had the same thing in mind.

"Going for a walk, Lucy. Back in a bit."

Lucy didn't acknowledge that, just waved for another drink. He got up, and Olivia followed. It took a bit, but they found a quiet spot in one of the far corners of the giant nightclub.

Olivia didn't waste any time once they settled into the waist-high wall shelf they found. She hopped up on the only stool and shrugged. "Sup?"

Fool looked at her again. Physically, he could see a little of his long-ago paramour in her features, but none of himself. Maybe a touch of his grandfather, if he squinted. He didn't think it really mattered. She clearly carried some of his genetics.

"You sure you want to do this?"

She didn't shrug, just nodded. "I'll miss the boys, but my family is gone. Land is gone… not just the stuff I was told was my people's, but everything. The trees, the animals, all the little plants and birds? Just gone. No legacy for me to carry on, and I don't see it getting any more back to the way it was, you think?"

Fool winced a little at the truth of that. "I suppose. Feels strange though. Almost like giving up."

"Can't fight the System. It's the same shit we've been dealing with forever, only this time they finished the job."

"Not running though, are you?"

"Nope. Figure it's time to start over. Gonna be lots of folks fighting here, but they're only gonna do so using the System, which means they've lost already. If we can make a new place somewhere else, maybe those people's kids can grow up some place better. Have a chance to be themselves."

That shook Fool. He'd found that his granddaughter was a bright young woman. Very strong, with an iron heart that was made to succeed in a Dungeon World. He'd figured she'd grow up to be one of the strongest on the Earth, maybe a leader of some kind. She just had that feel about her.

But even with all that, he hadn't really thought of her as especially wise. Or, to be fair, intelligent. That was clearly his own bias at work though. He'd always had a bit of a problem not taking people's choice of language at face value. Olivia's clipped way of speaking had led him to underestimate her, because she clearly had a better sense of the long-term development of things, and the consequences thereof, than he had.

She was right, but he wasn't sure it was the right kind of right for him. Didn't matter too much, not right now.

"So, you gotta dance for a spot or what? I kinda forgot to ask Lucy how that's supposed to work."

"Nah. I mean, I can break, but not like those dudes. They're hard. Pretty awesome. But maybe they could use a little help with the Mana thing too. They still got some habits, bit lazy."

"Yer shitting me. They look amazing to me."

"Well, yeah, but they can't be what they are, right? Lucy gave them a good set of Skills and a challenge in the dances that forces them to work outside the System, but they still got that whole idea of 'structure' and 'right and wrong' that gets in their way. Look. Check it out. You got that Mana Sense thing now, right?"

Fool nodded, curious about where she was going with this.

"Kay. So fire that shit up and watch this."

She cupped her hands in front of her, and Fool watched as she summoned one of the green flames he'd seen her use before, part of her Chaos Magic Skill set. Watching it this time with his nascent Mana Sense, he could see how the Mana was drawing into her as she used it and how it was being consumed by the Skill. As before, he couldn't really see it so much as see the distortions it caused in his visual field, but it was apparent now that he was getting used to how the Skill worked. It was different from how he'd been seeing other people use their Skills.

He glanced toward the dance floor and the crowd milling about. There were more than a few people using Skills, so he did a quick comparison. The dancers were using Mana the same way Olivia was. It was like an organic spiral that seemed to twist and coalesce into a shape as it got closer to the belly of the person using the Skill.

In contrast, watching someone in the crowd use a more "normal" Skill—they were showing off to someone by doing some kind of juggling trick—the Mana seemed to arrive in pulses. Regular chunks. As if it was being broken somewhere into discrete chunks and delivered in regular doses as the Skill required it.

He looked back at Olivia, who was playing with the little green fire. "Okay, I see that. And I see how people use it differently, but it looks like you're doing it the same way the dancers are. What's the diff?"

Olivia smirked, and Fool was afraid that smug expression was something that appeared on his face from time to time. It looked like it felt familiar. Good god, he thought, what a terrible legacy to pass on.

"I dunno how you see it," she said, "probably different for everyone, but this is using the Chaos Magic that the System allows. It doesn't like it, so it's rare and tricky to use. But it's still part of the System. Like a broken part that it hasn't learned to fix yet, or… I dunno. Feels like one of those hack things, right? Like how you can unlock games?"

Fool nodded. "In my old job, we knew every server had some weird things that happened from time to time. Sometimes they broke things, but every time we tried to fix them, it would just break the whole server until we had to restore from a backup with the bug intact. Eventually we learned how to work around the bug, wrote scripts that allowed us to get past it without really doing anything about it."

Olivia perked up with that description. "Right! Just like that. It's not supposed to work, but it does, and some of us have learned how to use it. The dancers have figured it out all on their own by going through the hoops Lucy set up with her dance comps over the last year and a bit. But check this out."

She dismissed the flame then fired it up again. It looked the same. Fool checked it out with his Mana Sense, then leaned forward to look closer.

There was no spiral of Mana. No pulse. Instead, he saw what looked like a fine mist that came from nowhere and seemed to coalesce into denser and denser fractal patterns until it became the flame in Olivia's hands.

"How the hell are you doing that?"

Olivia flicked her hands to dismiss the flame. "Dunno. Not really. I'm just learning to do this now. It was kinda how I started to do things when the System came. Just a fluke. I saw all those Skill things and didn't want to make a choice, but things were changing all around me, so I figured that whatever was making it all happen was already working, so… I just tried to make shit happen. You know, like in those superhero movies where someone gets told they have powers but they don't know what they are, so they try a bunch of things like jumping up in the air or yelling 'Power Bolt' or some shit?"

She stopped to take a breath. Fool hadn't seen her this excited or talkative ever, and it warmed his heart.

"Anyway, yeah, I thought maybe that was it. So I tried a few things, then it got weird. I got a hell of a headache, and the System screen glitched and went all weird for a bit. When it came back, it had assigned my Class without asking. But just before that happened? It felt like I was about to do *something*. When I got my Class and Skills, I went with them, figured it was the right way and I'd been trying it wrong before. The feeling never really left though, and I kept playing with it from time to time. The more I worked at it, the stronger my Chaos Magic got, but also some things got harder. Didn't make sense until DM showed up and told me to work on it. She told me to head down here and that it would make more sense."

Fool was surprised. "DM talked to you? When was that?"

"Just before she went away. Told me she had to go but wanted to give me a head start."

"Huh. I guess it worked. So is that how everyone is going to use Mana in this new place?"

"That's the plan. I guess. Lucy offered me a spot because of that. Teacher. Wild, huh?"

"Hm." That was about all that Fool could think of to say. It made sense, but it bothered him. He thought he knew why, but he didn't want to think about it at the moment.

They sat together for a moment. The place was quiet enough.

"You know you're supposed to come along too, right?" Olivia said.

"No one asked me."

"You only been here a bit. Finals aren't for a bit yet. Got anything else to do?"

"Supposed to be working for the Foundation. They've still got things to do."

That was true, but it wasn't quite true. From what Fool had been given to understand, the Foundation had been created as a way to build toward the Trickster's plan. And in a way, that was what Fool had been recruited for in the first place. Fight the good fight for humanity on Earth, but the secret goal was always to find a hidey-hole for some folk. Fool and Jackal had been sent out to recruit the right people for both missions.

Yagnar and Roger were on their way to being the leaders and backbone of a formidable military force, and in another few years of training, they'd be ready to step out on to the world stage… and the galactic stage. Protectors and champions for everyone on Earth, with an army and resources at their back. That plan was well in hand, and Fool and Jackal had more than done their job for that aspect of things.

For the backdoor backup? Fool wasn't sure about that. He'd never really discussed the plan with Professor Xi, but he'd always assumed it would be some kind of migration of spaceships heading to a distant world to settle it. But from what he'd learned since joining the Foundation, especially since learning about how the Galactic Council worked? There was no hope for that. The only chance was to follow the Trickster's plan to its end.

Problem was, Fool didn't really know where he fit into that.

Olivia echoed those thoughts right back at him. "They've got things to do, but they've got it all worked out. So what you want to do?"

Fool bounced his elbows back against the edge of the shelf to bring himself upright. "Right now? I'm hungry. Food?"

Jackal wrapped his arms around Nicholaus as he watched Olivia and Fool walk across the dance floor, making a beeline for the canteen. Or refectory. He supposed that was a more accurate label. He'd been there earlier when Nicholaus had taken him for a quick meal. Tasty burritos, drenched in a kind of molé sauce and served up in pairs in a flat bowl. He'd gone back for thirds, trying all the different kinds of sauces they had.

And now they were up on the catwalks, watching the action below.

Nicholaus had wanted Jackal to meet his friends. House Masque.

They'd been, even for Jackal, intimidating folk. At first glance.

All of them wore masks. There were two women who were almost a match for Jackal in height, both slim and with broad shoulders. They wore skin-tight dresses that covered every square inch of skin and expanded into sleek, flowing skirts that allowed for more movement. One was a matte silver tone, the other matte brown-gold. The masks of both were smooth and featureless until they erupted into horns. Silver had two thick horns that swept and curled in s-curves to gentle points, and Gold's horns were wide and thick, extending far past her shoulders. Gold's outfit was also more ornate, with a cowl and a bustle seemingly made out of a sword, all with tassels dangling from them. She was the leader of the House.

There was one other man, similar to Nicholaus in complexion, who wore an ornate, heavily embroidered renaissance-style outfit, topped with a golden crown. His mask was just a transparent veil that dropped down from the crown, stopping just above his nose.

The last member of the crew was clad in head-to-toe black leather and had on a half-cape with epaulets that became pauldrons over the deltoids and sleevelets that opened up wide just before the elbows. The capelet had a hood, and it mostly covered their head, but still exposed the heavily worked brass mask they wore, with an articulated brass gorget that rose up and into the mask.

They were intimidating to look at, but once Jackal had been introduced to them, that had faded away almost immediately. These were his people. They wore physical masks as a reminder of the behavior masks they'd been forced to wear for most of their normal, pre-System lives. The masks made everyone assume they were standoffish and remote, and they kept up a posture that maintained that impression. Once you started talking to them though? That went out the window.

The group was lively, ribald, ferocious, and outgoing in opinion, and Jackal found his normal reticence to speak, his movie-tough-guy mask, being dropped in their company. He couldn't remember a time he'd felt so relaxed, so comfortable, with anybody other than Fool.

And maybe that was why he was so reluctant to have House Masque meet Fool. He didn't think there would be any actual issue between them. The opposite, if anything. They were all erudite and sarcastic and deeply witty, and Fool would absolutely enjoy their company. He, like Jackal, also found it hard to relax and be himself in the company of others, often because his tongue would get away from him and cause misunderstandings. With this group, that wouldn't be an issue. They'd understand.

The problem was that they were also deeply passionate. The brief time Jackal had been with them, they hadn't held back from exposing their views on everything. It had been refreshing, but Jackal thought that Fool's innate cynicism would make for a rough fit.

At least, he thought that might be the issue.

He had to be truthful with himself. Fool had been his only real friend since the System, and for years before that as well. Jackal had always been an awkward outcast, and as he realized who he really was, his internal wrestling hadn't made him a great socializer either. He'd enjoyed the few LGBTQIA+ groups he'd sneaked out to or hung out on the edges of, but he'd struggled to feel as though he'd earned access to those groups. And still wasn't really sure where he fit.

Fool had been the first person to see Jackal as his new self and who had still seen him as his old self. The two of them had undergone their transformations right about the same time. At first, Jackal had thought that had been what had brought them together, but over time, he'd come to realize that Fool was one of those people who truly saw people for what they were under the skin and cared little for what they were on the outside. Probably because he'd been overlooked for so much during his life.

More importantly, the deep bond of their friendship had grown for another reason all together.

They both genuinely liked and appreciated each other, and the other fit into all the empty spots each one was missing. Together, they made a whole bigger than the sum of both their parts.

Only now? Watching Fool and Olivia go through the doorway and Fool patting his granddaughter on the shoulder? And feeling the sudden, aching comfort of Nicholaus in his arms?

Nothing had changed between Jackal and Fool. But in some strange, sudden, and unexpected way, Jackal felt as though he was growing into something new again. Something a little bigger. As though he had room to encompass more in his life without losing anything he had right now.

He just wasn't sure how Fool would feel about that.

Suddenly Lucy was there, standing right in front of him. "We gotta go. Now. Get Fool. We leave in two minutes."

Jackal had already started to move. The look on Lucy's face was all the alarm he'd needed. And her next words shook him to the core.

"McBride's under attack. They're going to take the Foundation out."

Chapter Fourteen

There was no time to collect anyone else or make any other preparations. Lucy had gotten word from Professor Xi that they'd caught scouts coming over the mountains from the south. Olivia had gone back to the mall to rally with everyone else in case there was a local follow-up attack. Alien mercenaries, no details beyond that, was all the Professor had reported. No actual idea of the size of the forces, but with most of the McBride Flying Cavalry in Vancouver, McBride was perfectly vulnerable to an attack. Someone had planned and timed it meticulously, and if an errant hunter hadn't stumbled across the spoor of the scouts and sent out a report in time, they'd have been caught badly off guard. Even Roger and Yagnar were out of the game for a bit, as they were training and recruiting out of province.

They'd thought they were in a safe window, but that assumption looked to be wrong. The Foundation should have been able to predict such things. That they'd been caught out like this was probably another sign of the Weaver's interference.

"Fuck," Fool said. "Any good news in all this? Or at least bad news?"

Lucy had rushed them through a tunnel and out to the top of the Queen Elizabeth Park right next to the Bloedel Conservatory. He took a glance to the side—the view was still epic, especially getting close to sunset. He remembered the parking lot used to fill up with people trying to get their golden hour photos of their cars.

"No good news." Lucy was scrambling to set up some sort of contraption. Jackal was keeping an eye on the surroundings, because they were out of the sphere of influence of whatever kept the Twisted Chapel hidden. Attack could come at any moment. "Fairly sure the System Knights won't be there though. That ain't good news because the reason they won't be there is that I'm going to be here keeping them busy, so I'm not going with you. Probably you won't need me, because I recognized the description of the mercs, and they won't be strong. Just plentiful. So you'll just have to deal with an army on your own. Yay you. Go you."

She didn't even grace that last comment with a smile, just kicked a recalcitrant strut into place. Fool looked at the structure she was building. It reminded him of a trade show banner setup. A flimsy aluminum frame with a near-useless tripod at the bottom.

"And this is going to get us there in time?" He'd already asked, but he couldn't help asking again. And Lucy hadn't replied the first time he asked. She'd been too busy swearing.

"Yes. Teleport. Instant. It's a one-time use, but…" She dug through the bag the frame had been stored in. She pulled out three items. Two small buttons and one large ball. "These are the recalls. When you're done with the shit, press the buttons. You'll pop back instantly to wherever this ball is, and I'm keeping it here, in my pocket. You fuckers return when I'm in the can and I'll kill you."

She flicked a switch on the side of the frame, and Fool smelled ozone. There wasn't any other change. He put the button in one of his pockets and saw Jackal do the same. The big man didn't look any happier than Fool did. Foundation aside, they'd grown to have a lot of friends in McBride. There was no way they weren't going to get caught up in the crossfire. Likely they'd lose some of those friends, and that wasn't something they looked forward to. The only hope they had, aside from getting there in time, was that the Foundation's stash of gear would be enough to put a stop to the attackers.

The contraption didn't look very… safe. And the ozone smell had taken a sharp turn into the hard plasticky reek of an electrical fire.

"You sure this is…"

Fool didn't have time to finish the sentence.

Lucy punted him through the gate.

And then he was standing in the middle of a field. A half second later, Jackal was next to him.

There was a beige building in front of them, with a street to the left. And behind the building was an expanse of rolling green mountains, with some stony peaks rising above them.

They were in McBride. By the library. Fool had a fleeting, reflexive spasm of wondering if he had any overdue library books.

"Well." He couldn't think of anything more clever to say. "That was… quick. What now?"

Jackal was looking around. "I don't see anyone."

Fool turned around and looked. The library was now the municipal center of the town. Still full of books, though anyone could get just about any book they wanted for a reasonable fee from the Shop. Even with the books occupying most of the space, and there being larger meeting areas available, the library had rapidly turned into the place everyone went to meet and make community decisions. It was always busy. Depending on the weather, there was usually even a fairly busy craft market out front, with Artisans selling all kinds of useful and interesting things.

Not today though. The library looked empty, and so were the streets.

McBride had turned into a ghost town.

It made Fool uneasy, but the likeliest explanation was that the Foundation had alerted everyone and they'd scarpered off for safer territory. The village had set up plenty of defenses—you couldn't live so close to premium monster breeding grounds and outdoor dungeons without them—but they were likely to be a stopgap against any kind of serious galactic mercenary force.

So where the hell were they? And what were Fool and Jackal supposed to do next?

If they'd arrived in the middle of a fight, no problem. Fool'd jump right in. In the middle of a group of people arguing about what to do next? He'd figure out what they all wanted and make it happen. Standing in the middle of a field in a ghost town? No sounds, no battle, no bad guys or good guys anywhere? This was way too complex for him to deal with. He turned to look at Jackal and raised an eyebrow.

"Find the bad guys?"

Fool nodded. "Good call. Things make more sense when I'm hitting them."

Jackal laughed. "And I'm the tough guy?"

"Shaddup. Things are weird. Let's find someone to hit."

"Fair enough. We can trust our guys to be doing something fun. Bad guys are supposed to have been on the other side of the mountains, and they have to come over them if they want to get here. Might as well head to them. Whatever Professor Xi has planned, I'm sure that will only help."

"Good a plan as any. Let's go."

They crossed the field and took a closer look at the library. The lights were out, which was only a little unusual. There were usually people hanging out way past dark, even in the summer. There wasn't any reason to turn the lights off, or lock the place, since the System and Mana ran it all much more efficiently than it had in the people-and-electricity days. The habit of shutting it down had developed to enforce people taking a break. The System had a way of throwing normal patterns of life for a loop, and restoring older habits had helped give everyone a common structure. So unless there was something specific going on, or enough people hanging out, the place shut down not too much later than it had pre-System.

There was no one in there though. The roads were empty of people, but not completely deserted. There were still a number of personal vehicles parked, and the village's communal ones were all parked in the usual places. Fewer vehicles than normal, for sure, but Fool thought they would all be gone if everyone had evacuated. That they were still there told Fool someone had a plan.

And they'd arrived too late to be a part of it, so Jackal's idea to take it to the enemy was probably the best idea. They'd never been any good at working with other people's plans, anyway. Best to just surprise the bad guys. Fool couldn't think of any way that would throw the village's plans awry. Probably.

The long walk down Main Street was more of the same. Nobody was around, but it didn't feel exactly deserted. Lucy had figured that the enemy forces would be in range and hitting McBride either in the evening or first thing in the morning, depending on who the enemy was. They'd rushed getting there because they couldn't take the chance of going slow only to find out the bad guys were believers in blitzkrieg. The Foundation, and McBride, had gained at least that much information. That was the only reason Fool didn't bother trying to check out the other meeting places, to see if some kind of last-minute battle planning was taking place.

The Foundation could move pretty fast when it wanted to. And McBride had been through its share of monster swarms, so they knew how to move fast when it was time. The most likely thing was that some sort of defensive line or trap had been set, non-combatants evacuated as best as possible, and Fool and Jackal had unluckily teleported outside of those preparations.

By the time they reached the railroad station, that impression had solidified. Fool had been looking up and down all the side streets and seen nothing, or any houses with lights on. And the train station and tracks were not only the first natural barrier between the village and the mountains, they were also the System boundary of the village itself. There were still more than a few farms on the other side, but no one had bothered to expand back out to reclaim them as yet. So it really was just wilderness past the tracks.

Nearly three kilometers, as the crow flies, before they hit the base of the mountains. Any really dangerous monsters had been cleared out, but it still was a risky place to go. Not to mention whatever beasties were left dwelling in the mountainside. It all looked nice and pleasant from the village, but those smooth green mountainsides hid valleys and ravines of surprising depth. No place for amateurs.

Especially not when there was an enemy force of unknown size, composition, and methods somewhere out there.

Nothing else for it though. It wasn't as if a massive army was rising over the crest of the mountains for them to charge at. Hell, a massive army could be covering the entire mountainside right up to the forest near the village and they wouldn't see it. That would have been true even pre-System.

Fool had an edge though.

He held up a hand to get Jackal's attention. The big man was clearly straining his Perception to try to make out any troop movements in the trees. He waited until Jackal noticed the hand.

"Gonna use Talent Scout. You ready in case it triggers anything?"

Jackal nodded. "Anytime."

Fool grinned at the eagerness in Jackal's voice. He was more than ready for a fight himself. So if using a Skill to find the enemy let them know he was looking for them, that was fine with him.

"Shit," he said a moment later.

Jackal glanced at him. "Is this a good news, bad news thing?"

"McBride news, yeah, both. Nothing shows at all. That's the bad news. The good news is the bad guys seem to have purchased some blocking, because there's an area that shows up as completely blank. So…"

Jackal nodded. "So we know where they are."

"Yup. And that's the other fun news. The area of exclusion has a border that ends… right there."

Fool pointed at the other side of the railway tracks. The message to Jackal was clear, and he visibly relaxed into his combat mode as he adjusted. The enemy could be a stone's throw away.

Time for talking was over, and without a word, Fool drew his hammer. Jackal pulled his twin swords, and that left Fool with a twinge of regret. He'd learned that Jackal had burned up most of his carefully hoarded uber-weapons in the scrap with the System Knights, and they hadn't had a chance for him to hit the Shop and replace even the least of them. As a result, Jackal was down to his swords and the Mana-generated weapon Skill that he had only taken a single level in.

Not that it would likely slow him down at all.

They hadn't won against the System Knights, but they hadn't been completely obliterated. And they'd faced an army before. They might be outnumbered and outgunned, but Jackal and Fool had enough confidence in themselves to know that barring any really strong opponents, they could handle a run-of-the-mill army.

Granted, with a ton of luck. And treachery. But that was what they were good at.

With that thought in mind, Fool stepped across the railway tracks and into the scrub on the other side.

There wasn't tingling or a change in sensation at all, but he immediately felt as though he was in enemy territory.

The scrub didn't last long, and they wound up in what looked like an old gravel parking lot. They cut across that, then through some more scrub, then across McBride South Road. Ahead of them, the only thing between them and the mountains was several abandoned farm fields, with fences in various states of disrepair.

They paused at that point, sinking down and looking around as carefully as they could. It wasn't completely silent. Much like in McBride, Fool could still hear the odd bird and the constant gusts of wind. There was an almost spiritual hush though.

The enemy was near. The fields weren't perfectly flat. Even before the base of the mountains, the ground rolled and ditched like the former riverbed it was. There was room for enemies to hide in the low points. And no way for Fool or Jackal to know where they were until they were in the enemies' face. Between the two of them, they at least had Perception scores high enough that they'd see anyone who stood up to take a shot at them, so they weren't so worried about that.

Still, there wasn't any point in being too obvious.

With a nod, Fool pointed out a different path to the left. It would take longer to get to the mountain, but there was more scrub and actual trees that way, giving them more cover. And if they were lucky, they might run into some bad guys trying the same thing.

Before long, they were deep in the woods and had to slow down. There was still no sign of any enemies, but there were none of the smaller animals or monsters that would normally be in the area.

Fool signaled a halt, and Jackal leaned in closer so they could have a quiet chat.

"I'm getting a little confused," Fool said. "Supposed to be enough army to take out the Foundation. Why are they sneaking in? Why not just pour in, guns blazing?"

Jackal didn't nod the way Fool expected. He glanced around one more time, then leaned in again. "Professionals. The scouts are in the area. They'll come in blazing when it's time, and when they do, the scouts will be in position to screw things up. Take out leaders, blow up things, stuff like that. We'd be surrounded when we thought the battle was just starting."

"Makes sense. Someone in town must be thinking the same thing then. Pulling back, trying to trap the scouts?"

Jackal nodded then froze in place. Something had caught his eye. Fool knew better than to turn and look, but he activated his Geas.

Jackal was a tree, and Fool was a breeze moving leaves around, nothing more.

Fool slowly turned and shrank down. He didn't need to explain to Jackal that he needed to stay still. They'd played this game enough in the last few months. Power leveling their Advanced Classes had required going up against progressively more dangerous monsters… and enemies of the Foundation. They'd had ample practice recently at being a stealth team.

Once Fool was aligned with Jackal's view, he slowly scanned the area. Nothing stood out, but since he knew there was something to see, he was able to more quickly break down what he saw.

It was subtle, but once he saw it, fairly clear. A patch of branches that didn't quite move right in the wind. Forest floor loam that was compressed in too regular a fashion. A tree trunk that was just a hair the wrong color.

The enemy scout has pretty good stealth gear on and was using it just right. It was hard to get around really high-level Perception though. At least without top-notch gear and Skills. Pretty good was good, but not good enough in this case.

There was more than one of them. A second set of aberrations was moving another twenty meters away, but roughly in the same line.

Fool turned around carefully to see if anyone was on the same line behind them, but there wasn't. Two-person team then, not a skirmish line. Must be the very lead elements. If he was running the other side, he'd probably have the next group coming about half an hour behind to keep down the odds of being detected.

Which meant that the enemy was hoping to hit McBride, and the Foundation, sometime overnight. Probably early morning, maybe three or four o'clock.

So they had a choice. Take out the scouts and get what information they could, or sneak back and let the Foundation know what they'd discovered.

Fool contemplated that for a moment while watching the two scouts inch forward. They were moving a little more quickly than he would have expected. A slow walk. That spoke to him of overconfidence in their gear. Perfect.

He wanted to know more about them anyway.

Fool didn't need to nod at Jackal—he just moved toward where it looked like the closest scout would be in about ten minutes. He had to pick up his pace to do that, but he didn't feel any extra draw on his Mana, so his Geas Skill was still keeping him and Jackal effectively invisible.

Bad scouts. That meant they weren't really looking for opposition. Instead, they were focused on getting into McBride proper. They didn't expect anyone to be out hunting them. Stupid.

By the time Fool reached his position, he noted that Jackal had already overshot and was nearly on the other scout… who was moving blindly forward. They'd hit their targets at exactly the same time.

Perfect.

Fool hunkered down and thought about being a shrub for a bit.

The vague discrepancies in what he expected to see and what he saw continued as the enemy got closer and closer. When they were about five meters from Fool, he realized the odd musky scent he'd smelled was coming from the same source. Very cheap stealth gear then, to not mask scent. It was also not a smell he had come across before. Clearly not human or any other race he'd been exposed to. He was rather glad for that, because he'd had a tiny fear in the back of his mind of running into Hakarta—or worse, more Hobgoblins. That would have sucked. Whoever these mercenaries were, if they were of one race, they probably weren't as formidable or he'd have heard of them or run across them before. And they'd have better trained troops, or at least better equipment.

Time for wonder was past though.

He saw Jackal spring into action, so he leapt up to face his opponent.

Or at least the vague outline of them.

Fool swung his hammer with all his System-enhanced speed and strength, but without using Hammer of Loki. If the enemy had any way of tracking

Mana use, that skill would pin-point them pretty quickly. If he could get away without using it, he would.

He judged the height of his opponent from the distance they'd covered and the outline of whatever he could make out. Fool hoped his swing would be a good enough estimate to aim for the head just below the rim of the helmet. He could have swung lower… but he was already swinging when he had that thought, and it was too late to aim for the ankles.

There was a light screech as he felt a shiver run up his arms. His hammer didn't bounce back, but he hit something. Without pausing, he dived forward and grabbed with his free hand.

Something smooth, slick. Something hard. A strap. He yanked on the strap hard, and felt a heavy weight lift up and drop. A body hit him, smaller than him, but only by about a foot or so. It felt bulky, crunchy, but also small. Didn't matter.

He spun around to the ground, still not sure if the body was face down or face up, but there was no experience notification, so it was still alive, even if he wasn't feeling any resistance. One more swift hammer blow to where he figured the head was, and the notification showed up.

And so did the enemy. He'd either smashed the cloaking device when he killed the scout, or it had been tied to its owner's Mana. Either way, he could now see the enemy.

A familiar enemy. Another creature out of human myth, although in this case, a more modern kind of myth. Smooth grey featureless skin, small jaw. Human features, but in miniature, except for the oversized black eyes without pupils.

The uniform and military kit weren't all that familiar, but its purpose was clear. Armor bits, ammo, lots of pouches with stuff in them, and a stubby little rifle with a banana clip. Fool wasn't surprised to finally see a stereotypical alien, but he was surprised to realize he hadn't even heard of any alien races looking like this. Then again, he didn't recall asking around about it much either. He shrugged off that thought and looted what he could from the body, then gave it a quick once-over to see if there was anything like a map or a code book.

He gave that up after a moment. There was just nothing useful. He tucked the body around the base of a tree and dropped some branches around it.

A shudder deep inside him wanted to come up, but he held it down out of fear that it might take him over for a moment.

He'd done a lot of things he wasn't proud of since the System arrived, but killing a sentient he couldn't actually see? He felt as if he'd broken something inside himself, but he couldn't for the life of him think why that one thing was suddenly hitting him so hard.

Maybe it was because he was imagining trying to explain it to Rebecca and having to see the look on her face when he did.

He shook himself. A little trauma, a little PTSD—that was just a part of daily life now. It was either going to go away or he would have a couple of really bad nights, but there was nothing he could do about it right now. If he didn't keep this up, there would be a whole hell of a lot more dead people, and those would be his friends. That wasn't something he cared to try to live with afterward.

Jackal padded over after Fool had dropped the last branches over his target.

"Greys," was all Jackal said.

"Right? What the hell? What's next, men in black?"

Jackal grinned, and it was one of his mean grins. He didn't show those very often, and Fool was glad to see it. It was time to get mean.

"Uphill?" was Jackal's only reply.

Fool nodded, and they started back toward the mountain. Taking out two scouts would buy the village another hour of prep, most likely. And it would probably be at least half an hour before the two scouts were missed, if everything went right.

They went at a quicker pace, with less caution about getting caught. Unspoken between them was the reason—the scouts they had killed. They'd both been fairly low level. The experience had been negligible, and the looted gear had almost been worthless. These were cheap troops.

Cheap troops against two Advanced Class aggressors? The best tactic for Fool and Jackal was no tactics at all. Hit hard and fast and don't stop. Tactics were for the side that needed them, and they had enough of a power advantage that they should be able to mop up anyone they came across.

There was no way that would be the case against whoever was leading these troops, but Fool and Jackal were no strangers to taking out heavy hitters. The same approach might not always work, but it had always worked for them.

Charge in, and take a chance. Do the stupid thing with your whole heart and trust that it will work out in the end. When in doubt, do something stupider. This was what they lived for.

Chapter Fifteen

Wherever the next line of scouts was, or if there had even been one, Fool and Jackal never came across them. They made it to the base of the mountain without running across anyone else, then about a hundred feet up the mountain slope before Fool abruptly slowed and knelt in place.

Jackal took note, hunched down, and crept over to Fool.

Fool cupped his ears and pointed in an arc up slope. Jackal turned and listened.

Rustling. Cracking. And faintly, from up the mountain, rumbling engines and more cracking sounds. Tree branches snapping off. Motorized vehicles working their way down the mountain slope behind a screen of infantry. Probably smaller vehicles. If anything up there was knocking down trees, they'd probably be hearing the rumbles from them falling.

The arc of the noise was pretty big. Considering how small the aliens were, and how cheap, it sounded like a fairly sizeable force was on its way down.

Which left Fool wondering what the next step should be for them. Keep going up the mountain and try to seriously dent the mercenaries, or skip around and try to figure out where—if—their big guns were hidden? They weren't likely to be any Master Classers. If they were swinging that kind of funds, why bother with the army? But an Advanced Class or two or three? That seemed likely.

Jackal interrupted his chain of thoughts. "Plan?"

"Dunno. Was thinking of just plowing through, finding the officers, and taking them out. But…"

Jackal nodded and looked up the hill again. "Too easy? They've got to have an ace in the hole."

"Right. But is it the leaders, with the leaders, or… on the other side of town?"

Jackal patted Fool on the back. "Don't overthink it. We hit them hard enough they'll reveal their trap to us."

That made sense to Fool. But he still wasn't too happy to just charge straight in. That was definitely Jackal's preferred plan. He was built for that kind of conflict, but Fool wasn't. This would be a much different story if they were even a few levels higher. If Fool had been able to access the next tier of Skills, they could completely kick ass. That Salmon Leap Skill, letting him flicker all over, would be killer. So would Mark of the Fool, boosting Jackal's luck, damage, and resistances.

Didn't matter at the moment though, because those might as well belong to a different Class for how accessible they were. He could really see the advantages of what Olivia had shown him and what the Trickster was aiming for. If Fool could freely use Mana to do what seemed right in the moment? That would be amazing.

The Class and Skills system made things neat and organized, and maybe worked for most people, but right now? Not being able to be as flexible as his Class had initially seemed to promise seemed like a brutal trap.

Fool held out his hand for a moment and watched the Mana flow. Pulsed stutters, the same way he'd seen it flowing to others back at the Twisted

Chapel. He activated Clouseau, changing the shape of his hand, making it a little bigger, then a little smaller. He pushed himself, trying to feel the flow of Mana into the Skill, and into his hand, and how it went into his body and was shaped through his will. For a moment, he changed the steady pulsing into the smoother, swirling flow…

Jackal leaned in. "Not sure what you're doing, but maybe not the best time."

Fool shook out his hand. Jackal was right, but this was something he wanted to play with later. There was no way it would aid them just yet though.

"Thanks, but I think I have an idea. This isn't the best engagement for us, but why are we playing by the rules? Why not change things up a bit?"

Jackal didn't say anything. He glanced up the slope to judge how much longer they had to plan, then looked back at Fool.

"What's the worst thing that could happen to them right now, that they'd be worried about? I'd guess a trap. Any moment now, they're going to wonder what happened to their scouts, and when that happens, they'll get paranoid. And when that happens, they start to second-guess themselves."

"So we make them think they're walking into a trap?"

"Almost. We make them think they've sprung a trap early. If they've got any training at all, they'll pour into what they think is an ambush, trying to overrun it. If we can get them to think that, then we can control where they go next. And if we can control their movements…"

"Then we can get a free shot at the head. So what's the plan?"

"Split up. I'll head to the left and draw them at me. When they start to press, I'm gonna book it down the hill. They'll follow. You swing over to the right, wait for the action to start, and take out the leaders when you think the time is right. That kinda confusion should prevent the troops chasing me from getting back in control. With any luck, by the time they get to McBride, they'll be so strung out that whatever the Foundation has got planned for them will eviscerate them."

Jackal's grin went feral again. "Done. Meet you back at the library?"

Fool shook his head. "I think I'm going to be running too fast for that. Bridge over the Fraser, maybe the guard post in Koeneman if I can make it. Not the worst place for a last stand if it comes to that."

Jackal nodded and headed off up the slope.

Fool watched his friend go and let a brief stab of fear run through him. There was no way he wouldn't feel that, so it made sense for him to let it run a little crazy. Once it had a good hold on him, all he had to do was put one foot in front of the other.

That was easier to say than do, but after a moment, with the aid of some deep breaths, Fool got his right foot moving, then his left. After that, it was all momentum, and he was able to put the screaming monkey in his head back into a safe room where it could hang out until the fight was all over.

The rustling of troops trying to sneak down into McBride felt as if it was only a few feet away, but that was just Fool's overactive imagination, and amped up Perception, at work. As far as he could tell, the nearest bad guys were an easy half kilometer away. He had a good thirty minutes or so before they encountered him.

Still, he picked up his pace and cut more around the right. Ideally, he could hit the line from behind a little. That should cause the most panic.

The terrain sucked, going that way, but he saw how it would work in his favor. The mountainside had a big bulge in it in that direction. His path was taking him up the steepest part of that bulge, on a ridge that sloped down into a vertical valley on the other side, with a creek running down the valley. Because of that ridge, the advancing line would be squeezed in from a wide spread-out skirmish line into a smaller and more compact knot of soldiers. With any luck, they were getting yelled at for squishing each other, and it was making everything more confused.

If he came down yelling from that ridge, the logical conclusion for the army would be that an attacking force had been hiding in the lee side gulley of that ridge and they'd walked right into a trap, leaving their backs exposed.

It was perfect for Fool's plan, and he doubled his speed. He was pretty light-footed, but the occasional noise he might have made would only serve to raise the paranoia of the advancing troops.

Ten minutes later, Fool was in the perfect position. He hunkered down behind a ancient cedar, wedging himself into the gap between the massive roots. He could have used Geas to hide himself better, but he wanted to save his Mana for the big show. Once he'd wedged himself into his safe space—hidden from casual sight, but also behind almost two meters of wood—he peeked around the side to see how the enemy was advancing.

It took another twenty minutes before they showed up. At first, all Fool could see in the fading light was a flicker of motion, and his heart dropped a little, thinking that the entire army had the same stealth devices as the scouts. That fear only lasted a moment.

The lead elements were all the same grey aliens as the scouts, though burlier in appearance due to heavier combat armor and weapons. Like the other mercenary troops he'd run across, they kept a uniform appearance, similar weapons, and gear across the board.

They weren't paying too much attention to what was around them, mostly looking forward or bickering with each other with high-pitched squeaks and fluttery sounds. As Fool had thought, they were bunching up. The bands of heavier tree growth and occasional steeper vertical sections weren't helping.

The first armored vehicle appeared a moment later. It was narrow, almost like a thick, armored motorcycle with treads, but it sat four troops in an open-topped compartment. A stubby artillery piece was mounted on a tripod in the middle. It looked to Fool like it was some kind of mortar, and the pile of shells in the back only helped that impression. One driver in the front, the loader in the back, and two troops on the side behind armored panels for protection.

It really looked like a stupid design to Fool. At least stupid for mountain or forest use. That open top was a disaster, and the narrow base wouldn't help with the rough terrain.

His impression was reinforced a moment later when the driver lost control, navigating around a stump, and the rectangle tank slid toward one of the steep drops. Despite the driver's best efforts, which included dropping angled supports from each corner, the vehicle tipped over the small cliff.

Everyone managed to bail out, to Fool's amusement, but the whole line of advancing soldiers was thrown for a loop when the thing crashed down the drop, hit the bottom, and rolled over and over until it crashed into a tree with a resounding bang. The troops that had been in front of it had only dodged at the last second, and one of them had taken a hard hit from an artillery shell that had been flung out in the spinning.

Fool couldn't think of a better time to attack. Everyone distracted, freaked out after being on edge, angry at each other, and trying to figure out what happened and what to do next?

It wasn't the right time for a big show though. Not just yet. Not while he could screw things up even more for them.

Fool carefully laid down his hammer, giving thanks he'd thought to bring his rifle with him. He hadn't used it much lately, but once Jackal had gained the hidden Ramstal storage space Skill, he'd talked the big man into carrying it for him. Fool figured he'd be able to put it into good use in a moment. All he had to do was be a smidge patient and watch carefully.

It didn't even take that long. The squabble was making it clear who the leaders were in this group. He saw two of the burlier soldiers separate themselves from the line and move toward the confusion. That was good to know. These aliens put their leaders on the ends of the line. Weird, but that would be why they were aliens. He watched for a second longer, seeing how the two burly sergeants kept glancing back up the hill, and that was how Fool found the next person up the leadership chain.

It was another grey alien, but this one had less gear, was wearing what looked almost like a business suit, and was notably taller than the others. Target one.

Fool brought the rifle to bear on that one, mentally nicknaming him "Tallest," and sited in on him through the scope. He had no idea where their vital organs might be, but with those big heads, he was happy to see what happened when he aimed between the eyes.

He centered the crosshairs on his target, then dropped the crosshairs just a hair to account for the relatively close range. Probably unnecessary, but he was a lousy shot and didn't want to take a chance. He let out his breath, tried to wait for a pause between his heartbeats, and squeezed the trigger.

The shot went right between the eyes. Dead on target.

If Fool had been aiming at the grey next to Tallest.

He settled for good enough, because Tallest turned a darker grey shade and dived headfirst for the ground behind another alien. Fool took his eye off the scope, found the first of the two sergeants, who were looking back up the hill in confusion, sited back in, and shot him through the throat.

Full of confidence after that shot, Fool turned to find the other sergeant and swore as he saw the alien looking right at him, screaming and raising his rifle. Fool got the first shot off, and it hit the alien's rifle, driving it back into his head and knocking him over.

Time for Skills. Geas first. Army of one.

The Mana draw, he hoped, would be less than he'd originally expected. All he wanted to do was feed into something the bad guys seemed more than ready to believe anyway. He was relying on the aliens having the same sort of mental reaction that humans would. Panic, fear, leaning into believing that things were worse than they were when things went in unplanned directions. For sure, some of them would stand up and take charge in opposition to him, but armies seemed to work by promoting those folks, so hopefully he'd already removed anyone that would make this difficult.

And hopefully the System would translate human norms to whatever was the equivalent for the aliens. If not, he was about to have a very short life.

Fool stood and screamed "CHARGE!" while emptying the magazine of his rifle, dropping it, and charging into the nearest cluster of screaming aliens, his hammer in hand. Geas was in full effect, and the contract he was enforcing with it was that he was just the vanguard of a much larger force that was also pouring over the top of the ridge and into the now-panicking aliens.

The Mana drain was severe. This was the closest he'd ever come to trying to cast a full-on illusion, and he felt the strain.

It was working. And it was getting easier every second, because the more the little greys panicked, the more they fed into each other's panic and the more their own minds struggled to find a reason for the panic and made up for that by making them see enemies piling over and onto them.

It was getting easier, but not easier enough. By the time Fool reached the first group of aliens, half of his Mana was gone. He was too leery of using it all up to summon Hammer of Loki, so he had to rely on old-fashioned fighting skills.

The aliens' panic showed in back-and-forth movements, a stuck decision loop that had them moving one way, then another. Some of them were even firing their weapons, but in patterns. Into the ground, then into the sky. Left, then right. More than a few friendly-fire casualties were happening, and Fool had a fleeting regret that he didn't have any actual troops behind him. With this kind of effect, even a handful of McBride regulars would have wiped out this wing of the enemy.

That didn't give him any confidence in how the actual battle would go. He knew his Luck was working overtime for him on this. He was dealing with a relatively small part of the army. The landscape had worked in his favor. His Skill was the perfect one for the situation. If any one of those factors changed, then he'd find himself surrounded by angry aliens, probably all shooting at him. He didn't expect he'd live long under that kind of focused fire.

A forehand swipe knocked aside the first of the greys. The next one was turning its panic to its advantage and swinging his rifle toward Fool, firing the whole time.

Fool ducked, gripped his hammer in both hands, and swung the hammer with a back fist blow right into the alien's waist. He hadn't reversed the head, so the pick end of the hammer punched right through the alien's armor. Fool had to kick the screaming and twitching grey off before he could get his hammer clear again. A second blow proved to be unnecessary as the alien promptly fainted.

He seemed to be in the midst of a squad of the little buggers, and there were all turning on him. His Mana was spiking again, which made him add a string of profanity to his wild ducking and dodging and random hammer blows.

This wasn't going to work.

The Mana was dropping faster than he'd planned. It was so damned close too. He'd attracted enough attention to keep the effect going for a bit, and he might be able to effectively take the end of this wing of the enemy line out of the battle, but this was a skirmish he could win. It wasn't the longer war he really needed to affect. To really make a difference, to give Jackal a chance with his attack, he needed to be hitting more than one section of the line. He had to draw as much of the army as possible out of position.

He just didn't have enough Mana to do that.

Or did he?

Mana Sense. The Mana was arriving in pulsed chunks, and he was getting the frustrating sense that the incoming Mana wasn't equal to the outgoing Mana of the Skill. There was waste. A lot of it. That made sense from what Jackal had told him about Dungeon Worlds and Mana use in general. The goal of all of this was burning up Mana, to stop it from getting past a certain critical point and doing something bad that Fool couldn't remember.

Especially not when he was getting shot.

Cursing, he spun about to find some eager beaver of an alien had emptied most of the magazine of his weapon into Fool's back. Fool's armor had given itself up to the cause, but it hadn't been enough and he felt things tearing that shouldn't be tearing as he spun around.

He must have been on a fair bit of an adrenaline rush though, because he didn't feel all that much pain, and his spinning hammer blow was hard enough to peg the head right off of the alien soldier. That made Fool grin. It was always cool when he achieved a Jackal moment.

Then Fool was tossed aside as something exploded next to him, and he slammed into a tree truck. Fortunately, the trunk was set into a bit of a rise, and when he fell down to the ground, he wound up in just enough cover to catch his breath… and be under the stream of fire that tore overhead.

If he was going to get out of this, he had to do something about his Mana.

Chapter Sixteen

Fool reached back to the feeling he'd had before all of this exploded. Take the Mana, open up to it, let it *flow* rather than *pulse*. Open up to the Mana, stop trying to fit it into neat little categories. Let it be, let it do what it wanted to do.

His perspective shifted, and he could almost see himself from the outside looking in.

Mana was all around. It wasn't pressing in. It was everywhere, and everything, and yet still somehow separate. He knew that something was a little off with how he was seeing things, and he knew he'd need a higher level of Mana Sense to really figure this shit out. For the moment though, he was getting a sense of what his backbrain had been trying to tell him.

There was no problem with the Mana. The real problem was the structure that had been built into his body. The Skills. They were a poor filter for Mana. They made it back up like water from a rainstorm trying to get down a leaf-clogged storm drain. Of course the Mana backed up. That was its nature. And he had felt that nature by interpreting it as pulses.

Something else explosive walloped his ears with a percussive blast of sound, and he felt little bits of stone drive through his skin like needles.

The image struck him suddenly that if he'd had the good sense to be dead, then he wouldn't care about the shrapnel. Hell, if he was a ghost, it would just pass through him.

Something clicked.

Willpower. Awareness. He had no words, not even a real mental image of what was happening, but somehow he stopped being. Stopped being aware, stopped being separate from everything. Stopped being a creature of then and now and next, and somehow, someway, he was just Mana.

It wasn't perfect, but the Geas trebled in power, and the Mana drain slowed to a trickle.

Little grey aliens were shooting each other.

Running. Yelling and clustering together.

Falling down on the ground as if shot.

Fool walked through it all, up the slope, with a grin.

Time passed, neither fast nor slow, and he was at the next group of aliens, and his Geas flowed all around them. The end of the line had been ambushed, the line was being rolled; they had to rush in to save them. There were explosions and gunshots and they were under fire. Run, don't let the day be lost.

Then the bubble popped, and Fool was back in his head. The stupid grin was still plastered on his face, and his Mana was nearly gone.

"That. Was. COOL!"

He regretted the shout almost immediately, as he saw more aliens up the slope turn down and face him. They were apparently some of the better troops, because they shot at him right away.

With his Mana reserves gone and no actual idea of what he had just done, Fool had to turn to one of his rarely used but more reliable skills.

He ran like hell.

One nice thing about mountain slopes is that you can cover a lot of ground fast. If you can avoid breaking an ankle.

Fool didn't break an ankle, but he twisted his at least three times before he caught up with, and passed, the first troops he'd attacked. No Geas was needed to encourage them to follow him, adding their gunfire to the other troops. One of the more universal and ancient truths of warfare was that nothing fires up a confused rabble of soldiers more than seeing their enemy's back.

The coalescence of alien squeaks sounded nothing like a roaring battle cry, but that was all Fool could hear it as. It was more goad than he needed, but he used it anyway.

His Mana was trickling back, so I Know a Shortcut and Oh God Don't Hit Me got activated, just long enough for him to figure out the right direction to go and to not get shot in the back. Too much.

There was no time for Mana or Health potions. He just had to keep running and trust his Perception and Luck to keep him alive. Even when he got out of the direct line of sight of the enemy, his speed downhill alone was enough to put him at risk of serious injury. No time to stop. He pushed himself to go faster, to run farther.

Fool had no idea how things were going with Jackal, or if he'd drawn enough of the bad guys away to complete his part of the plan. He'd at least done the best he could.

The flat-ish ground at the foot of the mountain surprised him. He had no idea he'd traveled so far. And even more surprising was that the sun still hadn't set. It had set in the "mountain" sense, in that the sun was below the mountain ridge, but the ridges of the Rocky Mountains on the other side of the valley were still glowing gold rather than pink.

That whole stupid encounter had to have lasted less than a few moments, not the hours of combat that Fool would have sworn he'd just gone through. He slowed and glanced back up the mountainside.

A big fire burned near the top of the mountain, creating two columns of smoke. That would be Jackal's work, but it didn't give Fool any idea of how things were going. The only thing he could do was head for their rendezvous point and wait. And keep an eye open for the McBride forces.

He was still running on a bit of a high from whatever had happened to him earlier. Long ago, when he was a teenager, he'd had a brief infatuation with Zen. He'd done the meditations, practiced reading and contemplating the koans, and done the daunting breathing exercises. After a while, he'd gotten bored, but the only thing he could think of that came close to explaining what had happened to him was something like the Zen "Satori" experience.

It was as if the gates of reality had opened, but just for a moment. And somehow they'd meshed with Mana, as though they were meant to fit together. Fool wished he had a pen and paper, or some other way to write things down, because he really wanted to remember to read some of the old Zen and martial arts philosophy books. Maybe those old guys were on to something.

He still had enough echo of that experience going through his head that he didn't really care that much. It just didn't matter. The "how" of what he had done was slipping away with the buzz, but he wasn't too worried about that. He'd had enough experience with how things worked to know that it would not be a simple thing to do again, but now that he knew it was possible to do?

He'd figure something out. Fool wasn't enough of a math nerd to work out exactly what had happened, but now that he was remote enough from it, it wasn't so much a revolution as much as a refinement. A lot of luck had played into the experience too.

It was a mark in Lucy's favor though. And a point for Olivia as well. Between the two of them, he'd been able to confirm and test their pet theories. The System was a layer on top of the Mana, and while it had clearly been developed and changed over god knew how long, it was like any computer system. Full of kludges, hacks, and holes that were too much for anyone to patch up. He'd just exploited one of them. It made Fool wonder if the System had any kind of System or Network administrators who had to run around and try to patch things.

For a moment, he considered how much work that would be, and a long and deep shudder passed through his body. Probably better for what he'd figured out if there weren't any. The thought made him grin anyway, because from his long-ago memories, he recalled that the computer systems he'd seen that were big and complex and screwed up? They were never run by the tech folks. They were always run by some pompous know-it-all jerk who thought they understood how tech worked and tried to crush their idea of proper protocol onto the techs. Fool figured that sounded exactly like the Weaver.

Which meant that a good hacker could run rings around their setup. Bit of shame, Fool thought, that he hadn't been a better hacker when he was younger. Still, he was willing to give it a try now.

It was always fun to stick it in the eye of the Man. Or whatever the Weaver was.

A weird little sense of euphoria sneaked up over Fool as he got closer to the village. He pulled up the list of all of his Skills. He'd always had a reluctance to use any of them until he accessed his Advanced Class abilities, when he'd "upgraded" that reluctance into relying on his new Skills almost exclusively. With his new little Mana hack, he was seeing that his reluctance came from what felt like the artificial tacked-on nature of Mana use. Now that he could pull things in a way that felt smoother to him, he could look over all of his Skills with a new eye. Some of those things might actually be useful.

The thought occurred to him that maybe what he'd figured out wasn't so much a new and unique hack, but a sign that he'd been doing the whole System thing wrong from the start. He'd certainly had that experience in the pre-System world, along with every other neurodivergent person. Things that were simple for normal people were twice as hard for him. Things like being able to read a book or listen to a conversation or lecture. When he'd gotten his brain re-wired, he'd had a few months of feeling like that alone was a super-power. Maybe this was the same thing.

It wasn't even close to what Olivia had shown him. He couldn't see how to get there from where he was, but he could at least understand how there was a path. And Lucy was right. Trying to get there for most people exposed to the System would be just about impossible.

Fool cut to the right as he got closer to McBride, hopping over the railway tracks. He was in line with where the creek ran through town, so he jumped down off of the road and followed the water. That way, he'd skirt most of the town. He'd cut back in through the greener areas to the south of the hospital, then come back out on the frontage road next to the Kilin restaurant. That'd get him to the bridge, and he'd figure out an alternative route from there, depending on what things were like there.

He still didn't come across any people on the way, and vehicles were scarce too.

From the frontage road, it was only a quick jog to the highway, then he was looking down the road toward the bridge. He let out a little sigh of frustration. Fool always forgot just how far away the damned bridge was from town. He'd walked, jogged, run, and driven it enough times, but for some reason, the map-view in his head always said it was just a brief walk from town.

He jogged down to the bridge and took a moment to stop scanning the road on both sides to enjoy the view. Beaver Mountain looked magnificent in the distance, the giant granite rectangle making up the peak glowing an amethyst pink as the sun went down in earnest.

Which reminded him to pick up the pace. No sign of Jackal ahead, no sounds of pursuit from behind, no gunfire or explosions or other sounds echoing off of the mountain.

He was on the bridge surface before long, and still no Jackal. He wasn't too concerned, not yet. It made sense to push on to Koeneman Park though. He was feeling pretty exposed on the bridge.

Something flickered in the park, just barely visible through the trees.

A motion.

Someone was walking across the big open grass field.

Fool picked up his pace, switching to the near-sprint speed that would have been impossible for him years ago. As he came to the end of the bridge and saw the small fort that had been built there, he realized where the townsfolk had gone.

It looked like most of the village's adult population had gathered in the park and had been organized into groups. The Foundation was out in force too. Fool waved when he saw Professor Xi. The old man had swapped his wheelchair for what was clearly a floating battle platform of some kind, complete with a bristling array of weapons to complement the armor he'd donned. It was a weird look.

The entire village had been outfitted with some pretty advanced gear. It looked as though the Foundation had emptied its considerable stores to combat the threat.

For a moment, as Fool got closer to the park, he wondered if he and Jackal had really needed to be here at all. That thought lasted until he got close enough to see the looks on everyone's faces.

He and Jackal had been out fighting monsters and fighting evil in all kinds of weird forms since the System arrived. The Foundation had been planning and preparing for humanity's future, but not doing any field work. They had people like Fool and Jackal for that. And the village folk?

Most of them hadn't even been living in the village when the System came. They'd been farmers, back-to-earthers, artists, preppers, and actual real hippies, mixed in with people who just liked the privacy of living in a remote spot in the mountains. They'd been driven into the village by wave after wave of monsters. That had given them some toughness and some experience with fighting, but mostly, they'd been happy to find a safe place, and their focus hadn't been on leveling up. It had been doing what they could to find a way back to their old lives.

Fighting an alien army backed by what amounted to supervillains?

As Fool hopped the highway railing and headed down into the park, he saw his favorite waitress, the one who always knew when he was in the mood for a cinnamon bun and a coffee. She had on a helmet and a combat vest, a high-tech beam rifle in her hands. Her very unsteady hands.

Fool gave her the cheeriest smile he could as he walked by. No one here lacked bravery, but that wasn't the same as having the confidence they needed to fight off even the motley army coming at them.

Professor Xi floated down to meet him. The old man looked a lot less ridiculous than Fool would have thought. He'd somehow seamlessly transferred his academic acidity into a bit of an aristocratic war face. It was the wrong time to twit him, but it was taking a lot of Fool's willpower.

"I was hoping you'd gotten our message. Where's Jackal?"

"Dunno." Fool glanced back up the mountain. The sky had turned a dark blue, and the odd flickering star was showing. The columns of smoke from the top of the mountain were still visible, as were the fires burning at the base of them. "According to the plan, that was probably him. He's supposed to meet me back here."

"Plan." Professor Xi seemed to be putting as much effort into not rolling his eyes as Fool had in not cracking wise. "And what was your plan? Did it work? And what exactly are we dealing with?"

"Little grey aliens, just like in the movies. Armed and about as effective as a stereotypical banana republic army. Some armor. Lots of them though. No idea on numbers."

Fool looked over the gathered villagers again. Some signal seemed to have passed to them, because they were already moving back toward town, and the motion seemed to gel them together into a semblance of confidence. They might have a chance. It was going to be close.

"Plan was to draw them out of position, have them come into town all strung-out. Figured you'd have some kind of trap set up. That part worked, and the first elements should come in around the train station right about now. Move quick and you should be able to wrap them up neatly."

Fool paused while Professor Xi held up a hand and barked out some orders. Some airborne units hopped up from farther down the way, out on Mountain View Road, hopscotching up and heading over to the town proper. It looked as though their original plan had been to form a defensive line and jump on the advancing army as they tried to cross the river. On a hunch, Fool turned to look back at the bridge, and sure enough, there were some suspicious-looking packages on the side of the bridge. They had been planning on blowing it. That was a good plan, because it was the only crossing for almost a hundred kilometers.

The professor finished with his orders and gestured for Fool to continue.

"We figured they'd have some Advanced Class support with the key elements. Jackal went up to deal with them while I played my games with the lead element. And that's all we had in mind. Figured we'd wing it after that."

Professor Xi nodded. "We'll just have to hope Jackal took care of any opposition up there. We've got no way to help him if not. All right. We've got spotters in town, and some of the better trained people have been stashed in makeshift redoubts and forlorn hopes around the village. Since you didn't see them, I can assume our camouflage worked as planned. That'll give us some strength in town, so I'm going to press the attack with most of our troops and leave the rest here for a reserve. Are you good to come with us on the attack, or do you want to stay and stiffen the reserve?"

"Been playing some war games, have you?"

The twinkle in the old man's eyes caught Fool by surprise. "Been playing *Squad Leader* since it came out. Make up your mind and get out of my way!"

Fool shook his head. That old dude had a manic gleam in his eye that almost made him feel bad for the greys. Those poor little schmucks were about to have a really bad night.

For a moment, Fool was tempted to leave the fun to the villagers. Give his head a chance to clear and be on top of his game. It wasn't the worst idea, because if they needed the reserves, they were going to really need Fool at his best. But he decided against it. It wasn't going to be an easy fight. No matter how good the planning, people were going to get hurt and probably die. If he wasn't out there with them, he'd never be able to live with himself.

Chapter Seventeen

Jackal could feel an almost electric tingle as the blast of power washed past him, his skin prickling from the heat of the near-miss. With every attack, the leader of the greys was showing how much stronger he was than the rest of the army. Taking cover seemed like a judicious idea, so Jackal took the energy of his dodge, added an extra kick step, and darted behind a handy rock to plan out his next move.

Jackal wasn't really surprised that Fool had been wrong. He usually was, but only in specifics. The general gist of whatever he planned usually turned out to be right.

The current case was the perfect example. Take out the leaders was the right thing to do. Find out what the ace in the hole the enemy had? Well, that was correct as well, but the unspoken thought that Jackal could take them out on his own? That was proving to be a bit of a challenge.

Jackal had sneaked his way up in good time, thanks to the judicious use of Skills. The lead element of the enemy force had been easy enough to find. They had already come over the crest of the mountain and were clustered up at the next ridge. That would put them over the slope and in a straight line down to McBride.

Two groups. The largest was an assembly of a few dozen mobile artillery pieces, and that group was idling, apparently waiting for orders. There was a smaller group nearer the ridge itself.

They were clearly the command group. A group of a dozen taller versions of the little greys. They were sitting around a table, gesturing at little holographic elements, and every once in a while, a shorter version would run off to another vehicle. Passing orders, Jackal had figured… until he saw the runners were coming back with snacks. Food or drinks, it seemed to vary.

Jackal had expected that the holographic table would be a representation of the potential battle area, and it was. But the aliens weren't using it the way he expected, for real-time tracking of their forces on the slope.

Instead, they seemed to be playing some kind of game, with each of them commanding a smaller army and trying to take down what was clearly a dragon flying around the town. He couldn't understand the language they were speaking, but the back-slapping and general attitude were the opposite of what he'd expected from a group of leaders.

The impression was solidified a moment later when the sounds of gunfire and explosions bounced up over the crest. The taller aliens all bolted upright, then sprinted over to the collection of smaller vehicles gather around. They all froze just short though, as a much taller alien strode out of the back of another troop-carrier-looking vehicle. That one yelled, and the others jabbered back then sprinted in different directions.

Jackal had grinned at the time, then sworn as all the artillery let go at once. He didn't have time to see where it came down. It wasn't hard to image the devastation any kind of artillery would have on the village. He had to take those out first.

The first one had gone down easily. The troops manning the gun had been focused solely on firing the next shot, manually loading heavy artillery rounds from a hopper at the back of the vehicle. Jackal had done his classic Death From Above, stacked on One Punch, and had basically punched the barrel right off of the artillery piece. Very satisfying.

That was when the problem started.

Another titanic blast pulled Jackal out of his reminiscence. He'd thought he was safe for a moment, but the dry-powder scent of shattered rock and the peppering stings on his skin as his hiding spot was turned into shrapnel showed him the lie of that. He didn't hesitate, diving and rolling across the tough mountain scree before the leader had a chance to fire a follow-up beam.

This would be a lot easier with Fool here.

The leader of the grey aliens, the tallest, was as strong as the army itself. A high Advanced Class mage of some kind, focused entirely on power blasts from what Jackal could tell. A smattering of rocks blasted into Jackal's skin emphasized just how much power this mage had. The rock he'd hidden behind was now a Jackal-sized crater.

The incompetence of the army made a lot more sense to Jackal now. Whoever had hired mercenaries to take out the Foundation hadn't hired the army. They'd hired the mage. The army was the mage's support. Probably a freebie that came along with the hire.

They may have been a crappy army, but they were pretty good at protecting their tallest.

Not with clever tactics, but just by being in the way.

Case in point—right now. He'd just gotten up after dodging that blast, taken three steps, and one of the little grey buggers was....

Then he didn't have to worry about clearing them, because the mage's power blast turned them both into burning husks and sent Jackal flying. His health dropped like a rock, and if he hadn't had his defense skills up for blocking, he'd be in a pretty bad spot right now. One more shot like that and he'd be toast. He had to find a clear path to taking out the mage.

The leader didn't take Jackal surviving well at all. A very human cry of rage ripped out of the alien's mouth, and he was clearly summoning some kind of massive power-up. Massive enough that he was floating in the air and glowing.

That new part of Jackal, the raging berserker part, wanted to rise up against the challenge. The confidence of that response made him grin.

This was joy.

Overwhelmed by a stronger foe? Hanging on by the skin of his teeth? This was the life he'd chosen, that he was born for.

He took the confidence, used it to fuel his plans. Now wasn't the time to take a chance. He loved himself best when he was confident, not cocky. Besides, cocky was Fool's jam. Jackal preferred to just win.

He activated The Wall, counting on the temporary invulnerability to keep him in the fight while he charged again at the mage. He was almost in range to use the skills he hoped would tip the fight in his favor. Almost.

The world went white. Even with the invulnerability, Jackal felt as if he'd blacked out for a moment. The Skill let him defy the physics of momentum to a certain degree, but against a Master Class attack, there was only so much it could do.

The angles were just right, so instead of Jackal being blasted halfway to space, he was instead blasted down into the ground, plowing a deep running crater for about thirty meters back and deeper than his head height. It felt as if he was being sandpapered to death against the mountain. Only when the force of the blast dissipated was Jackal able to recognize that he was still somehow standing upright.

It wasn't in him to even break a sweat under pressure, but he knew that if his now-depleted Skill hadn't been active, he wouldn't even be a greasy stain on the mountainside. And he had nothing left to take another shot like that. Or even one of the regular blasts the mage was dealing out.

He was getting angry. It was time to crush this mage. He couldn't let someone this strong beat him. Not here, not now. Someone this powerful was more than capable of taking out not only the village, but the entire Foundation.

Incompetent or not, the enemy was ready to exploit the mage's blast, and Jackal barely had time to blink the dots away from his eyes before he saw the greys swarming toward him. The still-floating mage was coming along with them, clearly looking forward to getting in a *coup de grâce*.

Jackal didn't move, just let the grin rise on his face, drawing the enemy in. He felt his body responding, the joy of combat rising in him, the sweet pleasure of his mind dropping away and leaving only the Warrior in its place.

He slowly straightened, moving into a combat stance just before the swarm of greys hit him.

Just as the mage came into range.

Blade Walking and Red Rover, to break the enemy formation and swarm into them, dancing through them, sending them flying when they weren't being sliced into ribbons.

Mr. Freeze to slow down the mage, just enough for the rest of his skills.

Narcissus to reflect damage back, Mana Steal to draw out the combat life blood of the mage, and finally Jackal's Advanced Class Skill, Punishment of the Bear, damaging and crippling the mage's Mana. The Skill was his current last-ditch favorite, used to cut the feet out from most attackers by making it impossible for them to use whatever last-ditch skill of their own they'd been relying on.

It was custom-made for mage-killing.

The fear on the tall alien's face showed Jackal that the leader realized that as well, as whatever Skill he was trying to activate—felt like a last-minute teleport—fizzled out.

The double blades buried in the grey's chest only added to his surprise.

The remaining aliens scattered as the green rain of their leader's blood spattered down amongst them, along with the top and bottom halves of his corpse.

Jackal landed from his leap and took a moment to swipe his blades clean before he turned toward the remaining artillery pieces. The crews of those weapons were still stubbornly firing, and they needed to be put down.

Jackal found himself pausing against his will.

The sun was setting rapidly, and he saw pink and amber streaky clouds in the distance over the far mountain peaks, as well as a hint of anti-crepuscular ray. It was looking like a beautiful sunset.

A sunset he shouldn't be able to see, because the long sloping ridge of the mountain he was on should have been in the way.

The mage's blast had punched a hole through the top of the mountain. The once impressive peak now looked like a bizarre negative space crescent moon.

Jackal let out a sigh then set about trashing the rest of the artillery.

A veritable glass cannon, and Jackal had nearly died from it. There was nothing he could have done differently, and he knew it was really luck alone that he was still alive.

If the mage had jumped to his big gun earlier, if Jackal had hesitated or used up his invulnerability earlier, he'd be nothing but a stream of plasma right now.

For some reason, that thought brought up a wave of shame. It only took a moment to realize why. He'd flung himself into battle, just like the heroes he'd always worshipped. The movie and comic book tough guys, larger than life, always winning by the skin of their teeth and brushing it off as though it was nothing. The System had brought the potential to be that, and Jackal had leapt at the chance.

But with all the crazy power of it, it was still real life.

This wasn't the real life he wanted anymore.

Nicholaus was amazing. His smile, the way he carried himself? Not just his confidence, but how he used that confidence to do things, to pursue his passion?

Jackal was smitten, and he knew it. The surprise on realizing that was profound. It wasn't just Nicholaus and his company. It was what Nicholaus was doing with his life. Jackal wanted to see what was next for him in life. What could he do outside of being the stoic hero? He wanted to be with Nicholaus, but he also wanted to *be* Nicholaus, and he had no idea how to do that. How to change his whole life.

He'd already made that massive transformation once, but the System had helped with that. The System had offered a way to make his internal vision of himself external, and it had only been a few Shop purchases. So easy. And wonderful. But now that he had what he'd dreamed of, why should he stop dreaming? Should he not want to have a life that just kept getting wider and wider in potential... while at the same time, maybe becoming more and more intimate and personal?

Most people never had this chance. And looking up again at that massive crescent in the mountain, he knew how close he'd come to being one of those people.

Jackal owed it to them to become something bigger, something different. Something new. Maybe he couldn't imagine what that meant right now, but that didn't mean he wasn't going to start moving toward whatever it was.

That brought a painful realization.

He stopped after having torn off the last barrel. The remaining soldiers had all fled down the mountain, and it was now up to the Foundation and the McBride villagers to do what they could with the army. And Fool.

That was the hard part. He had to change, and maybe… maybe Fool wouldn't be a part of that.

He'd seen the woman who had been the bait the System Knights had used to trap Fool. And he'd seen how Fool had looked at her. Probably, he'd seen more than Fool even knew.

Fool was, in a lot of ways, still a very broken person. He'd opened up a bit to Jackal after explaining the Rebecca thing. That discussion had explained a lot of the things Jackal had only previously assumed about Fool. The System had fixed up his disabilities, but that didn't make up for the decades he had lost. He'd thrown himself into the new world fast and hard to try to make up for it, but even just a glimpse of his old world…

Jackal had seen the pain in his friend, and tied just as strongly to the pain was hope.

Hope for love, for redemption, for a second chance.

Somewhere ahead of them, if everything worked out for the best, Jackal knew that his path and Fool's would diverge.

That thought hurt, but not as much as the thought of turning away from his own future, what he was just realizing that he wanted. While there was pain, there was also a brightness coming from inside him. It'd work out. Things were going to change, but he had to trust Fool. Somehow, they'd work it all out. He couldn't help but have faith in that.

Jackal looked over the battlefield again. The sun was going down, and it was a long way down the mountain. He didn't hear any more echoing shots or explosions from where Fool had been, but he didn't think that meant anything bad for Fool. Likely, he'd just pulled it off perfectly somehow, as usual, and was on his way to the village with the enemy vanguard hot on his ass. Which left Jackal in a bit of a quandary. He could follow the original plan or improvise.

"I see we had the same idea."

Jackal spun around in surprise. It should have been impossible for anyone to sneak up on him, yet he was suddenly aware that someone was behind him. Not within striking range, but within shouting range. Much closer than he would have expected anyone to get. And they weren't alone.

Then he saw who it was and grinned. "Looking good, Roger. Made some new friends?"

The young man was looking good. Jackal hadn't really noticed at the party, but a fundamental change had overcome the young man. It wasn't anything overtly physical—aside from the rough shag of a beard that was making itself known.

It was all in the posture. Living in a Dungeon World had a way of making people grow up fast. It wasn't always easy, but some people prospered. Roger clearly had. The cockiness was still there, but it was tempered into confidence. His grin was easy and welcoming, with no trace of the old arrogance in it. Roger's back was straighter, and his eyes… His eyes looked harder, his gaze more direct. It matched the firmness in his jaw. The boy was growing into a man, in Jackal's estimation. And a leader, judging from the companions with him.

The grin turned to a smile, and Roger turned and gestured to the surrounding folk. "My companions. Yagnar's been helping with the recruiting, and we're building a matching ground force to the Airborne Cavalry. These will be the officers. I'll introduce you when we've got all this settled."

Jackal nodded and glanced again over the Companions. They were a diverse group of eight—four human and four alien. Eric was there and clearly foremost amongst them. He looked to have put on considerable muscle since Jackal had last seen him. The Companions straightened a little under Jackal's gaze, moving together to almost stand in formation.

Jackal gave them a nod and turned back to Roger. "Competent. Well done."

The grin that crossed Roger's face knocked away all the maturity Jackal had seen, but it was only a fleeting grin. "We came up here to find the head and cut it off, but now that you've handled that for us, we should chase them down the mountain."

"Fool's leading them down, breaking their formation."

"Brilliant! We've set a trap. My team, if we could take out the leaders, was supposed to harry the troops and try to drive or draw them toward the town. The Professor has some armored units across the river to be an anvil for them to run up against, and Yagnar has another group hidden on the northwest end of town to be the hammer. I managed to talk the Professor into managing the reserves across the bridge."

Roger had not only grown up but was also becoming the tactical leader Jackal and Fool had been sent out to recruit. It was gratifying to see such a nice concrete result for all their work. So many of their previous missions had been to retrieve objects or help people in ways they never really saw any result from.

Jackal glanced down the mountain again, then back up at the big, empty crescent in the mountain. There was a distant rumble as some of the rock cracked loose and fell. With this new information, he could think of a few ways to be useful. Especially now that he knew there was a plan and Fool was far less likely to get in over his head. Extra troops were all around, and Fool's usual luck would probably work in his favor no matter what. So Jackal had a choice of what he wanted to do next.

But really, the best choice was to trust in the community he'd help build. "Where would you like me?"

It seemed to be the right question, because Roger just about glowed at the compliment. "Head southwest! Yagnar's group is mostly new recruits. I get to cherry pick from them, and the prof's group is all people comfy with each other. Yagnar's group will need the most backup. We can handle driving the army into the trap. If you make it quick, you can join Yagnar in crushing them. We'll hit them just after you do, with luck."

Jackal nodded and took off at his fastest pace, boosted by Skill use. He knew about a few trails, as well as a road, that he could use to get down the mountain without having to dodge trees the entire way. With only a little luck, the route would take him to Yagnar's position without having to cross or alert any elements of the grey army.

He was looking forward to seeing the Hakarta again. She'd been good company, and the first mission of what he was realizing was the Foundation's final chapter. Or, more realistically, the final chapter of its opening act.

After Lucy's competition was finished and the jump to the new world was made, the Foundation's primary mission would be complete. They would have established a foothold for humanity on the far side of the galaxy, out of the hands of the Galactic Council, in a place where they could prepare like no one else for the coming of the System.

The Foundation's work wouldn't be done, of course. From what Lucy had told him, the follow-up mission would be almost as important. That would be a two-part mission. The first would be to keep up the fight against the Galactic Council on Earth, but in a more above-board way. In some ways, to be a more direct target. The more obvious they could be, the more they could keep attention away from their actual goals. They'd come out into the open and rally who they could into an Earth Independence movement, finding the strongest voice they could make for Earth on the galactic stage. They'd push for a human-first coalition, but any aliens that had come around to thinking of Earth as their home would be more than welcome and treated like equals.

It was a good plan, but only had a tiny chance of succeeding. The secondary mission, the one Jackal felt he and Fool had been slotted into by default, was to keep up the secret war. Eventually, if it all worked out, there would be a colony ship. That ship would head toward the colony the competition winners would start, toward whatever world they had built for themselves. The Trickster had built a plan for that as well, in conjunction with the tech folk.

That was the riskiest part of the operation, not just because it would be technically difficult, but because of the time involved. At a best estimate, building the ship that could make the trip would take almost fifty years, though the trip itself would take less than five. At that point, the colonists would have only a year before the System caught up to the new world. They would have to rely on the leadership of the first group to survive and prepare. They wouldn't be able to take advantage of what the advance team would have learned, but their children would.

Jackal didn't know all the details. No one really did, outside of the Trickster. But it was a plan he believed in. One he was willing to sacrifice himself for. It was a foolish and desperate plan, but it was the only one there was. And it was a hell of a lot better than sitting back and watching the entire world slowly fall apart, ripped into oblivion and forgotten as nothing more than a series of increasingly dangerous dungeons to be exploited by off-world powerhouses.

He was willing to do anything to save what he could. At least he wasn't alone in that.

Jackal's bursts of speed took him down the mountain in no time and across the woods. He came out on the outskirts of the village and had to swing back toward the town. As a result, he came up to Yagnar's group from behind.

He'd expected a small army, given her inclinations toward logistics, but he'd forgotten that the System changed the dynamics of everything. Her group was larger than Roger's, but only by about three times.

Much like Roger's group, they were a mix of human and alien and, judging from their outfits and equipment, all experienced adventurers.

Jackal was wondering if he and Fool had really been needed so urgently.

"Jackal!" Yagnar roared across the remaining space between them. That at least let Jackal know that there wasn't any need for stealth as yet. "Glad to see you. We can use your help!"

He slowed down his sprint and walked up to Yagnar. She was at the side of the road, leaning on an armored vehicle. Most of her troops were gathered around her in a loose circle, with a smaller group down the road keeping an eye on how things were developing with the approaching army.

He gave Yagnar a nod in welcome, but the big Hakarta was having none of that and gathered him up in a bone-crushing hug.

When she set him down, she turned to everyone else. "This is Jackal. I've told you about him. If you want any loot or experience from those little grey bastards, you need to stay ahead of this guy. And don't worry about your backs, he'll have them covered. Now we can really kick ass!"

The hearty roar that came back was mixed with raspberries and jeers, but all in good humor. Clearly professional, with a sardonic and practical approach that contrasted nicely the earnest but deadly vibe that Roger's group had been working hard on broadcasting.

Yagnar leaned in before Jackal could say anything. "Actually, glad to see you. That you who took out the Primarch?" She nodded toward the missing part of the mountain.

Jackal nodded. "Wasn't too hard."

"Nice bullshit. I'd gotten a read on his stats finally. That thing would have cleaned all our clocks, no matter how much prep we had. You've saved the day for us. Where's the old man?"

His shrug didn't quite satisfy Yagnar, so he had to add, "Either on his way to the Professor or already there."

"Excellent. We've got an edge on the little bastards now, but as you humans say, 'quantity has a quality all its own' and they are still a lot of them. You up for a run with us? Roger let me know you know the plan."

His savage grin was the only answer Yagnar needed.

Chapter Eighteen

That plan fell apart, as such things do.

The greys, panicked, angered, and without leadership, should have chased Fool all the way down the mountain in a ragged, stretched out line. Then they would have run into the armored units the Professor had sent forward and been pinned between them and Roger's group, with Yagnar putting the finish to them. The villagers under the Professor would have swept in to pick off any strays and collect any that surrendered.

It was a good plan.

What actually happened was that the lead element chasing Fool lost track of him at the foot of the mountain and tried to backtrack, thinking they might get flanked and be cut off from their supporting elements.

The group still coming down the mountain behind them saw the artillery hitting the village and pushed downhill even faster, wanting to get in on the loot and experience.

The group farthest up the mountain was in full flight down, running from the monster that had crushed their Primarch and had been in the middle of tearing up the artillery when they'd decided beating feet was the wisest thing to do.

All three groups mashed into each other at the base of the mountain, still in the thick part of the woods. And as sometimes happened, one of them pulled his head together and recognized that a strong leader was needed. And then decided that he was the one to be the strong leader and continued on to rally the whole lot of them back into a cohesive fighting unit. It took them until nightfall to organize that, but they managed it.

Fool was okay with that. It was when they turned into a smarter fighting unit and set up a defensive formation within the woods that he took it personally. Not that he was anxious for a battle. Mostly, he was pissed that someone else had done the unexpected. That was his job.

A part of it was that he felt some urgency to get back to Vancouver. He wanted to make sure that McBride was safe, and the Foundation. That was important, and he knew he had to be here in case anything else unexpected happened. Vancouver though… there was unfinished business there. The longer he was away, the more risk that some other plan of the Weaver would crop up and ruin everything.

Sure, Lucy was more capable than he was of dealing with anything. More capable that him and Jackal combined, at least in terms of levels. Fool had been coming to realize that levels didn't count for as much as he thought they did. He'd certainly taken out more than his share of higher-level opponents. Hell, he'd been responsible for ending some kind of otherworldly god. Accidentally, but still. That was his primary tactic.

In any case, he didn't have any difficulty rationalizing his urge to return to the big city as someone else needing him.

The Professor was on something like a radio, talking to the other elements of the Foundation's "armed forces." Fool had at least confirmed that Jackal was okay, news that hadn't surprised him at all. They were working out a strategy, trying to decide how best to wipe out the opposing army.

Fool held up his hand, and when the Professor ignored that, Fool leaned a little closer, took out his warhammer, and landed a gentle, ringing tap on the Professor's floating conveyance.

That got Fool a look.

Not a friendly one.

"Back them up against the mountain. Surround them on the other three sides. Yagnar on the right, you on the left, Roger and Jackal right in front of them."

The Professor stared at him for a moment. Then he sighed. "Bad idea. Basic strategy. Give them no place to retreat, and they'll fight to the death. Best to leave them a way out, give them some hope. They won't feel like they have to fight as hard. More likely to surrender, and if they don't, they won't realize how bad their position is."

Fool nodded, but kept talking. "Right, I get that, but that's the old world thinking. System, remember? People heal up from anything short of death? They all have a chance of leveling up and getting stronger in the middle of a fight? Morale works differently. Lock 'em up in one place and let me talk to them. I can get them to surrender."

That got the Professor's eyebrows to rise, and Fool absently noted that one of the older man's eyebrow hairs had turned white and was getting noticeably long. Maybe they were the bad guys after all.

After thinking about it for a moment, the Professor spoke into the communicator to the other groups and let them know what Fool's suggestion was. It only took them a moment to respond, and Fool figured it would be a bad idea to comment on the Professor's sour look.

"They seem to trust you a fair bit. All right, we're moving out now. Follow along then." At that, the Professor turned around and flew off, waving to the assembled villagers.

In the distance, Fool saw the flying units lift up from the outskirts of town, still sitting low but advancing.

Everyone moved in good order, and Fool tagged along. There was a fair bit of shuffling and maneuvering. For a bit, it looked as if the greys would try a breakout, but they weren't very serious about it, and it was repulsed easily. A steady fire kept up from all sides, which slowed the advance. The Foundation forces were mostly firing, under the Professor's orders, to keep the enemy pinned in place.

Even with their careful advance, there were enough casualties that the grey focus on defense was proving to be a very sound strategy. The only thing that prevented fatalities on the Foundation side was that the greys seemed to have sub-par night vision equipment.

It took until dawn before the encirclement was complete. And with the sun rising from the back of most of the Foundation troops, the enemy fire slackened. When the Foundation responded in suit, a blissful silence settled over the morning, neither side firing nor making any sound.

That was Fool's cue.

He really had no idea what the hell he was doing. In the night, walking up to the enemy had sounded like the right thing to do, as did negotiating their surrender. But his stupid mix of confidence and ethical motivation had faded into a grumpy resignation. The insight was still there, but the assumption that he could do anything to change his life had faded.

Still, there was no choice about this. It was the right thing to do, and he was committed.

He could do this. He had the tools. All of Fool's Basic Skills had been built with this kind of thing in mind. So were his Ability scores. The automatically distributed points assigned at every level were all in aid of this. He'd spent so much time feeling like a useless appendage, because Jackal had all the fighting skills and Fool had had to rely on weapons to try to keep up. The only way he'd seen any use for his Skills had been in their earlier missions, when he'd been acting like a spy or running what amounted to scams on all of their targets.

He was the rogue. Jackal was the muscle.

It didn't have to be that way, but Fool could recognize now why he had been so reluctant to use his Skills. He'd justified it as being cautious about warping his personal sense of reality, worried about relapsing.

The truth was, his powers were entirely rooted in deception and manipulation, and he'd had a giant and deep-seated fear that the Skills were available to him because at heart, he was a liar and manipulator. That had been his barrier all along, his secret pain that'd he'd been the bad guy, the villain, and not the victim of unlucky circumstances.

He'd come to grips with that overnight. There was a truth to it, but by shying away from that truth, he'd blinded himself to the full story, to the honest intentions and hopes in his heart. That, and the painful realization that he'd failed at so much in his life, not because he was legit crazy, but because he'd been afraid to really commit.

At his core, Fool was a broken man, and the System hadn't fixed that at all. It had only patched up one of the things that had caused him to break. It wasn't the only thing though. And he wasn't fixed at all.

That didn't mean he couldn't do the right thing from now on, as often as he could.

His Skills lit, activating with a fire he'd never felt before.

His real Skill base wasn't just deception. It was diplomacy. It was leadership. It was doing whatever it took to spread the truth, while making sure that what he spoke was the actual truth.

He was an Acolyte and an Adept, a priest of the Trickster. And he was gonna preach.

Clouseau, to become taller, because the greys seem to respect that.

Pants on Fire, to tell an undetectable lie. Not because he was going to lie, but to mask any wavers or lack of confidence that might dilute his message.

Oh God Don't Hit Me, to lower the System-default reflex to violence.

Location Scout, to know the best place to stand and speak from.

Aziz!, to ensure that he was lit and visible to everyone.

Dry Hair is for Squids, to remove any lingering fear from the audience.

And finally, Geas, rising up with almost no Mana charge, because he knew, deep down in his heart, that what he was saying was the most important truth at the moment and that the greys needed to believe in him.

He walked into the woods, hands held up high. There was no worry about a white flag. He knew they would read his intentions clearly via his Skills. And his Charisma.

At first there wasn't any response, but he heard a rustling from the treeline. His Mana draw spiked up. His previous experience with controlling that via his Mana Sense was still strong, so Fool reached back to the same feeling he'd had before.

It worked again. He wasn't sure what he was doing, but it felt as if the rough edges of his Skills were smoothing out. He wasn't entirely sure if that was because of his tuning of Mana or just because his Skills were finally working in unison with each other and the synergistic effect was reducing the overall cost.

In any case, he only took a few more steps toward the woods before he saw the first grey step out. It looked awestruck, its weapon dangling in its grip. It dropped the gun a moment later and slowly stumbled toward Fool.

The first one out started a small wave, and the next thing Fool knew, he was surrounded by greys. The slower they came out of the woods, the less awestruck they looked. Clearly, some of them had higher resistances than others, but the follow-the-leader group effect seemed to affect them, regardless.

He kept moving forward until he was right at the treeline. He saw smaller groups of greys clustered all around, hastily built defensive positions clustered up around the base of the trees. All the eyes were focused on him, and weapons, at first raised, lowered.

After a brief pause, a slightly taller grey came out from farther back in the woods. He was a bit taller than all the others, and from the way all their eyes darted between him and Fool, Fool figured he must be the new leader.

For a moment, Fool was tempted to yank out his warhammer and end the whole thing. It was just a fleeting thought.

Less fleeting was the growing recognition of the soft mutterings all around him. Warbles, chirps, tweets, and hums.

He had no idea what the hell they were saying.

Fool had set himself up as the negotiator and had completely forgotten about not speaking the same language.

The little alien walked right up to him and talked. At least, Fool assumed it was talking. He tried nodding in response, and the flow of sounds continued. At least Fool's Mana wasn't spiking back up yet, so he seemed to be giving the right response. He had no idea what to do next. Walking back to the Foundation side of the battle, gesturing the little alien to follow, seemed like the best course. Someone back there had to have some language Skill or purchase or… maybe a more thought-out idea about what to do next.

Fool thought he'd try one more thing first. He pantomimed laying weapons down and then made a "follow me" gesture.

The only thing that happened was that his Mana use climbed back up. He did a masterful job of not swearing, then his Mana use did a quick tick upward and all the aliens glanced behind Fool.

He glanced over his shoulder, and there was Yagnar. It was likely not her size that caused the Mana spike, but rather her tusky grin. It was intimidating as hell. Fool at least knew her well enough to read it as her happy-go-lucky smile.

"Forgot to bring a translator, huh?"

Fool's cheeks didn't quite turn red, mostly because he used his Clouseau Skill to adjust his skin tone. "I may have. I take it you've got one?"

"Nope. No need. The Ir-Khan are not uncommon where I'm from. Learned to speak it when I was a kid."

He couldn't restrain the eye roll. "Of course. So what are they saying?"

She pointed at the Ir-Khan leader. "Sub-lieutenant Grim says that he trusts you, but he and his soldiers are ready to die rather than submit to your tortures."

That rocked Fool back. "Torture? Why do they think we're going to—"

Yagnar cut him off. "Ir-Khan like to exaggerate. This is pretty much a standard start to negotiations. They've already surrendered and are hoping to get more favorable terms than giving up all of their gear and are trying to find a way to get home. Want me to handle the negotiations?"

"Oh god yes, please."

"I got it. You just keep standing there looking like a benevolent, glowing target for a little longer, okay? I'll give you a nod at some point, and when I do, you head back to our side before your Skill wears off. How long can you handle it?"

"Ten or fifteen minutes. It's getting easier."

Yagnar nodded. "You just keep on then. I got this."

It took fifteen minutes, but by that point, Yagnar had the details wrapped up, and she took Grim back to talk to the Professor.

Five minutes after that, the Ir-Khan streamed out of the woods, dropping their weapons into a pile as they came.

Once all the kerfuffle was over, the villagers spread back out, mixed emotions clear on their faces. Relief, for the most part. It hadn't been clear at the start of this whether any of them would live to see the next day or not. Rage, as they saw the damage even a brief artillery barrage had done to the village. And sadness at the thought of all the work it would take to rebuild.

Fool watched all that, the play of emotions. He saw some people settling into one of the three, and he hoped that the usual System healing would help those folks cope and find some equilibrium. Without that, they'd be where so many other people had been before the System, stuck in the aftermath of war with unreconciled feelings that would linger and show up when they were least wanted.

Another lesson of the System. It brought pain, violence, and misery, but it also tried to make things better. Fool was seeing what motivated the Trickster. Millennia of seeing this? The only way it wouldn't break a compassionate person was if they felt as though they could make a difference, make some sort of change to it.

Violence and its consequences weren't anything new in the world. The worst part of the System was that it brought hope. Magical powers made real, the potential to make dreams become real. That was wonderful and beautiful, but it had somehow been warped into a hungry cycle of destruction and the craving for power.

Fool had once heard that each drug had a demon in it, and when someone's addiction to that drug became overwhelming, you could see them take on the face of that demon, like it peered out from the depths of their soul, showing itself to the world.

He wondered what the face of the System was, and he looked around to see what was peering out at him from the surrounding souls. What might peer out from his own face? He had a sure sense that it would be the face of the Weaver.

Another little tipping point clicked over for him. The Trickster. Lucy's mission, the goal she'd talked about? It wasn't all about finding a way to use Mana better. He knew that was what she believed, and in knowing that, he finally understood what an avatar was. A shadow of the real thing.

He knew that, because he knew what the real goal was. The real goal was not to fight or destroy the System. The real goal was to restore balance to the universe. To find a way to let Mana flow in a different way, to bring hope and love back into the equation instead of greedy consumption.

Have Faith. It was the strangest skill he had, the most overpowered, and the one he was most hesitant to use. And that was because faith scared him. Until now.

Now, he'd tipped right over, and he believed in the Trickster. What the Trickster wanted, Fool wanted. He could feel and see the strands of the Trickster's plan all around him, from every element of his past and extending into his unforeseeable future.

Whatever it was, he was ready.

He glanced up from his reverie and saw that Jackal was finally free of whatever had been occupying his time and had come to find Fool. And from the pensive look on his face, Fool knew Jackal had come to a realization of his own. Fool didn't have to ask to know the consequences of that realization.

Fool grinned at his friend and hugged him. Jackal was obviously surprised, but only for a moment before he hugged Fool back.

Fool stood back and looked up at the big man. "Ready to get back into it?"

Jackal nodded, and Fool activated the return portal that Lucy had given them. Neither of them felt like making goodbyes to the McBride folk. There was an unspoken sense that doing so would acknowledge a truth that neither of them cared to admit to just yet.

Fool didn't know if all of this would be worth it, but he had faith.

Chapter Nineteen

Lucy was right there waiting for them. Same stance and everything, just as she'd been when they stepped through the fixed portal in the first place. It was morning, just as it had been in McBride, but without mountains to block the rising sun, the glare of the just-off-the-horizon star was bright enough to make Fool and Jackal wince.

"Holy Pauper's Horns, what the hell happened to you two? You look like you got wrung out and run over!"

Fool glanced at Jackal. He didn't look roughed up at all. He looked pretty tired though. Come to think of it, Fool realized that neither of them had slept in over twenty-four hours. Their enhanced Constitution carried them pretty far, but even so, realizing how long it had been since Fool had felt a bed hit him all at once.

"Just tired. Lot happened, but it's all okay. Need bed." Even as Fool said that, he felt the sandpaper weight of his eyelids dragging down. Bed would be so good.

Jackal made a grunt that sounded like agreement.

Lucy collapsed the portal structure, but it had clearly been used up. It crumbled into dust, and she just looked at her hands as it turned into a silvery grey pile on the asphalt. "Well, that was expensive. Worth it? You two kick some butt?"

Fool nodded. "Bit of a trap. Another Master Class? I think? Jackal?"

Jackal grunted then stretched with a very contagious yawn. "High Advanced, maybe. Hefty gear though. Would have wiped everyone out. I got lucky. He was a glass cannon build and let me get in his range."

"Hole in a mountain," Fool added.

Lucy crossed her arms and looked at the two. "Can't let you guys out of my sight, can I? All right, follow me. Things are coming to a head, but you can crash for now."

She didn't wait for any kind of acknowledgement, just walked back to the entrance to the Twisted Chapel. She didn't stop talking the whole way, but neither Fool nor Jackal had any energy to reply. They just followed along and made grunts of acknowledgement when they could muster up the energy.

"Competition ran through the night. Prelims are over. Quarter-finals start this afternoon, semis in the evening, and the finals just before midnight. Portal opens at midnight. Winners and support crews go through then. Few minutes for the portal to be open, then that's all she wrote. System Knights have been rumbling about, but Vancouver City Council got together and stopped them from actually wrecking the city. Somehow. But we got word a few hours ago that we are *persona non grata* locally for making trouble, so that ban doesn't affect us. Those fuckers will be along eventually. Gotta figure the Weaver knows the deal by this point, and we can expect them to come and stomp us into oblivion. So." She finally led them through the doors and over to the stairs leading up to her personal quarters in the club. "So, you two gonna be ready to kick some serious ass? After your nap?"

Fool grumble-muttered something, and Jackal found one last burst of energy to squeeze out some coherence. "Six hours sleep. Wake us up with coffee, bacon, hash browns, and eggs. Lots. And cinnamon buns? Please?"

Lucy snorted. "Pretty please."

Jackal shoved Fool through the door as Fool slowed down approaching the threshold. "Pretty please. Sugar something top…"

They were both crashed out on the couch and asleep less than ten seconds later.

It wasn't the smell of coffee that woke Fool. It was the bacon, wafting through his subconscious, pushing past the strange dream about cats and a field of daisies. His stomach woke him, and he was almost upright before he woke up a bit more fully. Then he smelled the coffee. And cinnamon buns.

Lucy had a little den next to her office. Quite the apartment really. The office took the place of a living room, but there was still a small kitchen, a good-sized dining room, washroom, and her bedroom in addition to the den. The door to the den was open. Fool let his stomach guide his feet, and he found that the dining room table had been stacked high with breakfast foods. Jackal was already stuffing his face, and Lucy was sitting back and sipping coffee with a blissful expression.

Fool knew exactly what his priorities should be in a situation like this.

Cinnamon bun first. There was a plate of them with icing, and one without. He opted for the icing covered buns first, plopped one on his plate, and unfurled it.

The first bite was perfect. Butter. Cinnamon. Rich, rich caramelized sugar, and melted icing running through it all. So sweet, it overloaded everything else that might have been a flavor in his mouth. Still the perfect temperature too… just hot enough that you wished you'd blown on it before biting, but not so hot that you'd bother to blow on the next piece.

He ate the whole thing without looking up, savoring each piece in perfect bliss.

Then he reached for the bacon. The fatty, savory, smokey crunch was the perfect way to balance out the sweet butter bomb of the cinnamon bun. Two slices shifted the balance in his mouth most of the way over to smokey bacon, so he reached for the hash browns to get some extra crunch and some pleasant mass to satisfy any lingering cravings. Next, a slice of toast with some egg.

Nothing he enjoyed more than that run of tastes and sensations in his mouth. A solid breakfast spread like this was his ideal gustatory experience. All it needed was the final cap, then he could start the cycle all over, repeating until he was sated. He poured himself a cup of the coffee in the silver urn. The first sip…

"Mind-blowing, isn't it?" Lucy hovered her nose over her coffee, eyes closed, inhaling. "Ethiopian Guji Gabeta, roasted three days ago. That explosion of fruit flavors lasts through the first mouthful, and when you get through the next few, lavender and honey start to come out."

"This is a damned good cup of coffee." Fool couldn't quite make out the distinct flavor notes, but the explosion of sweet citrus in his mouth completely reset his palate back to a clean start. He took a second sip and hoped that the urn was fuller than it looked. This was going to be at least a three-cup breakfast. If he was being forced to rush, he'd skip more food and drink all the coffee himself.

Lucy grinned, seeing the pleasure on Fool's face. And maybe on Jackal's, but it was hard to tell because the big man was making an effort to eat enough for someone three times his size. There *might* be enough food for everyone at his pace.

"Enjoy it," Lucy said. "I've been saving this coffee for a special occasion. I've got a little bit more for the other side, but that'll be it. Not even sure if the farm I bought this coffee from is still around, in any case."

Fool wondered about the "other side" comment, but then he remembered. Tonight. Hours away. The portal opened. He hadn't been entirely sure that Lucy intended to go to the colony world, but it sounded now like she intended to. Some part of him had been wondering how that would work. She was born of Mana, but she was a real and separate entity now, like everyone else. But would that maintain in a world without Mana? He wasn't going to ask. She'd probably worked all that out already. Still, time was running out and getting some clarification was feeling important to him.

"So not just the winning dance crew going then? I know you mentioned support crew, but I wasn't sure if that included you or not."

Lucy took a long sip of her coffee. "Yeah, I'm going. Everyone here knows it now, and I've put things in place to give everyone else a good head start on the next few years of System shenanigans. This club will be a safe place for them. They'll be able to make a proper home here and do more than just survive. The dance-off is being picked up all across the galaxy, and there will be opportunities for all the dancers. Earth-style dance comps will be popular for a while."

She looked down for a moment, then continued. "And we still need to be fighting the good fight here. This is all about securing a potential future, but it's not the same thing as giving up and winning from within the System. That's still a goal. So… I thought about staying. When I mostly thought about though? If we're gonna be really ready to fight the System when it arrives, the colonists are gonna need to know how to fight, and having someone to train against will help immeasurably. Plus, they might need some Master Class muscle when the System arrives. So, I gotta plan on giving up coffee for a while. We're bringing a ton of supplies, but there won't be any Shops there for a long while."

She looked down again. Then she leaned back in her chair and looked at the ceiling for a while. Finally she puffed out a little air, dropped her chair down, and looked Fool and Jackal in the eye, in turn.

"Room for both of you too. I'm hoping you'll come along. We could use you."

Fool didn't react, just started on his next chunk of cinnamon bun. Chewed it carefully, then glanced at Lucy. "You need to know right away?"

Lucy rolled her eyes. "No, you can take your time. Seriously? The portal opens in, like, hours! Shit or get off the pot, dude!" Her eyes seemed to literally simmer for a bit, then she crossed her arms and leaned back again. "No. Shit, no. I don't need to know at all. Look, here's the deal. The portal opens at midnight. On the other side is a complete unknown. Unknown, but a fresh start. Make your own fucking world. I know you two have some connections here, but I guarantee you after tonight, they'll be fine. At least fine enough that you can't make any difference being here or not. So you have a free ticket to go without worrying about consequences. You will see the portal open. It will be only open for a few minutes, so if you decide to go, just walk on through. If you don't, stay put. And to be clear, you both should be right next to the portal when it opens. I don't care what else happens. That needs to be protected at all costs, and you two and me are the only ones strong enough to do that."

The glare in her eyes faded a bit, and she slumped a little. "Any case, enjoy the breakfast. Never know when it might be your last." She shook herself a little and led by example, grabbing another cinnamon roll.

Fool didn't need to read her mind to know that she'd hoped they'd agree right away, and Fool's reticence had come as a surprise to her. When he glanced at Jackal, he saw the same curiosity on his face. He wasn't used to surprising Jackal, not like that.

Honestly, Fool had surprised himself with his moment of doubt. He didn't have any strong personal connections to anyone aside from Jackal. And Jackal had been an easy lover to many, but not really a partner to anyone. Fool didn't need a giant blinking neon sign to see that Nicholaus might be the person to change all of that for the big man. He was slightly envious that Jackal seemed to have found someone, while Fool still felt a little too remote for such things.

It made sense to go. Why stay? Sure, they could keep on going the way they had. Level up, get stronger… maybe even strong enough to retire. Or make an honest difference in the world, leave some kind of legacy. That all sounded fine, but it felt like not quite enough.

There was something special about being part of a movement. Fool had to admit he quite loved being a literal secret agent. Shenanigans for a good cause was absolutely his thing.

That mission of the Foundation was over though. Fool had worked for startups before, and that was what the Foundation was. A startup. It had that dynamic energy and nearly impossible mission statement focus. They were in the transition phase now. All the craziness had served its purpose, and the Foundation was settling into what it was good at. The next phase would be an entrenching and focus of purpose.

It was gonna get all corporate. Things always did, in Fool's experience, and he'd learned to hate that. Mostly because he never fit in. He could fake it for a while, but the boredom would sink in, then the self-destructive behavior came. He never seemed to be able to move on, on his own, to the next startup. Had to cling until everyone, including himself, was sick of having him around, then he'd get canned and move to the next job. Had he been a clever kind of Fool, he'd have jumped ship before things gelled and had a happy life of always being on the cutting edge.

This was his chance.

Why was he hesitating?

A small square of potato bounced off of his forehead, and Jackal giggled. Fool looked up with a glare to see both of them staring at him. Lucy was clearly the instigator, and Fool could see her reaching for another hashed projectile.

"Quit thinking about it! Got more important things to work out. Eat!" Lucy said.

Fool couldn't even remotely stay mad about that. She was right. Sure, it was a once-in-a-lifetime decision, but… there was no point in fussing over it. Somewhere inside him, he knew he'd already made up his mind. Everything else was just second-guessing. When the time came, he'd do what was right for him. Thinking about it now was a waste of brain, and he didn't have enough of that to waste.

"The Knights," Jackal said while reaching for another cinnamon bun.

He seemed to be eating more of the un-iced ones, so Fool decided to give those a try. When Fool went to unroll the one he'd grabbed, he saw the appeal. These had extra filling, and it had caramelized into a crunchy little cinnamon brittle all across the bottom. More cinnamon too, almost to the point of spiciness.

Lucy nodded. "Kantele found this place once, so we can expect them to attack before tonight. At the worst moment, whenever the hell that turns out to be. I'd love to hang out and watch the competition, but we three are going to be dealing with whatever they bring. And no cavalry to save us this time. How do we handle it?"

The food tasted a little flat in Fool's mouth. He'd managed to put those monsters out of his mind for a bit. That had been pleasant.

"We aren't strong enough." Jackal said, settling back and patting his stomach.

Fool wasn't surprised. Jackal had eaten over half of the table so far and hadn't looked as though he was ever going to slow down. The big man didn't seem too upset thinking about the upcoming fight though. Or too full. He was reaching for another cup of coffee, after all. Fool grabbed another cinnamon bun, despite his bursting stomach. Just in case Jackal ate the last one and Fool somehow found more room.

Lucy tossed the hash brown in her hand up and snapped it out of the air on the way down like a lizard. Fool was reminded of a video he'd seen of a Komodo dragon snapping down a deer.

She held up a hand while she chewed it. Once. "I've got a solution for that."

She walked into the kitchen. There was a thumping and scraping sound. The closest Fool could figure out was that she was pulling out an appliance.

Then there was a *bang* and a chunk of wall came flying out into the office, just behind Fool. He turned around to look, and Lucy stuck her head through the hole and looked around.

"Shit. Wrong wall. Just a minute." She popped her head back, and the scraping and thumping happened again, and the bang, but this time no wall came flying apart. Instead, there was a muttering, a shuffling, some swearing, and finally an "Aha!" and silence.

After a moment, she came out of the kitchen holding two objects.

In her left hand was a sword taller than Lucy, so Fool figured it had to be at least seven feet long. It wasn't overtly thick, but proportional to its length. It was hard to tell what the shape of the blade was, because the whole thing was covered with a thick, red, leather-covered scabbard. The quillons that met the scabbard were almost as long as Lucy's arm, narrow and black. For some reason, the quillons were tightly chained to the scabbard, and there wasn't any lock apparent. It looked as if the chains had been welded shut. Someone didn't want that sword taken out of the scabbard.

Even with that, the thing gave off an air of menace that even across the room made Fool shiver.

Its hilt was completely covered as well, wrapped in layer after layer of some sort of leather densely etched with runes.

In her other hand were two metal bracers. Plain, but sturdy. At least that was what Fool thought they were at first glance. At second glance, he saw the heavy metal buckles that closed the bracers, and the short, broken lengths of chain that dangled from each. Those were cuffs that had once been used to imprison someone. Someone who had eventually broken free.

Something about those shackles felt oddly familiar to Fool. Familiar enough to make him shiver, and he had no idea why. He'd been arrested more than a few times, and the feel of being cuffed was a familiar one. This was something different. It felt like an *old* memory. Older than him. He knew that, yet somehow he recalled a damp darkness, rocks, and the hissing spatter of acidic venom.

He shook off the memory with a shudder and saw Lucy looking at him with an odd expression before she said, "Yeah, they hit me the same way. It fades pretty quick. Huh. I guess you got some of the Trickster in you, after all."

That made Fool sit upright, but Jackal got the question out first. "Genetic trait? How is that possible?"

Lucy didn't answer right away. She carefully leaned the sword against the edge of the table—the damned thing was so big that the hilt was almost directly over the center of the table—and dropped the shackles on the table after shoving her plate aside. "Don't touch. Not yet."

That was directed at Jackal, and he sheepishly pulled back his hand. Fool got the impression the big man hadn't even realized he was reaching for the sword. Lucy glared at Jackal until he shuffled his chair back a bit and sat upright.

Satisfied, Lucy dropped her elbows around the shackles on the table and rested her chin on her hands. "Thought you'd have figured that out already. Loki. Coyote. Raven. Reynard. Anansi. Lucifer." She winked at that last one. "The Mana bleed has given rise to a lot of your earth mythology, but the Technomancers and the Trickster have been around longer than that."

It didn't take long for Jackal to figure it out. "Huh. So the Trickster was on Earth. I guess that explains something. I was wondering why someone so powerful would have an interest in a new Dungeon World."

Lucy nodded. "Part of it, yup. Most of those memories are… hm… not accessible to me, but yeah, he was physically here for a while. Not surprised that he made a 'friend' or two."

That was a little too much for Fool to process, and it just made way too much sense. He remembered his grandfather getting very drunk one night and talking about the family legend that they were descended from one of the Irish High Kings, who was only supposed to be half-human, and that was why the Second Sight ran in the family. Fool had figured he had that—

until the DSM-V diagnosis came, much too late to make much of a difference to him. He stomped down on those thoughts and put them away in the back of his mind to deal with later, then spoke up to move the conversation on and away from that topic.

"So what are these things?" He gestured to the shackles and the sword.

"These?" Lucy was doing a pretty good job of sounding disingenuous, but she gave it up quickly. "These are the Trickster's personal weapons. And now they belong to you two. You've earned them. And you'll need them."

Chapter Twenty

"I guess the sword is for me then." The quip had the effect Fool had hoped for, but he trapped the giggle before it escaped, not even glancing at Jackal as he heard the big man make a choking sound.

Fool knew better than to reach for the sword. And he wouldn't have, even in jest. Even the thought of touching it gave Fool the creeps.

"Ha. Ha. Very funny, Fool." Lucy was leaning back now. "Too bad these don't work for their original purpose anymore." She gestured at the shackles.

"And what was that? Other than the obvious." Fool was really hoping it wasn't for some kind of kinky sex thing, because clearly Lucy intended him to wear those things.

"Just that. Back when he was just Heroic, some ancient Legendary decided Trickster was getting too big for his britches and bound him with them."

That rocked Fool, and Jackal let out a low whistle before saying, "Those were strong enough to bind a Heroic?"

Lucy raised an eyebrow, sucking back her lips before letting them out a pop. "Yup. Some history behind the making, but they sure did the job. Damped down all his Skills, all kinds of nasty. Bound for a long time before he found his way out. Took them with him when he escaped. Had them reworked, Became a symbol to him and a lot of other people back in the day. They used to call them 'The Unbroken,' but their real name is something like 'Honor's Friend.' And yes, Fool, they're yours. Don't touch them just yet. Wait till we're done. That means you too. Especially you!" Jackal had only barely leaned forward, but Lucy was jabbing a school-marm finger at him. "No touchy!"

She took a moment to shift the sword to the other side of her, which brought it closer to Fool. He shuffled his chair farther away from it, wishing the table was bigger.

Satisfied with the arrangement, Lucy nodded toward the sword. "Fool knows what's up. Jackal, you can have the pretty once we've discussed what it is, and what it's going to cost, and why you need to be very, very cautious… and most of all, informed! Before I can let you get any closer to this thing. You can feel it calling to you already, right?"

Jackal nodded. Fool was more than a little troubled to see that the acknowledgment was mixed with a little confusion, as if Jackal hadn't realized it had been happening.

It was Fool's turn to make the jump to understanding.

"Fuck! It's a Stormbringer!" Fool jumped up as he said that, knocking his chair aside and retreating to the far side of the table. "Like that damned spear, when we met DM for the first time."

Lucy held out her hands. "Chill, dude. It's safe. Ish. As long as it's secured. Mostly. But calm down, probably safer that way. I mean, don't worry. It's totally okay. It's a legendary, soulbound weapon. Yes. Maybe it eats souls, I don't know. It is somewhat sentient. Maybe. I don't really know, because it's not for me. Jackal, I'm going to tell you everything I know about it."

Jackal nodded, his eyes a little too hungry for Fool's liking. "It's got a name, I can tell."

Lucy pursed her lips. "Fool's gonna freak out."

"I will not! What's the stupid name?"

"Faithbreaker."

"I'm freaking out a little."

The hunger had faded a bit from Jackal's eyes and been replaced by amusement. "Faithbreaker. That doesn't sound well-aspected, you have to admit."

Lucy nodded. "I don't know who names these things. Probably the Artisan maker used a stupid name generator or cut his own finger off making it or something. These kinds of weapons are more than just unique. They grow and change over time and take on their own character regardless of how they were made or for what purpose. Although, to be fair, this was the Trickster's weapon. For a long time. That absolutely had to affect how it thinks about itself, and what it does."

Jackal was holding up his hand. Lucy seemed to like that and nodded at him. "Soulbound. How is it not still bound to the Trickster?"

"Because he has no soul?"

Fool choked at that and sputtered. Then stopped. Lucy was having fun pulling his chain today, for some reason. He decided to not be the butt of her digs anymore and carefully moved back, picked up his chair, and sat down. And did not glare at Lucy.

She glanced at him, and he felt her eyeballing him. After a beat, she continued on.

"Well, no, not that. But he's a Legendary. And an old one. You collect a lot of things over time, and one of those things gave him the ability to release a soulbond without destroying the weapon. The sword was leveling up with him for a long time, so it's incredibly powerful. It's been depowered a fair bit, but still. Fool's right, it's pretty dangerous."

"And what are the benefits?" Fool didn't mean to mumble, but trying to keep stoic meant he'd jammed his chin into his chest.

"We'll get to that in a minute. There's one thing in common between both of these that you need to be aware of. You get a boon as soon as you claim them, and I wanted to warn you both first so you can make a good choice. You each get one 'free' Skill from anywhere on your current Skill tree. Yeah, that means you can grab something you don't have the prerequisites for. It's only in effect while you have the item on you and active, but once you make that choice, it's locked in forever. And I know it sucks, but we're going to have to figure out the best Skill to defeat the System Knights. I know you have other Skills that might make things a lot easier in the future, but if we don't beat them, we don't have a future. So let's talk."

That froze Fool in place. "*Any* Skill?"

That was incredible. He'd been looking forward to unlocking some of his later Skills. Some real powerhouses in that lineup. And Jackal had some that seemed completely broken, like one that could shut down an opponent's System Regeneration. That couldn't be right.

Fool leaned back and crossed his arms. Then uncrossed them and grabbed the last icing-covered cinnamon bun. And poured himself another cup of coffee.

"So," he said after taking a bite, "do we get our toys now or what?"

Chapter Twenty-One

"Whoa." That was all Jackal said after touching Faithbreaker.

Then he sat back in his chair. He didn't remove the wrappings from the handle or break off the chains. Just gingerly touched the scabbard with one finger. That was all.

Fool waited until his patience wore out—about three breaths. "Well? What? That's it?"

Jackal sat up, started to say something, then closed his mouth and sat back again. After a minute, he leaned forward again, reached toward the sword, then leaned back in his chair. "Hm. So. This thing is *old*. And smart. I can feel it reaching out to me. I have to admit I'm a little shy about this. Lucy, am I right that Faithbreaker is going to bond to me—not like a contract, but more akin to becoming a part of me? Including my mind?"

Lucy didn't give a verbal reply. None was needed. The serious look on her face and terse nod was more than enough.

Jackal stared at the sword a moment longer but didn't make any motions toward it.

Fool had a pretty good idea what was bothering him. "Wanna swap? I'm a little more used to having another voice in my head."

He didn't expect to see the grateful look on Jackal's face. And he must have shown his surprise outwardly, because Jackal waved his hands in denial.

"No no no. I mean, I won't lie. It's tempting. It's just…"

Fool trusted his hunch. "You get used to it. And it won't know all your secrets. It'll just understand the source of any secrets you decide to share." He shrugged. "At least, if it's anything like what used to live in my head. No guarantee of how it will react, but… trust your own mind more. I was crazy because I didn't trust myself to be me. I know you have some idea what that might have been like, but you've already shown that you can maintain who you are even when your body was the wrong one for you. You're more than strong enough to deal with this."

Fool had forgotten how much younger than him Jackal was. The look that flashed across Jackal's face as Fool's words sank in reminded him. Behind that stern and stoic warrior was a young man still unsure of himself— not in battle, but in who he was inside.

The two friends smiled at each other, and they didn't need any more words.

"All right then. No point in delaying it." Jackal picked up the sword by its scabbard and slowly unwrapped the bindings around the handle and pommel.

The fittings for the blade were simple, but the construction was clearly the work of an Artisan of consummate skill. The lines and edges all curved into each other in smooth arcs, as though it had been poured in one piece— even the rough skin of whatever covered the grip. At the same time, the implication of mass spoke of endless hammering on an anvil somewhere. Fool half expected to see a burning eye for a pommel, but instead it was a small black orb. The thing was deep black, and Fool shivered when he looked at it. A clear, powerful, malevolent energy rolled off of the blade like the chill of an open door in winter.

Jackal stood, holding the scabbarded blade in his left hand, and grabbed the handle with his right. With a swift pull, he yanked the blade free. The chains shattered into dust.

For a moment, reality seemed to twist and bend, and Fool had the briefest sensation that he was standing on an endless plain. An all-encompassing presence was behind him, and a sound that was either the creak of a cart or the wailings of a world being put to death punched through his soul.

And then it passed, and he was looking at his friend holding a long black blade in both hands, with the biggest grin he'd ever seen Jackal sport.

The blade itself was a matte black, carved with runes that had an extremely faint red glow. Unlike the hilt, the blade looked rough from the forge, visible hammer marks all up and down its length. There was no perfection to be found, just rough shaping everywhere except the edge. The edge was a keen whisper of silver.

With effort, Fool pulled his eyes from the blade and looked at Jackal. The grin was fading into an easy smile. To Fool's relief, nothing seemed different about his friend. No maniacal gleam, no shiftiness hiding behind his face. If anything, he looked calmer than he had in a long time. Not his usual chill calm either. More... serene.

Jackal reached for the sheath again. Putting something that long into a scabbard was a bit of a production. Jackal placed the scabbard on the table, took a big step back to lever the tip in, then walked forward. Fool tried to recall how Jackal had pulled it out of the scabbard so fast, but his recollection was blurry, so he chalked it up to System shenanigans.

Once the blade was sheathed again, the serene look on Jackal's face turned again, and his normally subtle grin crept back. "Well… that was something."

He sat back down before continuing. "It's an old blade, and it's seen a lot. Given it a rather calm and relaxed outlook on life, and I think we'll get along just fine. Pleasant old chap, really." Then he leaned forward and looked up at Lucy and Fool through his eyebrows. "We are going to absolutely kick ass. The giant's mine. I'll take him out first."

Lucy let out a loud "Ha!" then turned to Fool. "Your turn."

Fool sucked in the corner of a lip and looked at the shackles. The Unbroken. He hadn't gotten another big flashback or anything since looking at them the first time, but he was still suspicious. If Jackal could get past the very real concern of touching and bonding with an intelligent, evil-looking, sword, then there was no reason Fool couldn't just reach over and grab those shackles.

No reason at all.

Any moment.

Apparently, the genetic memory was a bit strong, because he found himself recalling that oppressive sense of being bound and forgotten, and he didn't like it at all. Lucy had said they've been reworked into something new, but he wasn't getting any kind of flash of that.

Fool knew he was just being a bit of a wimp about it, so he grabbed the shackles without thinking anything more about it.

They clipped onto his wrists with no effort, sizing themselves automatically. They felt good. Comfortable. Safe.

Nothing happened.

Fool glanced up at Lucy, unsure of what to expect.

Then he saw the look in her eyes. The hidden laugh.

"Okay, very funny. So are these actually yours?" Fool's face was burning, but he was trying to play it straight.

She'd clearly pulled a fast one on him. These were System-generated shackles, but there was nothing really special about them. She'd built him up for nothing.

"No, they were his." She was grinning, but there was no cruelty to it. Fool was starting to understand what it might be like to have a bratty older sister. "Nothing that special about them really. Except this."

She squeezed the end of one of the shackles, then knocked on a discolored spot on the back of the right one.

At that point, things got a little confusing. The shackles activated with no further warning, and suddenly it was as if an entire world unfolded in front of Fool.

The next thing he knew, Jackal was shaking him and Lucy was in his face, yelling something.

Fool waved them both away, and his hands scrambled on their own accord until he found his barely touched cup of coffee. It was still hot enough to scald his throat, but he didn't care. He drained the entire cup, then sat back.

Lucy started to say something, and Fool held up a finger until his thoughts settled down. He started to talk and stopped. Took a few breaths, then let out a whoosh of air.

"Whoooooo. Okay. Wow. All right. First thing…" He stopped to fumble for the pot of coffee again, poured out the dregs, and chugged them. "Bleaugh, grounds. Yuck!" He spat those out, cleared his throat a few times, and then started again. "That was a fucking mistake."

Jackal and Lucy looked at him. Lucy made a "go on" gesture.

"Okay. First off? Should have gone with the 'use magic' Skills. Either one of them. Lucy, did you know… no, you wouldn't. He'd have hidden that. Ha. Oh god, I'm gonna be on the run for the rest of my life. I gotta figure out how to hide this shit. Or throw it into the sun. That would be the best."

"Fool." Fool turned to look at Jackal, and the big man's face had only gentleness in it. "You're babbling. Slow down."

Fool shook his head. "Not babbling enough, my friend. All right. Here's the deal. This shackle"—he held up the left-hand one—"is a stat boost. It's a good one. Intelligence and Perception, some defense, and resistance buffs. Pretty sweet for that alone. However, and this is where it gets fun, Intelligence and Perception almost *double* when you're accessing the right-hand shackle."

Jackal titled his head a little. "I assume that's why you sound a little different. Clarify? Doubles only when accessing the other shackle? That implies a few things."

Fool nodded and held up a finger. "Right. Absolutely right. Voice will go back to normal in a bit when I assimilate this more. Right now, I've got a lot going through my head. So the right shackle is a library. A very, very extensive library. It might be every book the Trickster ever owned, read, bought, or wrote. Lucy, did you know how powerful of a sorcerer he was?"

Lucy nodded. "Of course. His knowledge of Spells and Mana is the driving force behind everything we are doing."

"Right. This bracer is his spellbook."

"Happy birthday. One more thing for you." Lucy tapped Fool on the forehead.

There was sort of a slow motion explosion, and Fool felt his head stretching as Lucy directly implanted a new Skill into him. He felt the mechanism of it working, some unique connection between the Trickster,

Lucy, and him binding them all together for a moment. And then, with a sharp, painful mental pop, it was done. The shackles were still giving him a boost, and it all clicked together faster than it normally would.

He gave himself a quick hard shake and looked up at the other two. "I'm a Shapechanger."

Chapter Twenty-Two

By the time the three of them had worked out a plan to deal with the System Knights, it was dinnertime. Lucy's minions had been running the competition all day and managing the ins and outs of the last-minute plans. Olivia had sneaked into the room at one point, but Lucy and Jackal had made it clear that she was to be one of the last ditch defenders right by the portal and to throw herself right through if things looked to be going bad. Olivia had already decided she would be one of the first to go through. Alex had changed her mind and was going to settle in with the McBride Cavalry for a bit before heading back to McBride. She'd be the one to let everyone know what had happened to those who wouldn't be coming home.

One way or the other.

Fool couldn't help but feel on edge. Lucy felt confident that Kantele and her crew wouldn't show until the last minute, hoping to disrupt things at the worst possible time. That wasn't the worst tactic. It had worked for Fool not that long ago. Accidentally. It also felt like the most obvious thing.

While Kantele might think like Lucy expected, Fool was having a hard time shaking the feeling that the Weaver was operating on a different level. Sure, the Weaver had tried to interfere as early and as strongly as he could, but he was running under the same set of restrictions the Trickster was.

The proxies had been set in place, and the game had to play out with the pieces set on the board. That didn't mean that the other side wasn't getting orders from on high that might override their own inclinations.

By the time the slapdash dinner was wolfed down, the three of them had about played out all the planning they could effectively do. They had a good plan, and it was a good plan regardless of whether the enemy pulled off a last-minute surprise or not. The tricks they had up their sleeves should do the job.

Losing the first engagement would work in their favor in this case. As would the higher Levels of the enemy. High levels meant they didn't need to worry about the other side having leveled up in the last few days and coming in with new Skills. And having kicked the shit out of the three of them, Kantele and the System Knights wouldn't feel any need to do anything differently this time around. Probably.

None of which helped Fool get rid of the feeling that they were going to get jumped early. Sure, the best time to attack would be when they had all the pieces together. That would mean the Weaver would have the best chance to wipe the board clean of every bit the Trickster had in play for this game. If they attacked earlier, there would always be the chance that the Trickster could try this again. Surely the Weaver would want to do as much damage to his ancient enemy as possible? Unless…

Fool sat upright in his chair. "Guys. I just had a thought."

Lucy muttered something under her breath, but Jackal put down the last of his food and waited in anticipation.

Taking that as consent, Fool pushed ahead. "Weaver and Trickster have been at this for a long time. They know each other well. What if the Weaver doesn't expect this to be the final piece in the Trickster's game?"

Now it was Jackal's turn to swear, but Lucy hadn't figured it out yet.

She tilted her head. "And? If he thinks that, then he probably thinks this is some kind of false flag or ruse. Hell, it might be, come to think of it… no. No, it isn't. But if he's thinking that…"

Fool could see she got it, but he finished the thought out loud anyway. "Then they won't wait till the last minute. They'll try to trigger any trap early."

Jackal was already up and running out the door

Fool stared after him for a moment, then turned to Lucy. "I didn't think it was that urgent. Did I miss something?"

Lucy shook her head. "I may have more experience than you guys, but that dude's got the brains for both of us. I guess we need to follow him. I think he's heading for the parking lot, and that seems like the right place to go."

"And why would that be?"

"Firing up the portal. Slight chance it would be a bit of a signal about where we are. Wouldn't be entirely accurate, but… hm. Yeah. The attack on McBride might have had the secondary intention of getting us to reveal our location."

Fool took a deep breath and stood. "You said earlier that Kantele had found this place but couldn't find it again. How sure are you of that?"

Lucy laughed and headed for the door. "Not sure at all. The entrance to this place is always concealed. But the general location isn't. So she'll know it's Queen Elizabeth Park, but not be able to find the same entrance she came through last time."

"Where did she enter last time?"

"She would have thought it was through the waterfall in the quarry gardens."

They both went out the door and back out into the galley. The dance competition was still going on in full force. The only difference was that all the big crews were out on the floor now. If they weren't dancing, they were watching what the other crews were doing and prepping for their turn. It would be a shame to miss it, but they had a job to do.

Lucy was putting on speed, so Fool had to scramble to catch up to her. On the far side of the space, he could just make out Jackal heading for the plaza they'd come in on this morning, on the way to the above-ground parking. He'd apparently had the same idea as Lucy.

Fool wasn't convinced though. "Any reason they won't try the gardens again?"

Lucy didn't even slow down, bouncing down the steps four at a time. "Nope! But we gotta start somewhere, so to the roof!"

Fool wanted to complain that it wasn't actually the roof, but it kinda was. As soon as Lucy hit the floor, she sprinted, somehow finding all the openings between spectators and dancers to almost teleport across the floor.

Fool couldn't keep up and kept running into people and stepping on toes. He wound up bouncing off of one person, then finding himself in the midst of the vampire-dancers he'd first seen downtown. Up close, they were even more intimidating. Fool out-leveled them and could likely take them all in a fight. That didn't seem to make any difference to his guts when he turned around and found himself surrounded by hungry/undead looking dudes he'd clearly just offended.

For a moment, he wanted to try to say something clever, but he couldn't even remember the name of the house they were part of, so he just mumbled something apologetic sounding under his breath and raced to catch up to Lucy. He felt their disdain trying to claw at him from behind.

It was a bit of a race, but before he knew it, he was through the crowd, up the stairs, and out the exit onto the asphalt parking lot. Jackal was standing not far away, intently looking in all directions, but there didn't seem to be any immediate threat.

It was a pleasant and warm evening with the faint aroma of roses coming along with the wind. The sun was most of the way across the sky, but the evening was still a good distance away. A lovely summer night.

"Yeah, they're here," Lucy said. "I can smell 'em."

"Where?" Fool asked, waving Jackal over as the big man looked back at them.

"Dunno. I don't suppose… yeah. I'm not entirely sure, but I suspect they've done the stupid thing and let Kantele talk them into trying to get in through the waterfall. That'll keep 'em busy for a bit."

Jackal walked up to them just in time to hear that bit. "What's on the other side of the waterfall?"

"Basalt, and a lot of it. Nothing else. When Kantele made her entrance last time, I'd set up an undetectable portal that shuffled people from there to the real entrance. Still in effect, but it moves around every evening. That's why you have to know someone to get in. Anyone who leaves after the switch can note where they left and know they can come back the same way until the next day."

Jackal grinned. "So we can get the drop on them. Good."

Lucy's grin matched. "Maybe literally, if we move carefully. The old bridge is still over the top of the waterfall. Bit overgrown, but that will just keep us concealed. Shall we go screw up someone's nefarious plans?"

Fool rolled his shoulders. They might get crushed, but it was time for some payback. And what the hell? They just might kick some ass. "Let's go get 'em, boss. What's the plan?"

Lucy and Jackal turned and looked at him.

"What?"

Lucy threw hands up and stared at him. "What the fuck do you mean, 'what's the plan?' We just spent the whole afternoon coming up with a plan."

"Right. I knew that. But same plan? Now that we're gonna surprise them?"

"Why not? Same shit will work. We don't need that much more detail, do we? Scions of chaos, aren't we?" The grin on her face was the only clue she wasn't serious, and it took some of the sting out of her words. "Seriously, though. Both of you follow me. Stick close, and we'll see if they really are where I think they are. If so, we'll figure out how best to take advantage of that. In the meantime, in case this is some kind of crazy setup, you both keep an eye open all around us while we get to creeping in. Works?"

Jackal gave a short, curt nod, and with a sigh, Fool added one of his own.

It wasn't that Fool really preferred a plan all that much. It just always seemed like everyone else had a good one, and if there was one time when he was actually in the mood to listen to someone else's advice, this was that time.

So of course, they were basically going to follow his usual process: wing it, but act as if you know what you're doing. It had always worked in the past.

Lucy didn't wait for any acknowledgement, just stalked off to the west. The big glass conservatory geodesic dome was north, and between them and it was a sprawling plaza surrounded by trees. The dome itself overlooked the Quarry Gardens Lucy had figured the baddies were at, so Fool figured she intended to stick to the trees and sneak her way over.

There was just one problem with that, so Fool hustled to see if she'd forgotten. "Hang tight, isn't this entire area a dungeon? If we have to fight our way over there, isn't that going to give up the game?"

Lucy shook her head. "No worries. I make sure to cull the dungeon once in a while. As long as you stick close to me, the monsters will keep away. They don't like to play with big momma all that much." This time her grin was big enough that Fool could confirm that she did indeed have two sets of canine teeth. And he could swear her horns were just a bit taller.

They made it through the plaza with no issues, and Fool felt as though maybe he'd been a little premature in his worries about the bad guys. Lucy seemed pretty convinced though. She kept pushing, and the closer they got to the conservatory, the more her posture and walk changed. She wasn't slowing down so much as prowling, with the tiniest hunch forward.

Whatever she was doing affected Fool and Jackal as well, and they moved in unison with her, spreading out just a little, forming a triangle with good coverage for their skills.

Fool noted Jackal had Faithbreaker in his left hand. Still scabbarded, but he'd have it out in an instant if it became necessary. That made Fool itch to get his hammer out, but his part in their grand plan put a kibosh on that. He needed to be on his toes and not actively fighting for the first part of the festivities. That had made sense in the planning, but now that they were getting close to a potential battle with five Master Class opponents? His confidence had taken a little vacation and was in no rush to come back.

They weren't in the trees long. They hit the southwest curve of the dome, where there was still a concrete path. It was a narrow path, squeezed between the dome and a little drop-off to the side, where a stream was still somehow managing to trickle and babble in the summer heat. It must have been part of the Dungeon setting, because most summers in Vancouver got too dry to keep the stream running and it went dry.

Ahead of them was a last bit of the path through the trees, then they were at the end of the concealed part.

Ahead of them lay the usual epic view of the entire city, backdropped by the always amazing view of the North Shore mountains. The walkway they were on formed the main viewing area of the park, a high plaza that covered the entire cliff-side that comprised the western wall of the Quarry Garden. The garden had once been an actual quarry until a group of plant fanatics had decided it was the ideal spot to showcase tulips. That idea had been the seed that had burst into a full arboretum, the Conservatory, and a whole host of other fun things. It was really the gem of the city, perched on the top of the aptly named Little Mountain.

Ahead of them, the top of the quarry was surmounted by a low rock wall, planted with perennials and smaller shrubs of different kinds. To their left was the bridge that spanned a gap in the quarry wall, about three stories up from the quarry floor.

Lucy was approaching the closest rock wall, but keeping low. Clearly, she intended to peek over and see if she could spy the quintet of evil.

She crouched down and leaned over for a quick peek. Sat herself right back down and gestured to Fool and Jackal. She didn't need to hold her finger up to her mouth; they moved as quietly and quickly as they could. When she gestured with her head to look over the wall, Fool slowly raised his head and peeked over.

The wall at that point was over a meter thick, so he saw nothing when he first looked. He had to stand up and lean forward a precarious inch at a time. At first, all he could see were the trees, rock walls, and plants on the far side of the quarry. Then the quarry garden itself, which was still in its summer bloom. All the flowers and leaves were fully exposed to the eye, and weirdly enough, the lawn still looked immaculately groomed. There were also a bunch of new plants...

On second glance, Fool realized none of the plants or trees were originals. System mutations abounded, but he couldn't figure out in which direction. He always assumed System mutations leaned toward monstrous, but he wasn't always correct. The Hoary Marmots around McBride were mostly harmless.

His chain of thought was interrupted as he leaned a little more forward, and he ducked back before he realized what he had been looking at. As he sank back down, his brain was telling him that all he'd seen was the top of a tent. A tent made out of a thick, ancient black felt. That was just the first flash of his monkey brain telling him what it expected—what it wanted—to see. His Perception and Intelligence filled in the blanks properly by the time he'd half-finished his squat.

It was the head of the giant. The System Knight was right up against the wall that he, Jackal, and Lucy were on top of.

Fool spun back around as he finished his squat, and he settled his back against the almost-comforting stone wall. Jackal squatted as well, although he didn't have as far to go since he hadn't risen as far. He was still facing Lucy and Fool, but he said nothing. Verbally. His face conveyed several messages, and Fool agreed with all of them.

This was the ideal setup. What they had planned for was being surprised by the System Knights. That made sense because they had no idea what the System Knights were going to actually do or when they'd attack. They'd been pretty confident they'd be able to confuse Kantele's team, so the plan had always been about how to capitalize on that initial confusion.

Barring something truly unexpected happening, they were now going to get the drop on the bad guys. There wasn't really any decision to be made, aside from how to attack. The longer they waited, the more likely it was that something strange would happen and they'd lose the brief advantage they had.

Which meant that the best attack angle was to drop down on them from above. They were all tough enough to survive that drop unharmed, so that wasn't an issue.

The only issue that had to be solved—the one that wasn't made easier by attaining the element of surprise—was positioning. For the plan to work originally, Fool had to find a way to work his way into the enemy line, preferably getting out of their sight for just a moment. The original plan was for Lucy and Jackal to make a big showy distraction. That wouldn't work now, because that would draw all the attention to the three of them.

Nor could they risk taking the time to sneak down to the level of the System Knights. Despite Lucy's assurances, the woods were dark, deep, and dangerous. They might not have to fight their way through if they stuck together, but they'd need to separate for surprise to still be a factor. And going separately was a great way to lose surprise.

The only answer was the one Jackal was indicating with his eyebrows.

Fool had to be first over the top, and he had to somehow land behind all the System Knights without being noticed. Since there was always a risk that using Mana might provide a warning, raw muscle was the only way for that to happen.

Which meant Jackal had to toss Fool.

Chapter Twenty-Three

There wasn't really any moment of decision-making, no subtle chat or whispered discussion. They just all seemed to make the same decision at the same time, and the next thing Fool knew, he was flying over the wall.

It didn't look that high up when he was peeking over the edge. Flying over the wall was a different matter altogether. The queasy sensation started as soon as Jackal released him in a gentle arc. The ground receding away was never a pleasant feeling, but suddenly having the ground drop away from under you? System be damned, Fool had to bite back a full-fledged panic attack. He couldn't do anything else though. He had to relax, to just be a flickering dart over the enemy's heads—just a bird, not worth looking at.

Since Mana was important to their plans—specifically, his ability to maintain Skills against opposition—he didn't even try to activate Geas. He just had to trust in the nature of sentient beings to be focused on their task at hand and to ignore background noise, like a bird flitting around overhead.

Not that he had any focus to use Geas. It was taking all his self-control to not flail like a maniac for as long as it took him to get out of the line of sight of anyone looking up from below.

The little arc Jackal had given him was already done with its horizontal component, and Fool was dropping almost straight down. For a heartbeat, he saw what the enemy was doing.

They were gathered around the rough rock face of the waterfall. It wasn't a real waterfall, not the roaring water kind. More of a chaotic trickle of water meandering and splattering down little bits of the old quarry wall. It had a lovely array of plants all around it in a modern western take on a Japanese garden design. A little rock semi-bridge at the foot of it, and a pond with a lovely Japanese maple covering it. Kantele was gesturing at the edges of the waterfall, and the twins were feeling around it with their hands. The spear-wielder was off to one side. The giant was standing in the pond and causing even its low waters to overflow.

Fool's trajectory had taken him just over the head of the giant. If not for the creature's hood, he'd probably have been noticed. As it was, he was going to drop almost exactly down the back of the giant skeleton and land in the water behind him. At least he'd have a soft landing. Ish. The water, as it rushed up at him, looked to only be a few inches deep.

He was just past the shoulder blades of the giant, and his stomach had almost managed to crawl all the way up his ribcage, when Lucy and Jackal started their distraction.

For a moment, he thought the other two had flung themselves down after him, judging from the giant's sudden forward movement.

Then the sharp retort of Lucy's modified scythe echoed all around the quarry walls. Fool had had only a glance at the thing while Lucy had been using it the other day. It looked like a regular agricultural scythe, the stereotypical grim-reaper thing, but she'd strapped some kind of shotgun to the side of it. It was a weird setup, but she'd used it to good effect in their last encounter with the System Knights.

That was about all Fool had time to think about before he hit the pond. System enhancements, and the not-insubstantial boost from the shackles, meant he took basically no damage. No damage, but his Agility was pushed to the limit. And beyond. He'd tried to spin in mid-air and land on his feet, and succeeded, but he hadn't accounted for the surface he'd land on. Or rather, sub-surface.

The pond wasn't quite as shallow as he'd feared. It came up to his knees. The problem was that the bottom of the pond was a slick mud resulting from decades of debris and rotting leaves. There might have been a solid surface somewhere under there, but Fool didn't find out. The last momentum of his spin to land on his feet transformed into enough motion to whip his feet out from under him.

He didn't even manage the dignity of landing in the water. The giant had taken a step forward at almost the same moment as Fool landed, and his enormous foot had slurped out even more water, which meant Fool got dumped on his butt in the wet mud and cracked his head on the edge of the pond. Fortunately, that was soft grass, or he might have had to start the engagement with a hit of health potion.

Instead, he had a muddy butt and a bit of disorientation, which he shook off. There was no time to consider dignity. He had a job to do. He was on his feet in a second and saw that the System Knights were already moving in reaction to Lucy's attack and Jackal's verbal taunts. The twins were turning to sprint up the paths to the higher level, and the spear-wielder actually looked as if she was about to scramble up the side of the quarry one-handed. The giant wasn't bothering with any of that, instead advancing on to the wall with all weapons out, swinging madly toward the figures on top of the wall.

Time for him to get into it. His Shapechanger Skill, thanks to the quick tutorial and benefits from the shackles, activated with quick ease. It wasn't as hard as it had been at first, and not nearly as hard as he'd thought it would be. With his amped up Ability scores, the process amounted to flicking a mental switch between different shapes he'd memorized. Or could see right in front of him.

Mana cost was an issue. It scaled based on a few factors. Monsters or animals that were bipedal and about his size were cheap. Inanimate objects were expensive. Sentient creatures had a set cost that was high, but not too bad. He also had an option of paying an ongoing lower cost if he wanted to maintain it for a while… or make it semi-permanent. Changing rapidly was more expensive. He could even imitate some of the Skills of a sentient, if he wanted to pay a very high cost, not to mention that would only result in the illusion of the Skill, not the actual use of the Skill.

Taking on the shape of the giant took as big a slice of Fool's Mana pool as he'd feared. There was no time to regret that though. Or even time to enjoy how small everything looked from this height. Instead, he roared loudly enough for everyone to hear and shoved the giant from behind.

The shove was hard enough to send the giant sprawling into the quarry wall, an action that spun all the other System Knights around.

Fool had to grin at their shocked expressions as they saw a second giant staring down at them. The grin turned savage as he drew out the curved swords with the two lower arms. He had hoped to use the upper arms to yank out the scary-looking longsword, but even thinking about using those arms for tool-wielding dinged his Mana viciously.

The intended effect was made though. The System Knights had no choice but to focus on this new threat in their rear. Mixed with their confusion over what the hell was going on, they were off balance for a split second.

Long enough for Jackal to execute his part of the plan. The timing couldn't have worked out better.

The giant turned its head to see who had shoved it, and that was the opening Jackal needed.

Fool clearly saw Jackal leaping, posed perfectly against the flat blue summer evening sky. His body was bent backward, like a warrior on the cover of a fantasy novel, the long black blade overhead, the point trailing behind him. His mouth was open, and Fool could only imagine he was screaming some sort of battle cry.

The red runes on the blade left a glowing trail behind Jackal, a trail that arced as he swung the blade down on the back of the head of the giant skeleton warrior.

The effect was instant and horrifying.

The sword easily clove the skeleton's head in two and looked as though it would have done the same to its whole body if Jackal hadn't landed in the middle of its back. As it was, the runic blade only halted when the tip was just clearing the sternum.

The ease with which the weapon, in Jackal's hands, had bisected a Master Class opponent was horrifying enough. The other effect of the weapon was the true terror.

It keened. A howl leapt from the blade as it touched its victim, and there was a *sensation* of sucking that reached out even to Fool. It was as if the giant's marrow was trying to crack free from its bones and fly into the maw that was the heart of the blade.

The cut the blade made was not just a severing of one part of the enemy from another; it was a cleaving of space itself, as if somehow the blade was creating a linear black hole through existence that sucked whatever was near it into its trackless depths. The howl was partly from matter disappearing into that void, and partly from the blade itself, vibrating and pulsing with a darkly red light that leapt from runes.

It was hunger made manifest. Fool had no doubt that if the giant skeleton had a soul, it was now a part of the sword.

The name Faithbreaker made more sense now. Seeing it in action, Fool was losing all faith in reality.

He couldn't stand in awe though. The battle was still going on. He tore his sight from the horrible blade, and with another wrenching drain of Mana, he took on his next form, that of Kantele. This would be his last Shapechange for this encounter. He'd already spent more Mana than he'd expected, so he'd be relying on his earned Skills past this. It would make him the weakest person on the battlefield, but if he did his job right, then he would have done what he could to break the enemy up enough to at least even the odds.

As expected, the System Knights had first turned back to look at Fool in his giant guise. That surprise had started them off balance. The giant's sudden demise, and manner of demise, had caused them all to whip their focus back. Under normal battle conditions, they would have enough experience to overcome such knee-jerk reactions, but the raw impossibility of what they were seeing had thrown them off-kilter.

All according to plan. It was up to Fool now to charge forward, getting as close to Kantele as possible. All he had to do was get close enough to her for the others to have a moment of wondering who was who. That was all. In that temporary bit of confusion, Lucy and Jackal would be able to knock out one more System Knight. Worst case, they'd at least be able to disrupt any attack the other side had planned. It wasn't going to get better than this, and no matter how much they planned for this moment, they hadn't been able to figure out anything past this point.

Battle was chaos, and they all had enough experience to know that relying on anything past this point would just make them second-guess and wonder if it was the right time to pull off whatever they were thinking about. That wouldn't be too much of an issue in a normal fight, but being outclassed like this? Every nanosecond of brain power was necessary.

So they'd opted to just keep causing whatever chaos made sense in the moment, rather than go with even an inkling of a plan.

It was a simple decision. Being a pain in the ass came naturally to all of them.

Fool had thought he'd run up next to Kantele and shout some kind of order, but in that, he'd underestimated the System Knights.

The one-two punch of distractions had worked, but they weren't total rubes. The System was really good at teaching how nasty surprises could be, and it had the effect of weeding out anyone who couldn't respond rapidly to unusual situations. This was true at all levels, but more so amongst those who'd reached Master Class. They'd already had enough experience with traps and surprises to react properly to any new ones.

In this case, the proper response was to stop responding to new inputs. If the enemy was in a place to distract you and put themselves in the best place to attack you, then the enemy had already done the hard work of identifying the best tactical location in the combat. The right approach was to do whatever you could to occupy the place they were attacking from. Charge the threat.

As he charged up to Kantele, hoping to get close to her before the System Knights noticed he was there, she moved. She didn't just move though.

She leapt to the top of the quarry wall, where Jackal had come from and where Lucy was taking potshots at everyone.

Jackal landed while the corpse of the giant was still teetering, and the twins leapt on him. They didn't show any fear of the blade at all. The reason became apparent almost immediately. Jackal threw a wide sweeping cut at both of them, but they blocked the cut easily using some sort of energy shields that sprung up from their forearms. Then they swarmed him, and Fool lost track of what was going on. The trio was nothing but a flurry of fists, feet, and the great arcing black sword.

Fool barely ducked in time as the golden, glowing spear tip slashed toward his head.

He dropped the useless Shapechange as he ducked and sprang backward as fast as he could. Fool was counting on getting at least a whole or half-second free of the spear-wielder. He'd noticed that she'd planted the tip of her shield in the ground as she swung at him. She'd need to free it to follow him. He used the time to draw his warhammer and slam in a Mana boost.

That was all the time he had.

He didn't even see the spearhead. Just a flash of an arc. A glint of sunlight on a distant wave. A glimmer that shone and vanished. His warhammer had been in his left hand, while the right slapped the prepared Mana boost on his thigh.

Sometimes, when Fool got hit or slashed in battle, he didn't notice until after. That was normal for him.

This time, it was different.

He'd vastly underestimated his ability to deal with the spear-wielder. And vastly underestimated her danger.

He was screaming, he realized. Screaming, and his notifications were a wall in front of his vision, and the pain was a wave of flame that removed all his conscious thoughts for a moment.

Between the space of one heartbeat to the next, he found his way back. Focusing on the pain did the trick. It wasn't his whole body. It was only half of it. Only a quarter. Just his shoulder. Something was wrong. Something was missing.

He collapsed to his knees as he saw the backstroke coming in, again just dodging the spear blade.

His head dipped for a split second, and he couldn't figure out why he was seeing his warhammer on the ground.

It must have been the shapechanging. He must have done something wrong. It was the only reason he could think of for seeing his arm on the ground, his hand holding the warhammer.

The spear-wielder was a consummate warrior and already had a followup for the backswing that had missed decapitating him. An armored knee smashed into Fool's face and sent him sprawling onto his back.

The sky was beautiful. There were little fluffy clouds, and the sun had dropped low enough that the bellies of the little clouds were turning pink.

Fool thought he might Shapechange, but nothing happened. The spear was quite a weapon. Either that, or its wielder had some truly nasty powers. His Mana was gone. And most of his health.

One of the notifications stood out, flashing above all the others, and he laughed. Hell of a weapon indeed. The words didn't say curse. Something else, but it all came down to the same thing.

His arm was gone and would never regenerate.

The armored enemy was over him, spear raised, but he could still see the clouds in the sky. They kept him distracted as the spear flashed down, and they brought a smile back to his face.

Turned out it was a good day to die, after all.

Chapter Twenty-Four

Or not.

He had a brief glimpse of flashing armor as the spear-wielder was sent tumbling over him, then the ground and sky were a tumble and he was looking at the ground… upside down? Why was he upside down?

It all clicked suddenly for Fool. Jackal had saved him at the last second, scooped him by his ankle, and was now running toward the woods with Fool dangling from his hand like a soiled diaper on its way to the garbage.

Fool fought back the urge to complain—mostly because he was afraid that he'd accidentally bite his tongue off, and if the stupid "permanent amputation" effect was some sort of time-based thing, he really didn't want to be without a tongue.

There was a sudden flash from behind them—bright enough to make all the trees white for a moment. Jackal must have been expecting it, because he instantly dodged to the right, down another path, and into a miniature forest.

Some kind of mess was happening back at the quarry, and it was kind of noisy.

Jackal dropped Fool none too gently, then sprinted off.

And came back a second later with Lucy in tow.

"Well," she said. "That didn't work. Knocked one of them out. You forget something, Fool?"

"Fuck you," he croaked. Damn, he was thirsty.

Lucy's grin was more manic that ever, and Jackal was showing cracks in his stoic face. Fool got the impression they were worried about him.

He sat up a little. Or at least tried to. For some reason, his left arm wasn't pushing him. That threw him off for a moment, but he sat up anyway. Easier with a little less weight. He felt a little lighter in the head too. That part he recognized as shock, and he knew he would feel a lot more once that wore off. He hoped he'd get a chance to do a few more useful things than sit up before that wore off.

"We should keep moving."

The other two looked at him.

Lucy gave a small shake of her head. "We're good here for a bit. They won't find us here, and I set up a distraction for them up above. I'm running out of tricks, but that one should work for a bit." Jackal's raised eyebrow beat Fool to the question, and Lucy shrugged. "Just a little demon summoning. Won't hold them for too long, but enough for us to get a breather. I suppose we ought to see what we can do about that arm. I've got a regen potion here somewhere…"

"Won't help," Fool said with more confidence in his voice than he felt. "Whatever she hit me with has a permanent amputation effect."

"Oh. Shit. Well." She didn't seem to have any more to say.

Jackal dropped down and gave Fool the biggest, squishiest, calmest hug he'd ever received.

Fool patted him on the back. "It's all right, we'll figure something out later. No time to worry about it right now."

When Jackal pulled back, his face looked calm and composed, but Fool could swear he was a little damp from where Jackal's face had crushed up against him.

"All right," Fool said. "What now? Still gotta hold 'em off, right?"

Lucy gave a savage little grin. "Just for a little longer. But we need to get back as soon as we can."

Something in her expression made Fool realize she'd been holding something back. "I thought we had until… shit. The portal's opening early?"

"Not early as much as on time. Trickster spent a lot of his built-up Credits and Mana to give everyone the impression that the timing was midnight. I helped as much as I could with that. Sorry, had to keep you two out of the loop."

Jackal looked quite stricken all of a sudden. "The competition doesn't… it's already happened, hasn't it?"

"Yeah." Lucy added a curt nod. "They should have just wrapped the semis. It's not just one team going. It's the top four. They'll be going through the portal in about five minutes, and it will close in five more. So we better haul ass to get back there."

Jackal's face went white, and Fool knew why. It took all of his effort, but Fool stood and tried to look strong. It wasn't as hard as he thought. The Mana boost and healing boosts he'd taken had filtered into the rest of his body, avoiding the arm. It brought him almost all the way back to normal.

He walked over to Jackal and gave him a hard little punch in the arm. "Don't worry, we'll get to Nicholaus before he goes." Jackal shot a confused look at Fool, but before he could open his mouth, Fool cut him off. "I know, big guy. You deserve this, and I'm all in on your happiness."

"Cute," Lucy said. "Now let's get going. Because our little hiding window just ended."

She snapped her fingers, but Fool wasn't sure if that was to end whatever was hiding them or just for drama. Either way, they started moving.

The goal had changed, and it made Fool feel a lot more confident. They'd provided a perfect distraction and pulled the System Knights far off course. They just had to get back now. There probably wouldn't be any time for the System Knights to wreck the portal. Even if the System Knights caught up to the three of them, they should still be able to hold off the enemy long enough for the portal to complete its job and shut down forever. Everyone would be safe.

There was no time to ask questions, but it didn't take more than a few steps out of the little forest glade they'd been in for Fool to realize what had happened. The hidey-hole was clearly some sort of space-time pocket, because instead of coming out on the half-hidden path back into the Quarry Gardens, they were close to where the fight had started. Except instead of being near the bridge, they were on the plaza in front of the Bloedel Conservatory.

Lucy was already hauling ass toward the steps on the west side and the water fountain plaza, and it was easy to see why.

The sky split, a fierce violet beam crashing down soundlessly onto the far end of the plaza. On impact, a roaring ripping sound filled the air, and the beam split from its base to a skyscraper height, opening like a yawning mouth until it was about as wide as a barn door.

The portal was open. And only for minutes more.

As they vaulted up the stairs, Fool saw that most of the dancers and a big group of supporters were already there, having started moving up while the fight was happening. There was a pile of supplies next to the portal, and everyone was tossing things in as fast as possible.

Fool was wondering how in the hell they were all expected to survive for decades on an alien world with no System support, but the answer was immediately clear, in two ways.

First, the supplies being tossed in were some mix of advanced tech and System-enhanced. The minute they passed through the portal, they practically exploded into larger sizes. Exploded and floated, moving themselves to new locations. Some of the packages expanded into large buildings. No mud huts for the colonists.

Second, a shadow cut off the setting sun, and an enormous spaceship cut through the air above them. It flashed right into the beam, which widened at the top just enough to allow the ship to pass. At a cost. Afterward, the opening dropped until it was only a single story tall.

Fool could now see the top of the glowing violet beam visibly inching its way down.

The portal was closing.

An angry scream from behind was their sign that the remaining System Knights were on the scene and aware of the descending deadline. They only had moments to stop the Trickster's plan from completing.

And Fool, Jackal, and Lucy were the only thing between them and the portal.

As one, they skidded to a halt and spun about. No hesitation, they leapt into the attack. Lucy went after the twins.

Jackal, clearly motivated to avenge Fool's arm, went screaming after the spear-wielder.

Which left Kantele to Fool.

He couldn't see what was behind her mask, but he felt her sneer as she saw him cut toward her. He couldn't blame her for that. Not only was he one-armed now, but he was also weaponless. His trusty warhammer was back in the quarry, along with his arm.

A small, grey-haired old man with one arm, charging what most people would consider an armored goddess? Sure, she could afford to be dismissive of him. She'd already beaten the crap out of him once before.

Fool hadn't forgotten that.

He had an advantage now. Not just this new Skill, or the remaining, nearly useless shackle. No, his advantage was that he knew why he'd lost.

Fool had lost because he'd tried to fight.

He wasn't a fighter. He was a Trickster.

He used every single thing he'd learned in the fight against the greys. It was easier this time. He'd already experienced once how to make all his skills fit together.

Most importantly, he'd learned that being able to kick the shit out of someone wasn't always the right way to win. Almost as important was the realization that his Skills were designed to be of service to the Trickster and those who followed his path.

He became the raven, shifting seamlessly and flying above Kantele, just out of reach of Jackal's Plasma Spear she still carried. As he flew above her, he flared into light, drawing not just the eye of Kantele, but all the gathered dancers and others rushing into the portal.

Some of those folk had ranged attack skills. Or weapons.

It was no real reach for Fool to stack his Skills and use Geas to direct all those folks to fire on Kantele.

She was high Advanced Class, but all the dancers were high Basic or had just reached Advanced. Even combined, they couldn't kill her. What they could do was hurt her badly.

Fool released his Geas on them after they'd fired one brief but superbly coordinated blast of fire at Kantele.

One of the bolts of Mana-fueled fury that ripped into Kantele was familiar to Fool, and he turned to look as he released the Geas.

Olivia smiled at him, waved, and passed through the portal.

That was the moment. The release. He felt something let go inside him, a nagging fear so deep he hadn't dared admit it. With that fear gone, his heart and mind soared, and he knew what he had to do next.

He transformed from the raven into a gorilla. The transformation was not without pain. Part of it was that the gorilla form was close enough to his own form that he became one-armed again. He was also learning that his skill came at a unique cost. At first, it was a small and niggling thing—becoming something else meant letting go of what you were. From a body that still felt old and broken, into a soaring thing? Not too hard. But changing back into a creature of the ground? Surrendering flight? He felt a twinge in his soul, a little grief for the change, as if he wasn't just changing form, but dying and being recreated into a new form.

He knew this was the future of his path. The Trickster was a soul that existed free from any single form, any single life, eternal unto himself. In the moment, Fool accepted that. He'd deal with the repercussions later.

For now, he was a giant bundle of angry muscle. It was time to crush.

He dropped on top of Kantele with a single-handed smash, powered by his Hammer of Loki Skill. Even without the hammer, even with only one hand left, it was still enough to smash her into the ground.

She was too tough to be down for the count, but Fool wasn't done yet either. The joy was in him now, and it wouldn't be denied.

He became coyote and darted around his rising enemy, nipping at her limbs, crashing into her legs to throw her balance off. Even with three legs instead of four, he was nimble enough to dodge her savage return blows. His tongue lolled out in the thrill of being faster, more clever.

She screamed with rage, smashing all around her, until finally Fool darted between her legs, stopped in front of her, and froze in place.

He transformed back into himself and grinned at Kantele.

A moment of confusion. That was what it gave Fool. Kantele paused for a second, the briefest hesitation before stabbing the spear into Fool.

"Too late," he said.

Kantele didn't even really notice the black blade slicing its way out of her chest.

Fool got to look right into her eyes as the soul behind them blinked out of existence. For the briefest second, he thought he saw… something in her eyes, but his brain wouldn't let him recognize it.

Jackal didn't wait, ripping the sword out of Kantele, and raced off to help Lucy with the twins.

Fool didn't think it would take them long to end the threat completely.

He reached for Jackal's Plasma Spear. Kantele's hand was still holding it, but it slipped out of her grip with ease. Fool stood back and planted the butt of the spear into the ground, leaning on it a bit.

His left arm ached, though it wasn't there anymore.

Fool burst out in a brief laugh. He had a vision of himself, and he could see how wrong it was. The spear was right, but it wasn't supposed to be his arm missing. It was supposed to be his eye, given up in exchange for wisdom.

Figured he'd screw even that up.

He looked down at Kantele. He knew nothing about her, aside from her allegiance and what she'd been intending for him and his. They'd been soldiers on opposite sides, and he knew it could have been—should have been—him lying dead on the ground now.

There was nothing inherently evil about her. They probably wouldn't have been friends, or even done anything more than argue and hate each other under other circumstances, but that didn't mean she was evil. Or even completely wrong. Mostly wrong, but not completely wrong.

Even with all that though? She would have killed Fool and felt nothing. She would have killed Olivia. Lucy. Jackal. And all she would have felt was victory and righteousness.

She was a tool. A tool of the Weaver, who was on the side that wasn't just winning, but had already won, probably millennia ago. All of the Trickster's efforts today were to give them a chance to escape, a chance to have a future that had a hope of being different.

That was enough. Enough for Fool, and enough to settle the question that had been in the back of his mind.

He didn't want to be a soldier, but he wasn't ready to stop fighting either. He looked at the portal and saw that it was closing faster and faster, like a zipper shutting off one reality from another.

The twins were down. Fool couldn't tell if they were dead or not, but it didn't matter. Lucy and Jackal were yelling at him, sprinting for the portal.

Fool walked after them.

Lucy leapt through the violet opening with a loud, "Whoohoo!"

Everyone else was through, and from what Fool could tell, the opening would only be open for a few more moments.

Jackal was about to step through but stopped and looked at Fool.

The look on his face said he knew.

Fool stepped forward and hugged him. "I've got things to do here."

Jackal just held on to him, and it felt like hours and less than a second.

Finally, the big man stepped back and looked at Fool. His eyes were full of tears. "I love you, you crazy, wild man. Find your way to us, and if you don't, find love and be happy."

Fool couldn't see much more as his eyes overflowed.

He hadn't thought it would hurt this much.

There wasn't much else to say, and Jackal stepped through. Fool saw Nicholaus on the other side and knew that Jackal would be in good hands.

And Olivia was there suddenly.

She stood on the other side of the portal, looking at Fool. "Lost your arm, stupid."

Fool grinned at her, sniffed, and wiped his eyes with his remaining arm. "Gonna miss you. All my love goes with you, granddaughter. Be a shining star in the heavens."

She laughed and shook her head. "I'm not done with you yet, old man. And you're not done with me. We'll meet again before you know it."

She stepped forward and held her hand out, palm up, and Fool stepped forward, holding out his hand. She was right. He knew that even if he couldn't imagine how it would happen. He had faith.

Their palms almost touched.

The portal closed, and Fool was left alone.

Chapter Twenty-Five

Fool stood for a moment longer. He saw the suburbs off in the distance, and the towers of Burnaby and Coquitlam. SFU on its mountain. Richmond to the right, and the Fraser Valley ahead. He turned to his left, and there were the North Shore mountains, turning color in the sunset.

Then he turned all the way around. The sun was setting over the ocean, and he stood still and watched for all the time it took for the sun to drop lower and lower, kissing the island and the coast mountains before finally drifting down.

Later, Fool knew he'd feel sad. And convinced he'd done the wrong thing. Probably he had made the wrong decision. He wasn't entirely sure why he'd done it, but in the moment? It felt right.

Feeling right wasn't the same as feeling good though. He had a lot of work to do and no idea how to do it.

He was done with the Foundation though. They'd been a useful tool, and they had a good mission going forward. It wasn't his mission anymore, that was all.

Raven. Coyote. Monkey. So many other Tricksters. He was going to learn about them all, and become them all, as much as he could.

And then he would find all the people he could who needed chaos in their lives, for good or for bad. Somewhere in that thought was the realization that if he really wanted to embrace his class—which he did—he needed to build a little community of like-minded folks. Probably he'd have to follow the same process that Lucy had talked about. Get 'em before the System locked them into a habit and put the thinking blinders on them.

That brought a bit of a grin to his face. He'd signed up to be a Priest of the Trickster, kind of thinking that was just some sort of gaming title that didn't mean anything. Now he knew better. He'd never been a person of faith, but now he was. A sizeable chunk of his Skills were all about building and maintaining a healthy congregation, after all.

Since the System arrived, he'd been focused on building up himself. The literal leveling up had been a good marker of that process, and he still had a long, long way to go. It was time to build something else new though.

Maybe a kind of resistance. Not just against the System, but against the people and kinds of thinking that had been crushing people like him even before the System. Those kinds of people were also the kind who seemed to benefit most from the System, so there was some overlap.

His mission was going to be different though. Like the Trickster himself. Not a direct threat, but a nuisance. A nuisance that served to always remind people there was another way—a way that might lead to a better future that no one could imagine when all they could see was the threat in front of them.

It wouldn't be just him.

He intended to make an army of Tricksters.

A burst of enthusiasm ran up his spine when he thought about that, and he spun around in a circle, laughing, taking in the whole world around him.

He stopped, grinning, and almost stumbled.

He'd stopped and spread his arms out wide in joy, wanting to take in the whole world… but he only had one arm, and that dragged him off balance.

One-armed. That wasn't going to do. He'd have to head to a Shop and find out what kind of replacement he could find. He didn't have much cash on hand for that. Once he'd finished looting the System Knights, helpfully left behind by Lucy and Jackal, he figured that wouldn't be an issue anymore.

He brought Jackal's Plasma Spear with him, mostly for balance.

He was relieved, and strangely sad, to see that the twins and the spear-wielder had been finished off, not just wounded. The only actual surprise he got from the looting was that the spear-wielder's corpse was oddly aged and thin, as if something had consumed it from the inside. It was hard to tell, because she'd clearly been slain by the Faithbreaker. Her shield, as well as her torso, was in two different places. Apparently, her shield didn't have the same ability to stop the black sword as the twins' energy shields did.

He gathered what he could of their belongings into a little pile and walked over to the edge of the quarry wall to see if he could figure out the best path down to the giant.

To his shock, the body was gone.

There weren't any footprints or anything. Instead, there was a faint grey powder in the rough shape of the giant. As Fool watched, a small gust of wind picked up a patch of the powder and swirled it off into the distance. It didn't take much imagination to realize that it was the result of dying by the black sword.

Fool shuddered. He'd seen a lot of death and destruction, even at an epic scale, but what that single weapon could do was horrifying.

The most horrifying part of it was the realization that it was only a tiny part of what was out there in the wider universe. Everything he'd experienced so far was nothing compared to what the real heavyweights of the System could do.

He had to get a lot stronger, even if all he planned to do was be an underground resistance fighter.

That chilly thought kept him company all the way down the path to the center of the Quarry Garden.

He did his best not to look at his arm lying on the carefully manicured grass. It took a bit of effort to wrestle the remaining shackle off of it, and he was disappointed to see that even holding it in his hand, he couldn't access the library in the other shackle. Apparently it could only be unlocked by having the matching shackle on an opposite wrist, which made Fool curse out the lack of accessibility modifications.

He stuffed it in a pocket, then looked down at his warhammer. He didn't really need it to access Hammer of Loki. It just made an aesthetic sense.

After a moment, he picked up the hammer and rammed its handle down into the middle of the dust cloud that was the giant. Then he walked back and picked up the spear. That would be his weapon now, at least until he found his way back to Jackal.

If.

If he ever found his way to Jackal.

Blanking out that thought kept his brain empty until he got back to the pile of looted belongings. He gathered what he could, wrapping it into a bundle using the bits of cloth that were still connected to Kantele's body… which was also breaking down.

Once the loot was all gathered, he tied it to the end of the spear and hoisted that over his shoulder.

He looked like the vagabond he used to be.

And he was okay with that. It was time to go back to being a vagabond. A memory came back to him of reading mythology as a child. Vafudr or something. The Wanderer, one of the names of Odin.

He nodded. That would be his model from this point on. He wouldn't go back to the Twisted Chapel, nor to the McBride Flying Cavalry at Metrotown. Or back to McBride.

That brought him up a little short, because he really had no idea where to go.

Maybe he'd just pick a direction and see where his feet took him.

He was less surprised than he should have been when a weight thumped onto his left shoulder. It felt right, as if the light weight was a partial replacement for the weight of his missing arm.

He didn't turn to look. "I thought you might be back. Figured maybe you'd be a raven or something though."

"Nah," DM said. "Why change a classic? Besides, those old tales were due for some modernization."

Fool nodded and walked forward. He wasn't really paying attention to where he was going, but it felt the right way.

DM settled on his shoulder, and she lightly bumped the side of his head. "So, tell me about this Rebecca we're on our way to find?"

Fool just smiled.

The End

Status Screen			
Name	Fool	Class	Priest
Race	Human (Male)	Level (Advanced Class)	8
Titles			
Adept Priest of the (Redacted)			
Health	290	Stamina	290
Mana	760	Mana Regeneration	58/minute
Status			
Normal			
Attributes			
Strength	22	Agility	47
Constitution	29	Perception	116
Intelligence	76	Willpower	84
Charisma	90	Luck	212
Class Skills			
Closseau	1	Have Faith	1
Talent Scout	2	Pants on Fire	2
Transform Object	1	Kiss it Better	2
I know a Shortcut	2	Truth or Dare	1
Dry hair is for Squids	1	Oh god, don't hit me!	2
Mint?	1	Location Scout	1
Face Swap	1	No Fair	2
Geas	2	Feign Death	1
Aura of *	2	Regeneration	1
Hammer of Loki	1	That's Disgusting	1
Aziz!	1	Over 21	1
Friendly Fire	1	Mana Sense	1
Spells			
Sparkles			

Status Screen			
Name	Jackal	Class	Bearshirt Warrior of the Claven North
Race	Human (Male)	Level (Advanced)	8
Titles			
(None)			
Health	920	Stamina	9240
Mana	750	Mana Regeneration	124 / minute
Status			
Normal			
Attributes			
Strength	97	Agility	86
Constitution	92	Perception	128
Intelligence	75	Willpower	189
Charisma	25	Luck	10
Class Skills			
Pain don't Hurt	2	One Punch	2
INTIMIDATE	1	Mana Steal	1
Knock back	1	Mr. Freeze	1
Only a flesh Wound	2	Death from Above	2
Neo	1	Indomitable Will	2
Maestro	2	Blade Walking	2
Red Rover	2	The Wall	1
Eye of the Tiger	2	Boomstick	1
C-C-C-Combo	1	Just a Scratch	2
Lead Zeppelin	1	Potooooooooo	1
I Found Dis	1	Gugnir's Wrath	1
Punishment of the Bear	1	Ramstal	1
Spells			
(None)			

Epilogue

It was a beautiful world.

The temperature was perfect, as was the light. A sun that looked the same as Earth's. The air was a delight, a mix of tangy caramel floral from the nearby jungle, with a touch of salty ocean.

It made sense, since the portal had landed them on the edge of a vast plateau. The edge they had arrived on broke down in a series of gullies and terraces to a broad beach. The far side of the plateau was ringed with a mountain range that spanned the length of the horizon, as far as the eye could see.

There were birds flying about. And insects. Things that looked like butterflies. Something like a deer had been watching them when they arrived, a herd of them. They'd stared curiously for a bit, then sprinted off into the trees of the jungle.

At least, what Jackal figured was a jungle. The trees were enormous and had wide-spreading roots. They looked like mangrove trees, but the tops looked like pines or cedars. Long vines hung from all the trees, almost reaching the ground, and each vine was festooned with pink, purple, blue, and yellow flowers.

The plateau soil they'd landed on was a hard scrub, big patches of hard-packed dirt, with low shrubs all around that looked identical to heather.

It didn't take long for Jackal to get a sense of the place. More detailed study would have to wait. They had to get settled first.

The buildings had all settled out into a pre-arranged pattern, so that part was taken care of. Jackal didn't really know what the buildings did, but he figured they'd be getting a tour soon.

When he finally looked around him at everyone else, they were all doing the same thing as him. The entire group burst into smiles, then he saw people reaching arms out and looking confused.

He went to pull up his stats and understood the confusion. There was nothing. The System was gone.

All his Skills were gone.

He had a brief panicked moment, wondering if he was suddenly going to revert, but he felt the same. He'd been warned to empty anything kept in storage by a Skill, but everything he had stored was Mana-based and probably wouldn't have been usable or accessible in any case.

This was going to be weird. He was going to have to figure out how to move, how to do… everything. He'd have to learn all over again how strong his body was without Mana fueling everything.

Then he noticed Olivia.

The young woman had ditched most of the bone fetishes she'd been wearing when Jackal had first met her, but she was still the epitome of a fantasy shaman otherwise. And she was grinning. Widely.

It wasn't much. Just a tiny sliver of a glow. A tiny, tiny green glow that Jackal would have been tempted to say was just a trick of the eye, but it was real.

Olivia caught him staring and grinned at him. "Mana. Not much. A trickle. Just a faint trickle. But it's here. We can make magic."

Others heard that, and a roar of jubilation rose all around them.

Dinner was a sparse affair. It wasn't due to lack of supplies—they had decades' worth, even if nothing on the planet turned out to be edible. The problem was that no one had cooked without using System Skills for years. It was made worse because Lucy, and the Trickster, had selected crew for youth and minimal exposure to the System. As a result, instead of having a population of broad interests, they'd accidentally self-selected for people who had relied less on the System for Skills, but more for providing the basic necessities of living.

Jackal had enough experience that he'd been pulled into a few chores, including helping on the cooking line. Nicholaus had laughed at that, but when the first meal was over, he'd shown Jackal his appreciation and promised to learn how to help for the next meal.

He'd abandoned Jackal shortly after though. The dance crews were all eager to see what they could do, but much like the food, music was another issue. They'd brought stored music and music players, but they'd been built to use Mana for power. The Technomancers that had come along were working on alternate power supplies, but it would take them another day or two to get it all set up. Which left the dancers trying to figure out how to play the various instruments that had been brought along.

After only a few minutes, Jackal had to walk away from the cacophony. They'd get it eventually, but he was rather hoping he'd find a way to be elsewhere while that happened.

He was standing on top of a small cliff, watching the sun creep into the ocean, when Lucy found him.

She walked up next to him and was silent for a few moments, taking in the view with Jackal and enjoying the peace. "Not too shabby, eh? Too bad we couldn't keep the portal open. Woulda been a nice vacation spot."

Jackal nodded and rolled his shoulders. There was a comforting warmth to the place, and muscles he didn't even know were knotted started to release. "I think we'll make a home here. But how much do we know about this place? The Technomancers found that it was suitable, but how much did they learn?"

"Not much. Too distant for them to really do anything like a survey, but they've got some pretty good science, anyway. Biosignatures are all compatible, which means we need to be aware of poisons, plagues, predators, and all that fun stuff. No way around that. And we need to keep tough to be ready for the System in any case."

"Fair. What about the big threats? Solar flares, plate tectonics, asteroid belt, all that kind of thing?"

Lucy gave a quick shrug. "Planet's about the same age as Earth, sun is roughly the same, solar system as well. Portal wouldn't have connected the two points unless a whole bunch of factors were roughly the same. So same risk as Earth. Some. We'll need to prepare for that. We've got the spaceship, worst case. It can evacuate all of us with no issues. We can't live in it forever, but if we need to run for a while, we can do that. And for the other threats? Tomorrow we'll start surveying the planet. That'll go on for years, I suspect. You up for some science? They'll need help."

That brought a big grin to Jackal's face. He'd missed science. Having an opportunity to explore a new world wasn't in line with his precise training, but it was absolutely in line with the kinds of dreams that had brought him into science in the first place.

He looked down at his feet and an interesting bit of rock. Then he paused and looked at it again. And looked up. "Lucy."

She stopped, looking a little chilled by the tone of his voice, and looked at him.

Jackal nudged the rock, and it came completely free from the ground. He looked up at Lucy. "Aren't we supposed to be alone here?"

"There weren't any signs of advanced tech, but I guess that was wrong."

"Apparently." With his foot, Jackal nudged what looked like a discarded soup can. There wasn't a label on it, but something like writing had been etched into part of the metal.

"Oh." Now it was Jackal's turn to look up at Lucy, startled by the sound of her voice. "Yeah, very wrong."

She was looking over Jackal's shoulder, and he turned to look at what had caught her eye.

He couldn't see anything at first. There were a few little islands out in the ocean, and a few clouds, but nothing else…

Except… what he'd taken for an island out near the horizon. A bit of a mirage warped the view of it in the distance, and for a moment, the atmospherics altered enough to highlight the shape of it.

The angular, artificial shape of it. It looked almost exactly like a World War II era destroyer, like the model his grandfather had had in his study that Jackal had loved to look at when he was a kid. After another moment, he saw it moving, even through the faint shimmer of the ocean mirage.

There wasn't any going back now. Perfect time to find out they weren't alone.

Jackal and Lucy looked at each other and grinned. Friend or foe, they'd be ready for this adventure.

THE END

Want to read one more adventure with Fool and Jackal?
Download the free short story, Tower of Doom!
https://readerlinks.com/l/4350577

Author's Note

Hey Reader,

Thanks for walking alongside me as Fool and Jackal's trilogy played itself out. It's been one hell of a journey!

Now that this story is done, I'd like to thank Tao for giving me a chance to play in his universe. The System Apocalypse was my introduction to the genre and researching for this trilogy meant I'm now a regular LitRPG reader. When I read the first System Apocalypse book, my first thought was that it was such a rich and deep setting that you could tell almost any kind of story. It reminded me why I spent so much of my youth in tabletop RPGs. Telling all kinds of stories, and helping to shape my friends' stories? Those were some of my best teenage memories.

I wanted to tap back into that feeling. I wanted to share the kind of imaginings that were going on in my head when I read about John's adventures. The way I felt like I might have reacted under similar circumstances. At first, I imagined something like the real old-school fantasy of Fritz Leiber, and that was my first short story.

Something about those two characters changed from that first little tale until I started to work out how this trilogy was going to go. I didn't really want to write a three-novel throwback adventure story. And I also didn't really feel like I had the gaming chops to manage the more complex leveling up staples of the genre, at least not in a way that would be interesting for readers.

Instead, I wanted to tell a more personal story.

Fool is a very broken person, and when the System and the Trickster fixed him, they only patched him. But the patch was enough for him to start to work out his own way into healing. My own life has had its moments of interest, and I've tried to fit some of that into Fool. There is a longing within him that comes from me, and when I think about where he goes in the future, I see that longing fulfilled. Perhaps someday that story will be told, but I also think that maybe he'd prefer it to be private.

Jackal also holds a special place for me. I've watched a lot of friends put in the hard work to make similar transformations, and that process has always looked heroic to me. I figured Fool needed a friend who'd reshaped themselves into their dream as a role model for reshaping himself. There is also a lot of me in Jackal, which is why I'm glad he found a way to settle down in the same way I have.

As for what's next? In the short term, I'm heading back to my first love. I've got an epic fantasy trilogy that will launch soon. I've also started to work on a cyberpunk book that is somehow a prequel to the fantasy series. That's going to take some time to develop. I've completed a sequel to my first sci-fi novel and am waiting for feedback from early readers.

Will there be more Fool and Jackal? Not planned. I wanted to leave their story with a completed arc, but open-ended enough that you could spend some time imagining where they go next. I have notes written on two more follow-up trilogies, so who knows what the future holds. For now? I hope these two rakes have found at least a little space in your head for their dreams.

They'll always be in mine.

- David, from the mountain village

About the Authors

David R. Packer has been a full-time teacher of historical European swordplay, a high-tech wizard, and a security professional. For a few years he was a for-pay bad guy working in police training, which once had him on the run from the entire police force, across the whole city.

Aside from that, he lives a cozy life with 2 cats and a real-life she-hulk for a wife. He has many books and likes coffee far too much.

You can find out more information on David's books by visiting his website: https://boxwrestlefence.com

Tao Wong is an avid fantasy and sci-fi reader who spends his time working and writing in the North of Canada. He's spent way too many years doing martial arts of many forms, and having broken himself too often, he now spends his time writing about fantasy worlds.

For updates on the series and other books written by Tao Wong (and special one-shot stories), please visit the author's website:
http://www.mylifemytao.com

Want updates on upcoming deluxe editions and exclusive merch? Follow Tao on Kickstarter to get notifications on all projects.
https://www.kickstarter.com/profile/starlitpublishing/created

Subscribers to Tao's mailing list to receive exclusive access to short stories in the Thousand Li and System Apocalypse universes.

For more great information about LitRPG series, check out these Facebook groups:

- GameLit Society

  www.facebook.com/groups/LitRPGsociety

- LitRPG Books

  www.facebook.com/groups/LitRPG.books

- LitRPG Legion

  www.facebook.com/groups/litrpglegion

About the Publisher

Starlit Publishing is wholly owned and operated by Tao Wong. It is a science fiction and fantasy publisher focused on the LitRPG & cultivation genres. Their focus is on promoting new, upcoming authors in the genre whose writing challenges the existing stereotypes while giving a rip-roaring good read.

For more information on Starlit Publishing, early access to books and exclusive stories visit our webshop: https://www.starlitpublishing.com/

You can also join Starlit Publishing's mailing list to learn of new, exciting authors and book releases.

Glossary

Anti-crepuscular Ray: Not a laser beam. My wife told me to write that. These are cool shadow-beams that show up under clouds around sunset if you are very lucky. Yes, I learned what they were called and I am always looking for an excuse to say "Oh! Look! Anti-crepuscular rays!" because I am insufferable.

Aura of *: Area effect mental attack Skill that's not really defined. More specifically, it has the effect of making the targets feel increasingly uncomfortable and out of touch with reality. It builds a feedback loop off of whatever the target initially interprets this as, and rapidly spikes it up into overload.

Aziz: Yeah, I'm a huge "Fifth Element" fan.

Bacon: Look, I don't know why Americans call back bacon "Canadian" bacon. We don't really eat that stuff, and absolutely not at breakfast. Sometimes we put it on pizza with pineapple, but we call that "ham." I assure you that we all eat the same bacon at breakfast, unless you are English, in which case you have "Streaky bacon"

Beau Geste: Classic 1939 Gary Cooper film about the French Foreign Legion. The actual fort in the film is Fort Zinderneuf. Fort Whisky is the fort that gets swamped by bugs in the "Starship Troopers" movie. Did you know there is also a book called Starship Troopers, and it is also good? Probably someone will make a movie out of it someday.

Bloedel Conservatory: Giant geodesic dome with an actual jungle inside it! So cool! My dad told me that folk were once told to hide out there in a hurricane, and I thought he was pulling my leg, but…there actually was a hurricane in Vancouver before I was born, so I don't know what's real anymore.

Blue River: Blue River is too small to be a village.

Caracol: Yeah, I spent a lot of my 20s and 30s in the SCA, and developed a deep love of renaissance military tactics.

Cariboo Mountain: Next door neighbours of the Canadian Rockies, and contain the Selkirk, Monashee, and Purcell ranges. These were my stomping grounds as a kid and the reason I get confused when I go to other places and they refer to hills as "mountains."

Children: Small humans that shouldn't read this book because there are swears. Wait. Did I remember that I'm allowed to swear in these books? Dammit.

Clouseau: Inspector Clouseau was of course, the master of disguise. This skill makes Fool almost as ingenious as the great man himself.

CPP: Canada Pension Plan. You get money when you decide you are just too damned old for dealing with people's shit. It't not much money, though, so it's best to suck it up as long as you can.

Crisp Meat (beef) Burrito: The greatest food in the universe, if eaten correctly. More properly a taquito, I suppose. Taco Time is the restaurant chain, the source of the best Classic Canadian prairie food that we sometimes call "Mexican" but we know better. It's just easier to call it that so that people don't freak out over how hot the hot sauce is. I'd kill for a crisp beef burrito with a dipping cup of hot sauce right now. Seriously. I'm on the edge of tears as I write this.

Darling Nikki: Prince song. Look it up. Our English 11 teacher asked us to do an analysis of song lyrics as poetry, and I chose this song. Felt pretty smug about my choice until I realized I had to recite the lyrics in front of the whole class.

Dunster: They have an ice-cream social once a year!

Dry Hair is for Squids: Jack Deth is cool. Cooler than you. "Trancers" is amazing.

EI: Employment Insurance. In Canada, a part of every paycheck goes into a fund. If you lose your job, this fund is used to pay you a portion of your wages until you get a new job. It's usually six months worth, but it can be extended if you are taking the right kind of classes, or working part time. Super handy.

False Widows: Steodata, generally Grossa. Big black shiny spiders that might live under your sink. These are great spiders. They will eat Black Widows and Brown Recluse spiders, as well as all the other pests in your house. They also stay put, so if you see one, you can safely ignore it and it will always be there doing it's job for you. Don't try to touch them, their bite stings like a hornet.

First Nations: The people living within the Canadian legal boundary called British Columbia. Despite popular misconception, most of this land is still completely owned by them. They have a serious issues with squatters. Please note that the author is not First Nations, and everything he has to say related to First Nations people, practices, and namings is not to be trusted or assumed correct. Hopefully this encourages you to go and find more reliable sources, as there are many. Here's a great place to start: https://www.bcafn.ca/

Friston: Karl Friston. Jackal is trying to explain how Friston's Free Energy principle might apply. You can look it up. It's a deep rabbit hole of very hard to understand stuff, but will give you a better sense of how the world works.

Fool's Warhammer: Not really a warhammer. The head is based off of a museum piece, but the whole thing is closer in weight and usage to a Hungarian Fokos, which is kind of a walking stick with an small axe head or hammer head on one side. Lightweight, fast, and real handy for troll smashing.

Foundation: Professor Xi chose the name because he is a giant nerd.

Fraser Valley: This is where corn, potatoes, and the smell of manure come from in the Lower Mainland. Half the food in the province comes from here. It's also the most northern point in the entire world where rice is cultivated.

Some super interesting wars have been fought here, and it also used to be a lake. Sometimes it still thinks it is.

Geas: I've been afraid to say this word out loud since I was twelve and got my first D&D set. I still have no idea how to pronounce it. I guess I should listen to the audiobook. Narrators research this kind of stuff, right?

Gitxsan: Coastal First Nation that no longer lives on the coast. Sort of like the Canadian version of Normans, who were descended from viking raiders that thought "oh gosh, wouldn't this be a nice spot for a winery. Let's learn to make croissants!" Alex is not Gitxsan. Fool is really, really bad at faces but really good at assumptions.

Halkomelem: One of the First Nations in the BC lower mainland area.

Have Faith: Fool can ask the Trickster for a favour. Any kind of favour. In exchange, the Trickster will ask something in return from Fool. The Trickster doesn't need to really be asked the question, though, since he always seems to know what Fool needs. And Fool never has any idea of how the request will be fulfilled.

Hoary Marmot: Squeak!
https://www.youtube.com/shorts/WC5NnBFvfdw
Seriously, Marmots are very cool. They will truly ignore you, to the point of walking right over you to get to something else, unless you bother them. Then you get to see a whole different creature.

Hope: Cute little town in the Lower Mainland. It's at the very, very tail end of the Fraser Valley, and acts as an unofficial boundary between "northern" BC/the Mountains and the city of Vancouver, which most people think is the entirety of BC.

Jumping Spiders: Did you know they make good pets? Very playful! So cute!

Kerfuffle: Commonwealth for SNAFU. I think. A muckery. A skibbiddy-doo. A thing. You know what I mean.

Lanza Spezzate: Literally "Broken Lance." Kind of a 15th century Italian ronin. A lance was a cohesive unit of armoured knights and their support train. The lanza spezzata were professional soldiers who had left their previous units to act as free agents.

Lower Mainland: The southernmost point of BC, and the most western point (if you ignore Vancouver Island and Victoria, which everyone does unless they are on vacation or work in the government.) Fun fact: Vancouver is the Southwest of Canada. That means there is indeed a North in Canada. BC is quite huge. You can squeeze California and Texas into it. Or most of Great Britain and some extra bits of Europe. It's also mostly unpopulated and unexplored by anyone other than extreme cartographers. There is a lot of First Nation's history in some of those empty places, and a lot of that history is "Dude. That is a tough place to get to." Heck, we only found the source of the biggest major river a few decades ago. It's not even hidden in a jungle or anything. It's just waaaaaay up there in the mountains.

Maker: Alex is a nerd, and likes the book with sand and giant worms.

McBride: A tiny village in the Robson Valley. Has a pretty good coffee shop, and a town's worth of facilities. Really. It's quite strange.

Metrotown: The mall. You know what it is, even if you've never heard of it or been there. Just a mall like any other, but bigger. Same life cycle as all the rest, somehow staggering along. No one likes it, no one goes there, and yet somehow it's still packed every time you get a touch of nostalgia and think about wandering through and window shopping.

Opilione: I am one of the few humans to have been bit by one of these. It hurt. Very pinchy. I also had the terrifying experience of crawling through a quartz tube (abandoned small gold mine) waaay up in the mountains when I was a kid, and looking up at the ceiling and realizing it was a few inches thick mat of these guys. I got over the fear eventually, which is good because these things are seriously weird and fun to look at. They are probably the most alien looking thing that you can see commonly, and probably ignore.

Orcabear: I used to dream about this thing. Brrr.
A monster with top half of an orca and the bottom half of a grizzly bear.

P. Craig Russell: Elric. Killraven. I really disliked his art when it started to appear in my comics reading, but…wow did it grow on me. His run on Elric really defined the whole tale for me.

Piobaireachd: Traditional form of bagpipe music. Also called ceol mor or "big music" as opposed to ceol beag or "party tunes." It starts with a simple melody that is repeated, and then gets more complex variations added. This was the first music I learned to play on the pipes. Sounds great echoing off of the mountains…if someone else is playing it, because I suck.

RCMP: Royal Canadian Mounted Police. Sometimes called "Mounties" but only if you're buddies. Militarized FBI with horses and cool dress uniforms. Most police in Canada are RCMP, and they go through substantial training. They are expected on occasion to be the only law enforcement for a very, very large territory.

Salish Sea: The sea between Vancouver and Vancouver Island. If you are of the right age and used to live in Nanaimo, you will know that people used to race bathtubs across it. Seriously. Bathtubs.

Sheriff: You rarely see or hear of Sheriff's in Canada. They have strictly limited duties, and no political connections at all. They occasionally provide extra security, but mostly they only handle prisoner transfers and courtroom duties. A Deputy Sheriff is someone who only works in the court system, so the usage of "Deputy" in Valemount is incorrect, but is the sort of thing some Canadians would think is right because they spend all their time watching American TV and have a hard time figuring out which country they live in. Sheriff Barnes is one of those people.

Simpcw: First Nation that also has ownership of the area this book takes place in. First Nations don't use the same border system theory that the settlers did, and this caused a lot of confusion for people try to assign ownership to things because it makes them sleep better at night.

Six-Step: Basic break dance move, somewhat like a crab on a hot tin roof.

Skytrain: Light rail/Rapid transit. Visitors call it a subway train sometimes, but it's mostly above ground. Probably the best way to see a big chunk of Vancouver, honestly.

Sto:lo: Fool's pretty off-base here, as are most of the people. Sto:lo is used in the lower mainland, and the usage of this word has spread a bit, but where Fool is located it would be slightly more proper to use either the Dakelh word: Lhtakoh, or the Tsilhqot'in word: ʔelhdawox. Locals use this word currently, anglicized to "Eldako" for some areas, but never to the river for some weird reason. Fool is Metis, but he was raised without any real education of his ancestry, so while he has a keen interest in First Nations lore, what he knows is spotty and often wrong. He sure tries, through.

Sunbeam Ecological Reserve: You can see this from McBride. It's lovely. I haven't been up yet because I don't own a 4x4.

Talent Scout: Fools most used skill, but it's not that great. Probably could have bought a basic identify spell from the Shop that would replace this.

Taxes: We pay these in Canada in the hopes that the CBC will eventually find a new comedy group as funny as Kids in the Hall. Or even SCTV. Someday.

Technocrats: This was a real thing! My grandfather was a member. Very strange days.

Tete Jaune Cache: Local's sometimes pronounce this "Tee Joan Cash." Tete Jaune means Yellowhead, as in the Yellowhead highway. Or "Blondie's road" if you are feeling catty. Tete Jaune was the nickname of a Metis scout in the area when it was "discovered." It's very pretty. Don't take my word for it. You should visit it sometime.

Tom Cody: "Streets of Fire" If you haven't seen it yet, you're in for a treat.

UBC: University of BC. The rich kid school. Has actual fraternities like it's on the east coast or something. SFU (Simon Fraser University) is where all the hip kids go, it's on a mountain top and has a borg cube for a library, and one of the best pipe bans in the world. There is also ECU (Emily Carr University) which is a unique art school that utterly hates artists while thinking it loves them. The UBC downtown campus is a strange underground post-apocalyptic sort of setup, and I once met Mandy Patinkin there when I had a rapier in hand, and it got pretty epic. I have photographic proof.

Valemount: You go through this on the way to Jasper. If you want to save money on Jasper hotels, you stay here instead. Cheaper hotels but still overpriced restaurants.

To learn more about LitRPG, talk to authors including myself, and just have an awesome time, please join the LitRPG Group!

https://www.facebook.com/groups/LitRPGGroup/